Running an independent bookstore in small-town Hazel Rock, Texas, doesn't sound like a high-risk pursuit. But when a fundraiser reveals a story with a truly killer ending, Charli Rae Warren will need to scramble to sort out the deadly plot...

Sponsoring the literacy drive to benefit the foster care system should be a feel-good endeavor, but one of Charli's helpers is definitely on another page. Charli's dad is distracted and keeping something secret, which Charli suspects is a harmless flirtation with an attractive county clerk who offered to lend them a hand. It's nothing to worry about—until the same clerk winds up dead...

When nosy locals begin pointing fingers, Charli finds herself entangled in a race to uncover the killer's identity—and to get to the bottom of a shattering family secret that could rewrite her history in alarming ways. Suddenly Charli is facing her worst fears and her childhood nemesis in order to unmask a murderer—before he silences her for good...

The Book Barn Mystery Series
by Kym Roberts

Fatal Fiction

A Reference to Murder

Perilous Poetry

Lethal Literature

Lethal Literature

Kym Roberts

LYRICAL UNDERGROUND
Kensington Publishing Corp.
www.kensingtonbooks.com

LYRICAL UNDERGROUND BOOKS are published by

Kensington Publishing Corp.
119 West 40th Street
New York, NY 10018

All Kensington titles, imprints, and distributed lines are available at special quantity discounts for bulk purchases for sales promotion, premiums, fund-raising, educational, or institutional use.

Special book excerpts or customized printings can also be created to fit specific needs. For details, write or phone the office of the Kensington Sales Manager: Kensington Publishing Corp., 119 West 40th Street, New York, NY 10018. Attn. Sales Department. Phone: 1-800-221-2647.

Lyrical Underground and Lyrical Underground logo Reg. US Pat. & TM Off.

First Electronic Edition: May 2018
eISBN-13: 978-1-5161-0658-5
eISBN-10: 1-5161-0658-X

First Print Edition: May 2018
ISBN-13: 978-1-5161-0660-8
ISBN-10: 1-5161-0660-1

Printed in the United States of America

For all those fighting the good fight

Chapter One

I knew better than to arrive at a bachelor's house early in the morning, but I'd been happily oblivious to the possibility that I might look like I was checking up on him—like I wanted to catch him in the act. I should have remembered that key word before I'd decided to surprise him with breakfast from the diner. He was a *bachelor*.

And the *last* person on earth I wanted to catch in the act.

Yet there he was . . . standing in his doorway wearing a T-shirt and jeans with his bare feet announcing to the entire neighborhood, make that the entire world, that he'd just rolled out of bed. The situation couldn't get worse. At least, so I thought. Until I noticed his hair was tussled and Ava James gave him a tender kiss on the cheek—with matching sex-mussed hair.

I stood on the sidewalk, surrounded by the spring fragrance of the wisteria bush growing over the white picket fence around his front lawn, my mouth hanging opening. Our to-go order breakfast was in my hands as Ava turned around and saw me for the first time. She immediately averted her gaze and jammed a pair of sunglasses onto her face. Their endearing moment over, I watched completely dumbfounded as her hand grasped at the neck of her button-down shirt, and her knuckles whitened as she held it together. I did not want to notice the missing buttons on the top of her blouse as she bowed her head in the traditional walk of morning-after shame.

We were all adults. We could handle this. It wasn't that big a deal. Their age difference wasn't shocking, nor was their potential of being a couple out of the question. It had just taken me off guard, and that was what I found most disturbing.

At least that's what I was telling myself.

Ava and I passed on the sidewalk and I tried to establish eye contact through her mirrored lenses. "Good morning, Ava," I said and smiled at the woman fifteen years my senior.

She mumbled a good morning without raising her head. I wouldn't have been able to see her eyes anyway, but I didn't want her to think I harbored a grudge. I didn't. They were consenting adults. I had no reason to judge them or be upset.

"Are you ready for the literacy drive for the foster care program?" I asked.

Ava nodded but kept walking right past me. "I'll call you," she said without looking back.

"Sure thing. Whenever you get a chance, I'm flexible."

I don't think I fooled anyone. I wasn't *that* flexible about any of this.

I looked up at the door where he stood watching the whole scene unfold. His jaw was tight, and his eyes narrowed as he scanned the street to see if anyone else witnessed their indiscretion. Then his gaze returned to me, and I could tell it wasn't a proud moment for him. He sensed what neither one of us wanted to admit—he'd just fallen off the pedestal I'd put him on shortly after I'd returned to Hazel Rock, Texas, my hometown of 2,093 people.

That however, wasn't what I found most disturbing. There was something in his eyes that said, "Don't ask questions; don't ask for an explanation." If I did? My inquiries would be ignored.

I reach the steps with the warm paper bag and two paper cups of sweet tea in my hands. "Are you going to let me in?"

He looked like he had no idea how to handle the situation. That made two of us, but from the look on his face, Ava James wasn't just a one-night stand—she meant something to him, and I needed to suck it up and accept the fact that the man had moved on. He stood back and held the door open for me to enter, but his gaze followed Ava as she walked down the sidewalk, past Mike Thompson, who had apparently started running to work off a few pounds, or fifty, before she rounded the corner.

"Daddy, you don't have to keep your love life a secret."

Bobby Ray Warren closed the door without saying a word, and by the time he turned around, he'd hidden that lost look in his eyes. "I'm glad you brought breakfast. I'm starved."

If he noticed the shudder he sent through my body with that comment, he didn't say anything. He grabbed the bag from my hand and walked into his kitchen without another word. I followed him into the perfectly designed kitchen of his old Victorian home. His last girlfriend, who had died the day I return to town a little over a year ago, had decorated and remodeled the century-old home.

Sometimes I wondered if he stayed in the house in memory of her. Today I wasn't so sure. After all, this was where he laid his head at night; it had his touches just as much as hers. Especially when it came to the industrial coffee station for his Colombian brewed coffee he enjoyed so much. Most mornings he waited for a cup of joe until he got to the bookstore; on the days he didn't open The Book Barn Princess, he had a cup of fresh brew at home in his state-of-the-art kitchen.

I looked down at the two plastic cups of sweet tea in my hands and wondered why I'd bought two. Two empty coffee cups were sitting on the kitchen table. I set the tea on the table, picked up the coffee cups, and carried them to the sink.

Dad had just shared a cup of coffee with Ava after their night together—though I really didn't want to think about his night with Ava. But it was stuck in my brain like the sound of a greased pig squealing in an arena full of kids. Nipping at this end of my brain and screaming at the other, sending it straight through my right lobe into my left, it wouldn't shut up or disappear.

"So . . . is this the beginning of something new?" I asked.

"Are you planning to bring me breakfast from the diner every morning?"

I rolled my eyes at his attempt to hide what I'd seen. "You know what I'm talking about, Daddy."

"I think you're stepping into waters you don't belong in, Princess." My nickname rolled off his tongue with more than a hint of irritation.

I searched his face and could see he was dead serious. He wasn't going to discuss Ava James with me. I didn't know if that meant they were serious or if it meant they were less than serious. His face was a mask of discretion. He was not going to discuss her with anyone. Ava James had his ear . . . and more.

"You're right. I'm sorry, Daddy. I was out of line questioning you about your love life. When you're ready to talk about it, I'm here."

Dad reached over and squeezed my hand. "Now let's see what you brought for breakfast. At this point, I'm pretty sure I could eat the bag and think it tasted good."

We ate our breakfast of eggs, bacon, and waffles made out of Texas Toast while discussing our upcoming fundraiser for foster kids. Ava James had pitched the idea to my dad and he'd been all for it. I was too, but now I wondered how personal that pitch had been.

Ava had been a customer of our family bookstore for as long as I could remember. When I was a kid she used to come in every now and then with Isla Sperry, the old sheriff's wife. When I was a teenager, she was a dispatcher at the sheriff's office, working for the same sheriff who spouted scriptures every time I so much as breathed in the direction of trouble. When the sheriff brought me to the station after a wild night of leading a cheer from the top of the town's water tower, it'd been Ava James sitting at the one-person phone system in the sheriff's office who tampered down his lecture straight out of 1 Peter 3:3–4.

"'Women with unfading beauty of a gentle and quiet spirit are precious to God,'" Sheriff Sperry had said.

Ava had turned around and looked at him with one eyebrow raised. "You can't tell Princess to be quiet and gentle, then turn around and quote John 10:10 to me. Princess is literally stopping 'the thief who comes to steal and kill and destroy' by sharing her joy with the world. Remember? 'Jesus came that they may have life and have it abundantly.' Princess has life—abundantly."

At that moment, I'd felt like I had a big sister looking out for me. It was wonderful. I'd never be able to quote scripture in an argument. But Ava could, and she did it effectively.

The sheriff's authoritarian attitude had turned into a pained expression as he looked between the two of us. Even at my tender age, I knew there was something important hanging in the air between them. And when the sheriff walked down the hallway to his office, I'd dared to complain to Ava about the old coot.

That had been a mistake.

My big sister disappeared. Ava had practically raised her claws in his defense. He'd been like a father to her when she'd aged out of the foster care system. Without him, she wasn't sure what street corner she would have been sleeping on. It was the last time I'd complained about her boss. At least to her. It also explained why she went to work for Sperry when he became a judge, and it explained her passion for collecting the books we couldn't sell, to give to foster children every month.

My dad broke into my memories. "When are you leaving for Dallas?"

"Tomorrow evening after I get off at the bookstore. I'm going to stay for the weekend and do a little shopping."

Dad's lip quirked. "I hear Mateo has the weekend off as well."

"Oh?" I began clearing the table to avoid any further comments. The last thing I wanted to discuss with my daddy was Mateo Espinosa. Mateo and I hadn't told anyone that we were going to a concert in Dallas together. For him, it was a privacy issue. For me it was complicated. We were taking a big step I wasn't sure I was ready for. During the past month, I'd found myself questioning my intelligence. Mateo was the current county sheriff, and I'd already had one bad relationship with the lead law enforcement officer in town. What if things went south between the two of us?

Would he quote the Bible to me as well? Would he be there every time I went two miles over the speed limit? Come running when I didn't cross the street at the intersection and tell me I was jaywalking? Or would he focus on first-time offenses I hadn't been old enough to experience with the old sheriff? Like shake his head at the "wild girl" in town when I came out of the Tool Shed Tavern a little tipsy after a Monday night football game, then arrest me for public intoxication. Those fears were very real . . . to me, anyway.

When my thoughts went in that direction, breathing became difficult, and as the weekend drew closer, those moments of panic seemed to be increasing. I finished clearing the table as my dad leaned back and patted his belly.

"Is Ava still working as Judge Sperry's clerk?" I asked.

Dad stiffened, the way he always did when I talked about the county judge who used to be my archnemesis. Unlike Ava, my relationship with Judge Sperry didn't contain fond childhood memories. They consisted of the man who had been sheriff looking for every reason in the world to spout the Bible to me. If I breathed a hint of rebellion, I somehow ended up staring at the gold star on his chest, saying "yes, sir" and "no, sir" before I'd even made a nuisance of myself. It always ended with Sheriff Sperry telling me my evil ways would send him to his grave.

I never quite understood why. Maybe that type of tough love had been a saving grace for Ava. For me, it'd been a pain in my backside and his nickname "the Judge" seemed to fit very well since the man had been evaluating my behavior since I stepped into town at the age of eight.

"Yes, but that may change soon," Daddy answered.

"Why?"

"Ava said Isla Sperry's Alzheimer's has taken a dramatic turn for the worse in the past month. She keeps wandering away from the nursing home and making wild accusations about the people she cares most about. The Judge is thinking about retiring."

"What? I had no idea she was suffering from Alzheimer's disease. I'm sorry to hear that. Isla Sperry was always good to me. I hate that she's going through that."

Dad cleared his throat, and I could have sworn there was a shimmer of tears in his eyes before he stood up and turned toward the hallway. "Me too. Me too, Princess."

As he walked down the hallway I couldn't help but wonder if I was missing something once again, but then his voice turned loud and clear when he said, "I'm going to take a shower. You better get to the store and open it. We don't want the customers busting down the Barn door."

We both knew there was no threat of our customers breaking down our doors. We also knew that something was bothering him, and my daddy wasn't about to talk about it . . . yet.

Chapter Two

I made my way to the Barn and slammed the truck door closed before approaching the store. My lighthearted mood had turned sour. Princess number two greeted me on the porch with a little hop in her step. I couldn't help but smile.

"You know how to turn my day completely around, don't you?"

She squeaked, then snuffled my bare leg, tickling my ankle. I couldn't help but laugh. "You just want breakfast," I scolded.

My accusation caused her to jump straight up in the air. It amused me no end to see our thirteen-pound pink armadillo prance around happily. Princess was unique when it came to armadillos. Her shell didn't just have a touch of pink at the ridges of her bands, like most armadillos did that were considered pink in color. Princess was pink *all over*. Almost like she was a combination of a fairy and a nine-banded armadillo. I liked to think we had a lot in common with our mixture of cultures and our names—because of my love for everything pink, Daddy named her after me when he found her as a baby.

I unlocked the door and she scurried in ahead of me, running straight for her bowl in the back storeroom. I followed her and smiled as I emptied the bag of mealworms into the pink ceramic bowl the two of us had made the previous week. Most people wouldn't understand how an armadillo could help make a bowl, but Princess was the one who had the inspiration for it. She'd chosen the design by chewing up a Jan Fearnley's children's book, *Milo Armadillo,* and forced me to turn what was left into a piece of book art instead of reading material. The inside of the bowl had the cover art depicting a pink armadillo with a backpack. Princess had conveniently chewed Milo's name out of the title, so no title graced the bowl. Instead, it was as if Princess got to look in the mirror and see a caricature of herself every time she ate, while the script chased around her image on the outside of the bowl.

I placed the food on the floor and she scurried to it, hoping for the best. The scent of the natural product, however, displeased Princess. She huffed, and I could have sworn her beady little eyes glared.

"Sorry, girl. You heard the vet. Cat food is bad for your health. From now on you're going organic."

I think she may have growled before she turned around and brushed through the pink velvet curtain that closed off our storeroom.

"Suit yourself!" I called out to her. "But this is the only breakfast you're going to get. It will be waiting for you."

I left the bowl and got to work. A few moments later as I pulled out a box of books donated for our literacy drive, I heard the buzzer on the front door and then the swish of the doors opening and knew Princess was on a rampage. I cringed. She was probably going to wreak havoc on the neighbor's garden for breakfast.

Thankfully, the morning went by quickly, but my thoughts were still focused on Isla Sperry being trapped in the clutches of Alzheimer's. I'd known Isla since I was eight years old. Even when I moved away to Colorado at seventeen, Isla had tracked me down. She'd sent me birthday cards every year and graduation cards when I graduated from high school and then college. When I returned to Hazel Rock, she was still a regular customer at the Barn until she'd fallen and broken her hip. At that time, she moved to a long-term care facility, and I'd only visited her a few times. Each time she greeted me with a smile and a kiss. Looking back, I realized I should have questioned the times when she appeared confused. I had no idea Alzheimer's had been the cause; I'd thought it was the pain medication she'd been given, coupled with fatigue, that had caused her lapses. Our conversations were warm, and she'd always seemed coherent, even if some of our topics of conversation were repeated a couple of times.

This morning's news, however, was a game changer. I needed to see her before I went away for the weekend. Isla was the only grandmotherly figure I had in my life since both sets of mine had died before I was born. The little old lady who came into the Book Barn a couple times a week to see me as a child deserved better from me as an adult.

Daddy came in just before noon, and I'd already made up my mind. I needed to get out of the Barn for a couple hours. "I'm going to go out for lunch. Do you mind?"

Daddy looked up from the computer screen that he was using to log in to our new inventory program for books. "Are you meeting Scarlet?"

"No, I think I'll head into Oak Grove and pick up some barbecue."

"It's Wednesday, the diner is having barbecued ribs."

"I know, but I have another stop to make."

Dad got an all-knowing look in his eyes as he smiled and let out a puff of air through his nostrils. "I got it. You're meeting someone and you don't want me to know about it. Your love life is your business, Princess."

There was no doubt Daddy thought I was going to meet Mateo. My love life, however, had nothing to do with it. My guilt did. I wasn't sure why I was holding back where I planned to spend my afternoon from my dad, but for some reason, I felt the need to hide that I was going to see Isla.

It didn't seem to make sense. Over the past year my dad and I had buried many of our differences and misunderstandings, but some things we could not discuss. The Sperrys and our love lives were on top of that list.

I grabbed the stack of cozy mysteries I'd set aside for Isla and left the Barn without any further discussion. Since I'd returned home, I'd been using my daddy's old beat-up Ford pickup that bore more rust than paint. The heavy metal door squeaked something awful when I opened it and jumped up onto the worn vinyl. I winced as the day's heat burned through my clothing and slammed the door with a loud *thunk*. The truck's old seat was cracked and covered with duct tape, but it could still peel the skin right off the back of my thighs in the relentless Texas heat. The gas gauge didn't work and the windows cranked down manually, but somehow the truck seemed fitting while I was living in Texas.

On my way down the road I could smell the spring flowers in the air and I could hear the birds singing and the sound of children's laughter at the only daycare we had in town. The truck bounced and rattled its way across the bridge over the river as I headed into Oak Grove. The drive was about as uneventful as my typical Saturday night, and I made it to the long-term care facility in record time.

I parked in the small parking lot off the circular drive next to the entrance. I'd always thought the sprawling ranch looked a lot like the funeral home in Hazel Rock, and it creeped me out. The similarities always made me think about moving from one place to the next, and I wasn't sure how the residents could stand it. Then again, maybe it gave them comfort—their surroundings wouldn't change much.

I approached the entrance feeling like I was one step away from death's door, especially when I got a closer look at the man to the left of the doors, sitting in a wheelchair under the covered porch, his chin resting against his chest. His skin clung to the bones on his hands and face with no meat between his skeleton and the pale covering that looked like it hadn't seen the sun in a century, despite the fact that the man was sitting outside. He was wrapped in a blanket while wearing a coat, and I felt the need to sweat for him in the warm breeze. The soft snoring sounds he made were the only indication he was still breathing. I walked by quietly, trying to be respectful and not disturb his sleep as I entered the front door. Off to my right was the reception desk where a skinny woman I guessed to be in her late forties was laughing and talking to three elderly gentlemen sitting against the wall in chairs lined up like they were ready to go into a doctor's office. On the opposite side of the foyer, an elderly couple sat holding hands across the armrests of their chairs. They were staring straight ahead in silence, as if somehow, they could see a better view than the white tile floors and beige walls the facility afforded. I imagined them looking across the shadowed elevations as the setting sun painted a spectacular view of the Texas Hill Country at dusk. I liked that view better as well.

I said hello to the couple who nodded in my direction as one, then I turned to the woman at the reception desk. She had kind eyes and a weathered face that I suspected made her look older than what she actually was. Her thin brown hair stopped at her chin in a blunt bob hairstyle. The name tag on her shirt read *Joan*.

"Can I help you?" she asked.

Guilt washed over me. If I was a regular she would've recognized me, but she didn't. "I'm here to see Isla Sperry," I said.

"Is she expecting you?"

"No. Should I have called?"

She quickly smiled to ease my uncertainty. "Of course not. We love surprise visits. I'll just call her room for you."

One of the men sitting in the chairs next to us pulled himself to his feet, his joints creaking with the movement. "I'd be happy to get Isla for you. Just give me a minute and I'll bring her back." Shoulders straightened as far as nature would allow, the gentleman disappeared down the hallway to my right. The sound of his whistling a military hymn grew softer as he progressed.

"Are you related to Mrs. Sperry?" Joan asked.

I shook my head. "No, she's just a good friend, but she was like a grandmother to me when I was growing up."

"I would have sworn you were related. You have her eyes . . ." She scanned my face further before saying, "And her chin."

The fact that Joan could see similarities in our features said something about the woman behind the desk. Even though I rarely ran across racial issues in Hazel Rock, my darker skin tone tended to differentiate me from the rest of Hazel Rock. Going outside my small hometown, however, was hit or miss with my biracial ethnicity. I glanced at the men sitting against the wall, and they nodded in agreement with Joan.

"You know what they say about husbands and wives gaining similar features as they age. Maybe the same can be said about grandma figures." I looked at the men. "And grandfathers."

The older of the two snorted. "God forbid anyone takes on Frank's nose."

I couldn't help but look at the man sitting next to him. Frank's nose was large and bulbous. Not a nose I would want to inherit, but it had a certain amount of character that looked good on Frank.

Frank laughed, loud and deep from his round belly. "Child, if you got my nose, I'd pay for the plastic surgery."

I instantly loved Frank and winked at him. "I'd be honored to have half your nose."

"If you had half his nose, you'd need collagen injections just so people could see your lips."

Frank elbowed his partner, and Joan and I laughed.

"Those are two of my three amigos," she said. "Hopefully, the third can find his way back to the lobby with Isla."

Since things were going so well, I decided to break every HIPAA rule in the book and see what I could find out about Isla's current condition. "How has Isla been doing this week? Is her memory still slipping from time to time?"

"This week has been particularly difficult for Isla. Tomorrow is her birthday, you know." She looked at my hands like my shopping bag full of books wasn't quite wrapped well enough for a present. And it wasn't, because I'd had no idea when Isla's birthday was. Another sign of my self-centeredness. I'd never thought to remember her birthday like she had mine. Even for my thirtieth birthday, she'd sent a birthday card and written a wonderful note about my mom despite having only known my mom a couple years before she died when I was a child.

"I can't come by tomorrow, but you can be sure, there will be a delivery for her in the afternoon."

Joan's smile slipped from genuinely friendly to merely polite. She didn't like me staying away on Isla's birthday, but I'd had a date scheduled for months. There was no way I could cancel now.

"We'll put on a show for Isla." The two men sitting against the wall bumped elbows and winked at each other, a little snicker passing between them.

"I don't think the Judge would approve of the type of show you two would want to put on," Joan warned.

Frank rubbed his nose with the back of his hand. "Aw, the heck with old Sperry. The starch in his robes cut off the blood circulation to his brain years ago."

I couldn't help but laugh. Judge Sperry had enough starch in his robes to keep his body standing up straight long after the man died.

Joan shook her head as if she were tolerating the antics of a bunch of three-year-olds. "You leave Isla and the Judge alone, or you'll have me to answer to."

"Sometimes I think he's starched your shirt as well, Joan."

I thought that comment might irritate Joan, but she smiled and laughed as Isla entered the foyer on the arm of the gray-haired gentleman who had gone to retrieve her.

At five foot two inches tall, Isla Sperry was a force to be reckoned with, or at least I'd always thought she was. Standing next to the third amigo, however, she seemed slightly lost and confused. Her smile wasn't quite as bright as the last time I'd seen her. Her gray hair was pulled back in the ponytail she always wore but seemed messier than usual. Strands of hair hung loose at her neck, and the ponytail was off-center.

She'd never been a fancy woman, but she'd always been put together perfectly. Today, as she walked in leaning heavily on her cane, she was a completely different person. When she released the man's arm, she immediately began fidgeting with her button-up blouse that was slightly wrinkled, while her khaki capris hitched up on one side. Instead of her everyday bright white sneakers, Isla was wearing slippers.

Maybe if I hadn't been looking, I wouldn't have noticed the difference in her appearance, but today I was aware of the changes. And it hurt.

I smiled through the pain and walked over to hug the only grandmother I'd ever known. We may not have been blood, but she was still very dear to me.

"I can't believe I warrant two visits in one day," Isla said as she pulled back and gazed into my eyes.

"Two?" I asked.

Isla smiled. "Your father was here this morning."

"Really? I had no idea."

"I think that's the way Bobby Ray likes it." Isla nodded to the man who walked her from her room before grabbing hold of my arm. "Would you like to walk in the gardens?"

"That sounds like the perfect place to show you the books I brought today." Luckily for me, it was breezy enough that the heat wouldn't bother me, because the odors from inside were beginning to wreak havoc with my mind. Cleaners mixing with a hint of urine had to be the worst kind of reminder of our mortality.

Isla and I made our way to the rear of the residence, passing by a room with a handful of white-haired people playing bingo. A few seemed to enjoy it, while the others appeared to be passing the time minute by minute, hour by hour.

Isla squeezed my arm. "It's not as bad as you might think." I tried to hide my skepticism, but she saw right through my blank expression. "Really, it's not that bad. As you age, your sense of smell deteriorates. Your eyesight isn't as sharp, and your mind . . . well, I think everyone knows what's happening to mine."

It was my turn to see right through Isla's attempt to minimize her condition. There was fear in her eyes, and I wasn't sure how anyone could accept the knowledge that everything was slipping away while their body remained healthy. "You have one of the sharpest minds I've ever known," I said. Isla smiled up at me, and I changed the subject before she could argue. "What was Bobby Ray doing here?"

"Your father comes to see me a couple of times a week. He's a good boy. I couldn't ask for a better one."

I tried to hide my shock and failed. I covered with bland conversation. "A couple times a week? I had no idea you guys were that close."

"When you left town, your daddy needed family. I knew what it was like to lose a child. I didn't want him to think he was alone. At first, he resisted all my attempts, but on one particularly hard day, he broke down in my arms."

We walked through the garden to our normal spot under the large cottonwood tree at the back of the garden and sat down on the bench. I wasn't sure what to think of this conversation. The raw emotion in her voice caused tears to well in my eyes. Was it real? Or was it a figment of Isla's deteriorating mind? Accepting that I'd caused my daddy so much pain he'd turned to a virtual stranger for support was like breaking a bronco—my emotions went on a wild ride that I wasn't particularly fond of. Running away at seventeen was one of the worst things I'd ever done. But I'd landed on my feet thanks to my destination at my aunt Violet's house in Colorado. She'd finish raising me when I shut my dad out of my life over mistakes neither one of us could take back.

I'd been lucky to get the second chance at a relationship with him. Looking back was the last thing either one of us needed to do.

"He never told me the two of you were close," I confessed.

"There's a lot of things Bobby Ray hasn't told you."

Before I could ask her what she meant, Isla asked, "What brings you to Oak Grove Manor today?"

I set the bag of books on my lap and smiled. "I know tomorrow is a special day, but I'll be out of town for the weekend and I wanted to make sure I wished you a happy birthday."

The wrinkles on her forehead drew together. "Tomorrow's my birthday?"

Talking to Isla had always come easy. Today, it was hard and stilted. We seemed to be on very different wavelengths. "I saw Ava this morning. She told me tomorrow was your birthday." I lied. The last thing Isla needed to hear was that I'd just learned about her birthday from a virtual stranger.

"Ava? Do you mean Ava James?" she asked.

"Yeah. You know, the Judge's clerk?" Confusion passed over her face. Maybe now was the time to find out if my dad ever talked about Ava. Part of me wanted to know I wasn't the only one in the dark about the relationship; the other part hoped Isla had some information to share on the topic and our conversation would go back to the way it'd always been. "I ran into her at Dad's house this morning."

"They weren't fighting, were they?" she asked.

Confused, I shook my head.

"I'm so glad the two of them are getting along. Your daddy was always jealous of Ava James."

"Jealous?" That was the last thing I expected Isla to say. What could possibly cause my daddy to be jealous of Ava? Biting my lip, I waited for Isla to fill in the silence. I watched as she picked a flower and twirled it between her thumb and forefinger.

"Bobby Ray didn't understand the Judge's relationship with Ava. It bothered him more than you can possibly know." Isla's gaze snapped from the flowers to my face. A look of pure panic widened her eyes and caused her jaw to drop open. I squeezed her hand, unsure of what caused her agitation but eager to make her feel at ease.

"Are you okay?"

Isla dropped her head and began rubbing my hand with both of hers as if she was afraid I'd pull it away. "I think I did something horrible this morning," she whispered.

Before I could ask why she believed that, footsteps crunched against the pebbled path leading to the bench. Mason Andrews, the director of the retirement home, appeared from the other side of a red-china rose bush, his face flushed with both concern and relief as he took in Ava. Like me, the tall slender man in his late thirties with thinning hair and slightly droopy eyes noticed Ava's unkempt hair. He catalogued the wrinkles in her shirt and slacks then focused on the way she desperately wrung my hand. Isla glanced at him, but her gaze immediately shot to the ground in what looked like a combination of shame and embarrassment.

Mr. Andrews spared me no more than a curt nod before he squatted down in front of Isla and peered up into her down-turned face.

"Are you okay, Isla?"

Isla nodded.

"I'm sorry I wasn't here for you. I should have been here," Mr. Andrews said.

"Is it true?" Isla asked, her voice barely a whisper.

I wasn't sure what was going on, but I knew better than to interject. Mr. Andrews cared for Isla; that was obvious. I also knew she had a soft spot for Mr. Andrews, who'd always treated her with kind regard in my presence during the few visits I'd made.

Mr. Andrews nodded, then reached up and wiped the tear from her cheek. "When I came to work this morning, you weren't in your room. I came outside thinking you were in the garden, but you weren't here either. I called the police, and they said they'd look for you, but . . ."

Isla gave a faint, wry smile, then released my hand. "I think they found me."

Mr. Andrews chuckled and I got the distinct impression he was trying to lighten the mood. "The way I hear it, you found them."

I couldn't hold my tongue any longer. "What happened?"

Mason smiled apologetically in my direction. "Isla decided she had something to tell the Judge this morning that couldn't wait."

Isla nodded in agreement. "It couldn't."

"She took off on her own without checking out at the front desk." Mr. Andrews turned to Isla. "You had all of us scared half to death."

Isla's cheeks pinked as she waved her hand in dismissal. "Nonsense. The courthouse is just a few blocks away, and that nice officer brought me back."

"You walked to the courthouse with your bad hip?" My disapproval may have seeped into my tone.

Isla sat up straight and threw back her shoulders with pride. "I reckon I did, and I gave them all a piece of my mind when I got there . . . including that cheating husband of mine and that tart, Ava James."

Chapter Three

The front doors to the Book Barn Princess swished open on their automatic tracks, but the little buzzer didn't ding as my best friend came running into the store. If Scarlet wasn't so frantic I might worry about the stupid doors being on the fritz again. Instead, I focused on the high pitch of her voice as she yelled, "Bobby Ray's in trouble!"

I slammed the register drawer closed and came out from behind the counter. "What kind of trouble?"

"I don't know," Scarlet panted. Barely over five foot, Scarlet had the kind of body I dreamed about as a teenager—all curvy and luscious—the kind high school boys got tongue-tied over. Except in high school, Scarlet was a book nerd with glasses and dull brown hair who wore oversized T-shirts. Absolutely nothing like the ginger bombshell who was now grabbing my arm and pulling me toward the door.

"Where is he?" I asked as I dug my store keys out of my pocket.

Scarlet barely slowed down for me to set the alarm. "I got a call from Daisy. She said you weren't answering your phone."

"I left it in my apartment."

That earned an eye roll from Scarlet. "You need to carry your phone with you, Charli."

"Hello? I'm working at the Barn. We have a phone. Why didn't either one of you call me here?"

"Daisy was a little flustered, and I thought it was better I came to get you in person."

Scarlet was one of those people who talked a hundred miles an hour. I couldn't stop her, couldn't make her yield to get a comment in edgewise, nor could anyone else. In the past, I'd wondered if she would ever turn off her nonstop dialogue that covered topics ranging from gossip to fashion to politics to scientific studies about beauty products. Apparently, tonight was the night. And it kind of scared me. "Scarlet, what's going on?"

Scarlet paused and turned to face me. "I'm going to tell you something, but I don't want you to freak out."

"You're already freaking me out. Just tell me."

Scarlet's words poured out of her. "Bobby Ray is over at the Judge's house, and there's a body on the ground."

When my eyes nearly bugged out of my head, Scarlet rushed to tell me the rest. Her voice, however, was muffled by overflow of blood pumping through my veins.

"I don't know who it is. No one does. But Daisy said it's definitely a body lying under a yellow police blanket."

My hand shook from adrenaline as the wind blew my hair in my face and made locking the Barn door that more difficult. By the time I had the store secure, Scarlet had the single front door to her little BMW Isetta open and we hopped inside. I slammed the door harder than I meant to and immediately apologized. "Sorry."

"Don't be." She grabbed my seat belt and buckled me in before putting on her own and starting the car. I don't know if it was the buzz of her little engine or the word *police* reverberating through my head that woke me out of my temporary shock, but I had to know if the sheriff was on the scene. "Is Mateo there?"

"That's what Daisy said."

I nodded but was immediately distracted with thoughts of the conversation I'd had with Isla earlier in the day. Isla was close to my daddy, but Isla had accused the woman I'd seen leaving my father's house that morning of having an affair with her husband, the Judge. The woman my daddy was interested in, was also apparently the other woman in Isla and the Judge's marriage. And Daddy and I had a mutual hatred for Judge Sperry—the old man who'd been the town sheriff when I was a kid. The same sheriff who was present every single time I made a mistake in my youth. He'd put handcuffs on me once, taken me to jail, and put the fear of God in me as he spouted numerous verses from the Bible. My daddy never took kindly to the Judge preaching to his daughter.

No one could anger my daddy the way Judge Sperry did.

I sent a prayer up into the universe, hoping God was more forgiving than vengeful. *Please don't let the Judge be dead at the hand of my father.*

Scarlett drove the ten blocks to the Judge's house, taking the corners faster than I thought her car could handle. It seemed every turn was made with divine intervention. As we approached Tenth Street, the strobe of emergency lights bounced off the houses throughout the neighborhood. People lined both sides of the street. Huddled against the increasing strength of the spring breeze, they peered toward the crime scene and talked to their neighbors.

Access to Tenth Street was blocked off two houses away from the Judge's by a patrol car parked at an angle. I could see another patrol car at the opposite end of the block, barricading the entrance to the street at the intersection. A white van marked *CSU* was parked across from the Judge's house in the midst of the area the police had marked off as their crime scene. The back doors were flung open and two crime scene techs were digging in bags in the back of the vehicle. Three uniformed officers stood guard at different sections of bright yellow tape that seemed to encompass a large amount of the normally quiet neighborhood.

An unmarked black Dodge Charger police cruiser was parked on our side of the *POLICE LINE DO NOT CROSS* tape. I scanned the scene looking for a familiar face, but it wasn't the sheriff's face that turned my already flopping stomach. It was the long lump covered with a yellow blanket that I spotted on the manicured front lawn in front of the Judge's house, and I prayed it wasn't anyone I knew.

As if my prayers were answered by a warped universe, I saw him. Dressed only in a dark colored robe with his gray hair unkempt, Judge Sperry was kneeling on the grass in front of his house, his face a mask of grief. I shouldn't have felt an overwhelming sense of relief when I saw the old man, but I did, because it meant my worst fear hadn't come true. Daddy hadn't taken out years of pent-up anger and killed the man. No, my daddy stood a few feet away talking with the current sheriff and owner of the Dodge Charger, Mateo Espinosa.

Who was lying dead in the grass?

Scarlet double-parked her car and turned off the ignition, effectively forcing me out of my frozen state.

"You can't park here," I told her.

Scarlet rolled her eyes and opened the door. "That cop guarding the crime scene tape closest to us is Sally Ferguson. She's got an appointment in the salon tomorrow morning. I don't think she'd like her blond locks turned green."

My head snapped back toward Scarlet as she pushed me out of her car. "You wouldn't."

Scarlet pulled herself out of her vintage car and closed the door. Dressed in a long-sleeved blue floral print pencil dress, she looked as amazing at nine o'clock p.m. as she had when she opened up her Beaus and Beauties hair salon at seven o'clock that morning. She was still wearing her five-inch heels that made my feet hurt just looking at them. I was also envious of her perfect ginger-colored hair that didn't block her view on a windy day like the mass of curls I brushed off my face for the third time since we'd exited the vehicle. My attempts to keep my curls from obstructing my view were fruitless.

"Of course, I wouldn't, but she doesn't need to know that. Besides, no one is leaving this street anytime soon."

I wanted to go to my dad, but he was busy with Mateo and hadn't seen us arrive. We approached Daisy and her husband Jessie by walking through a couple front yards. We reached their position in the middle of their driveway in a matter of minutes. The older couple was holding hands like teenagers until Daisy saw us approach.

"Young lady, I've been trying to call you for the past thirty minutes," Daisy scolded.

"I'm sorry. I left my phone in my apartment."

Jessie came up and put his arm around my shoulder. "Don't give the girl a hard time, Daisy. Can't you see she's worried half to death?" Jessie winced as soon as the word left his mouth, and Daisy pushed him away to wrap me in a tight embrace.

"That's my husband," she whispered in my ear, and a lock of her gray hair blew across my face, hiding my view of my father on the other side of the holly hedge that divided the Mahans' yard from the Judge's. A tall metal arbor stood in the middle of the long row of bushes allowing access between the yards. A yellow piece of crime scene tape, however, blocked our entrance. "Everything is going to be okay, Princess. Mateo will take care of your daddy."

The last thing I wanted was comfort. I needed answers . . . yesterday. I gently pushed her away.

"Do you know who died?" I asked. Deep in my gut I was hoping some stranger had just keeled over from a heart attack or an aneurysm or had tripped and broken his neck—anything was possible.

"No, dear. By the time we came out to see what the ruckus was all about, the officer had already covered the body."

Scarlet asked the question I was dying to hear the answer to, "Was Bobby Ray already here?"

"He was when we came outside," said Jessie.

"Nobody else?" I prayed there was someone else. Someone Daddy had cajoled into giving him the smoking gun. Someone he disarmed in hand-to-hand fisticuffs. Someone he'd taken out with his pocket knife a moment too late to save the person under the blanket . . . but then there'd be two bodies.

"The Judge was with him and they were arguing," Jessie explained.

I winced. That was the last thing I wanted to hear.

Daisy shook her head. "That's my husband, always stirring up the women."

If I could find some humor in this whole mess, I'd think Daisy's comment was funny . . . but I wasn't laughing. I was worried my daddy was in over his head. If he and the Judge had been working together to save whoever was under the blanket, it would look better for my daddy—the Judge too.

I grasped onto that. The two of them would never work together to kill someone, that much was certain. If my dad ended up being a suspect, that made the Judge just as big a suspect. Unless there was another witness. I gazed down the street lined with neighbors.

"We should go talk to people," I suggested to Scarlet.

She pointed at the two men in wrinkled suits standing directly across the street from the crime scene. They were taking notes on identical steno pads as they spoke to the residents, one at each end of the front porch. "I think the detectives are doing that now."

"That's them. This is us."

Jessie tried to stop my mission before it began. "Princess, I don't think your daddy—"

"Would want me to do anything? If I was over there standing next to a dead body, he'd have made his way through the crime scene tape to stand by my side no matter who stood in his way. I'm just going to ask a few questions."

I turned toward the street as a gust of wind rustled the trees and blew something through the arbor that flattened against my leg. I looked down to see a piece of paper wrapped around my shin like a pair of skinny jeans from the force of the wind. Grabbing it, I began to ball it up, until I saw dark splatter marks running across the face of what appeared to be a letter in the dim lighting.

"What's that?" asked Scarlet.

Something told me the piece of paper was important, but I couldn't make it out in shadowed driveway. "I have no idea. I can't really see it."

The four of us huddled together as Jessie lit up the piece of paper in my hands with his cell phone and a collective gasp passed through us. Dark crimson splatter marks covered the letter, which was addressed to the Judge.

"What's it say?" asked Jessie.

Daisy's voice seemed to echo through the neighborhood even though it was barely above a whisper. "Is that blood?"

"Read it, Charli," Scarlet urged.

I cleared my throat and looked around to see if anyone was watching, but everyone seemed to have their eyes and ears glued to the Judge's house. "Judge," I began to read, "I can't take this anymore. I'm causing you problems with Isla, and John Luke is demanding I choose between him and you. I'm so sorry to disappoint you. I know this is a bad time, you must feel like you're losing everyone, but please know you will always be in my heart. Ava."

"O.M.W. you don't think that's Ava under the . . . under the . . . you don't, do you?" asked Scarlet.

I looked up into her troubled eyes. "I don't know." I thought of the woman I'd caught making the walk of shame that morning from my daddy's front door. "Jessie, take a picture of this."

"What in tarnation for?"

"I . . . I . . ." What could I say? That my dad was having an affair with Ava and was mixed up in some kind of ugly triangle between the Judge and Ava?

"That's my husband." That was Daisy's favorite phrase. She used it to claim Jessie as hers and to tell other women to back off her man, to make fun of Jessie's actions, or to ridicule him no end. At the moment, I was pretty sure she was using it to shame him into doing as I asked. Especially when she pushed Jessie's hand that held his phone over the half-crumpled note from Ava and said, "Do as you're told and take the picture."

Jessie snapped the picture as we all huddled over the letter. The sound of a masculine throat being cleared outside our circle caused us to jump in unison at the intrusion.

"Charli Rae, please tell me you are not interfering with my homicide investigation." Normally, his voice warmed me from my core out. Today, Mateo's voice sent a shiver through my body . . . and it had nothing to do with chemistry.

Chapter Four

My investigation hadn't started as planned. Mateo was immediately irritated that I'd read his piece of evidence, and when I questioned how I could have known it was evidence in the case without reading it, he immediately warned me not to meddle.

"This case belongs to my detectives," he said. "Keep your nose out of it, Charli Rae."

Mateo never used my middle name unless he was irritated or being all sheriffy. By now, he should have known all that did was raise my dander—like I'd raised his. We stared each other down like a pair of prickly pears—heat rising to our necks and sharp barbs ready to be thrown if one of us said the wrong thing. Then he pulled out a pair of gloves from his back pocket and took his anger out by snapping them on his hands with a pointed glare in my direction before he took the letter.

"Where did you get this?" he asked.

"It smacked me in the leg."

When he looked at me dubiously, Scarlet backed me up. "All she did was bend down and pick it up. It must have blown through the arbor."

Everyone turned and looked through the arbor that linked the two yards.

"Did anyone see the letter before it hit Charli's leg?" Mateo's tone told all of us he didn't have time for games. Jessie buckled and started to confess our crime of photographing Mateo's evidence before turning it over.

"I—"

A pinch from Daisy on Jessie's backside kept her husband's mouth shut as he rubbed his rump and glared at his wife.

"Did you want to add something, Jessie?" Mateo asked.

"No, no. I just think it's a tragedy."

"Yes, it is. But we'll find who did this." Mateo turned back to his crime scene with his piece of evidence in hand.

Up until that point, I wasn't sure if he'd seen Jessie taking the photo of the letter before he'd walked up and scared the bejeezus out of all four of us. I had no doubt Jessie would have confessed if not for Daisy's warning, and I was happy she'd interfered. Yet if Mateo ever found out about the photo, he'd be more than prickly.

In my defense, I'd planned to turn over his precious piece of evidence as soon as I identified it as an important piece to the puzzle in the murder of Ava James. Granted, if I'd been alone when I found it, I probably would have held on to the letter for a little while longer. I was well aware that would have put a hitch in his chain of custody for that particular piece of evidence, but I was worried about my daddy. I still wasn't sure if he was a witness or a potential suspect. He wasn't in cuffs, which was a good sign, but he wasn't making any effort to walk across the lawn and come talk to me either.

Knowing that Mateo's loyalty was to the job—to the law and to justice—no matter what the cost, made me fidgety. My loyalty was to my daddy. Period. If that meant I had to clear his name, or God forbid, build his defense, then so be it. I would do what it took to take care of him. But there wasn't a smidgen of doubt in my mind about his innocence. We'd been down this road once before when his girlfriend had been killed a little over a year ago. Now he was facing a second murdered girlfriend. The man had to have the worst luck with love of anyone I'd ever known, and I was more than a little worried about him.

Watching Mateo walk away with the letter suddenly seemed unacceptable. I needed more information. I ducked under the yellow crime scene tape, ignoring its bold message, and took off after him.

"Mateo, wait!"

Sally Ferguson, the nearest uniformed deputy guarding the yellow tape border, made a quick turn in my direction, but Mateo stopped her by raising his hand. He didn't immediately turn and face me, and that little pause suggested he was bucking up for an argument. Or maybe he was contemplating all the different charges he could use to take me to jail. I followed his path across the lawn despite a feeling of doom creeping down my back. I had questions about my dad and figured Mateo would have to get over me crossing that line in the sand, even if it was plastic and yellow and flapping in the breeze with bold letters telling me not to cross it. I also knew he didn't like being hounded, but I *needed* answers.

He turned around with a heavy sigh and a pointed look at the crime scene tape.

"I need to know if you're holding my daddy for questioning."

"Why would I do that?"

Why indeed. "I don't know why. Tell me why he seems to be glued to the ground near the Judge."

"That's a question for him, not me."

His response threw me off guard. "You didn't tell him he had to stay over there?"

Mateo shook his head, and I looked past his shoulders to where my dad was awkwardly patting the Judge on the shoulder.

"Bobby Ray is a witness, Charli."

"Oh."

His lips thinned and flattened in an I-told-you-not-to-meddle expression.

Part of me still couldn't believe Daddy would willingly stay beside the Judge. "He's just a witness?"

Mateo nodded.

That was great news—except I felt like an anvil was going to drop out of the sky. I held the one bit of information tightly inside my chest that would change Mateo's perspective about Daddy's status in the case. If Mateo had seen Ava leaving Daddy's house that morning the way I did, he'd be questioning my dad a lot longer than he already had. And until the moment Mateo found out about the two of them, I really didn't want to talk to *Sheriff* Mateo. I could screw everything up with one slip of the tongue.

For now, as far as I could tell, I was the only one with that tidbit of news, and I didn't plan on sharing it with anyone anytime soon. Not until the real killer was behind bars.

The faster that happened, the better off my daddy would be and the sooner I wouldn't be holding back information in Mateo's case.

Which left the other man across the yard who was on his knees quoting scripture as the only possible suspect.

Yesterday I wouldn't have thought the Judge capable of murder. Today I wasn't so sure. Yet I had to acknowledge that my bias against the man could be building the case up in my mind against him. I didn't care for him. His wife seemed to think he was shacking up with Ava. And if I had to choose between my daddy or the Judge being suspect number one, hands down I'd say the Judge killed Ava James.

But I'd never seen an ounce of violence from him either. I would, however, characterize him as being under a lot of stress with his wife in a nursing home losing her memory of him and their life together, which could have caused him to turn to another woman for comfort.

I shivered at the thought that my daddy and the Judge could have been seeing the same woman. The age difference between my daddy and Ava made me cringe. The age difference between Ava and the Judge made me want to barf.

As hard as it was for me to picture, the Judge could have been looking for a comforting touch, and everyone knows that anyone can kill under the right circumstance. It remained to be seen, however, if these were the right circumstances to push the Judge over the edge.

Better people than Judge Sperry had buckled under less stress.

"If that is all?" Mateo's question wasn't really a question. It was more of a polite statement to bug off and get out of his crime scene.

I pushed anyway. "Is that Ava under the blanket?"

"You have five seconds to get out of my crime scene before I have Deputy Ferguson arrest you."

"But, is that—"

He pointed in the direction of the arbor.

He wasn't going to tell me a dadgum thing. When I hesitated a bit too long, Mateo grabbed my bicep and led me to the tape. "Good night, Charli Rae."

I swung around and was about to demand the victim's identity when my daddy looked up at me and said something to the Judge, and the two of them stared in my direction. It wasn't lost on me that they had to look over the top of the body to see me. I could hear the Judge spouting a verse. Not literally, as we were too far away to hear his actual words. But in my mind, his voice was loud with reverence for God. The man may not have known it, but I held the same respect for our creator. I just didn't preach it to others.

I held my biting retort for Mateo and nodded at both of them. My dad said a few parting words to the Judge and headed in my direction, passing Mateo on the way.

Looking older than his fifty-some years, my daddy stopped in front of me. I hugged him, swift and strong. "Are you okay?" I asked.

"I will be."

"Is that—" My voice cracked and I cleared my throat. "Is it Ava?"

Daddy took a deep breath and nodded but wouldn't meet my eyes. For a lean man who always held his head up high and spoke in a straightforward manner, he seemed completely out of his element. Quiet. Uncertain.

If you didn't know him, you might read shame into his expression. As it was, I wasn't sure what emotions he was feeling. There were no tears in his eyes. No waver in his voice. Just a clenching of his jaw as he looked around the neighborhood like he was seeing all of the bystanders for the first time.

"I'm sorry, Daddy." I guided him away from Daisy, Jessie, and Scarlet and lowered my voice. "I know how much she meant to you."

"You need to go home, Princess."

"I'll wait for you."

"My truck won't be released from the crime scene for quite some time. It seems I parked right in the middle of it without even knowing." My gaze followed his, and for the first time, I noticed the trail of blood crossing the sidewalk. Ava had apparently been attacked there and staggered onto the lawn before she died.

I forced away another shiver wanting to snake up my spine. "Scarlet can take you home," I offered. I had no doubt my best friend would take him home and then come back for me since all three of us wouldn't fit in her Isetta. Scarlet was that type of friend, the kind who would go into debt to bail you out of jail if you needed it—or drive you to a crime scene when someone you loved was in trouble.

A sad smile graced Daddy's face as he cupped my cheek with a weathered hand. "Jessie has already offered to give me a ride. Go home. There's nothing you can do here."

"But—"

His head shook and I knew there was no point in arguing. "Go home, Princess."

I leaned into his palm and clasped it against my face. "I love you, Daddy. I'm here for you . . . no matter what."

"I know. Now go." He turned me toward my best friend with a gentle push. "Scarlet, I'd appreciate it if you'd take Princess home. It's been a long, hard day."

"Anything you say, Bobby Ray."

"Jessie, I'll take you up on that ride in just a few moments."

Jessie nodded and my daddy headed back across the crime scene, making a wide detour around Ava's body and the path of blood we couldn't see from the sidewalk to her final resting place.

I made note of who was standing around the crime scene tape so I could contact them later. One face caused me to stumble as we approached Scarlet's little white two-seater.

"Are you okay?" she asked.

I waved her off. "Yeah, I'm fine."

But I wasn't, because on the opposite end of Tenth Street stood the town mayor, Cade Calloway, my old high school sweetheart. Tall, commanding, and Texas tough, Cade always made my heart skitter when I saw him. Tonight, however, it was the man standing next to him who sent my heart into overdrive. Not as tall by any means, and more on the plump side than muscular, his hands were on his hips as he bent over and breathed heavily. Gauging from the running shorts, clinging T-shirt, and wet tendrils of hair falling out of his man bun, I suspected he'd been out for his second run of the day on his quest to lose weight.

My chest tightened with unease at seeing him—here with Ava and my daddy—because Mike Thompson was the only other person who could place Ava James at my daddy's house that morning.

Chapter Five

I spent a fitful night tossing and turning while images of Ava, bloodied and battered, walking out of my daddy's house, haunted my dreams. I woke up with Princess curled on the pillow next to me. Her eyes opened slowly as if she sensed me watching her. We stared at each other for a bit and then she yawned.

"You have terrible morning breath."

She snorted as if to say it was my fault for making her eat grubs last night for dinner, then closed her eyes and went back to sleep. I was definitely going to need a new pillow. I probably went through more pillows than the bed-and-breakfast in town.

It wasn't that I didn't love my pet armadillo; I loved her dearly, but I really didn't want to share a pillow with her. There were some things not made for armadillos. My bed was one of them.

I pulled off the covers and stumbled into the bathroom for a long, hot shower. As good as it felt, it didn't erase my unease. I finished my shower, got dressed, and texted my dad.

Ru okay?

It didn't take long for him to respond. *I'm fine. I'll be at the store a little late this morning, but I'll be there in plenty of time for you to leave on your trip.*

My trip. I'd completely forgotten about my trip. I'd gotten a mani-pedi on Wednesday for my first romantic weekend in ages. It'd been so long, I wasn't sure I remembered the last one. Not that I had a ton of them, but this one was supposed to be special. For my birthday, Mateo had given me a pair of tickets to see the Tony Bennett concert in Dallas. He'd told me I could ask anyone I wanted to go with me to the concert since the drive meant at least one night in the Big D, and I'd finally gotten the nerve to ask him to go with me. Since then, he'd confessed if I'd asked anyone else other than Scarlet, he might have arrested the guy for jaywalking every day just to make sure he'd have a warrant or he'd have to figure out another charge when it came time for us to leave for the concert.

I was pretty sure he'd been joking.

But now it felt like a weekend getaway was impossible. Not only did I have people to talk to, Mateo didn't exactly seem like he wanted to go anywhere with me last night. I sighed and gazed at the suitcase sitting in my living room. I'd packed in the beginning of the week, anxious to really identify this thing between us as a relationship.

As if reading my mind, my phone rang with his special ringtone about bad boys.

"Hello?"

"Hey. How'd you sleep?"

"Probably better than you."

He chuckled. That was a good sign. "Listen, about tonight . . ."

That was a bad sign.

"Can we postpone our weekend?" He didn't wait for me to balk. "This case has us pretty busy and—"

I didn't give him time to explain further. "I understand."

"You do?"

"Of course I do." I didn't, but my defensive walls were building. "I should have given you the opportunity to back out last night. I'll let you get to it." I started to hang up, but his voice stopped me.

"Wait, Charli! I'm not backing out."

"You're not?"

"No. I'm asking if we can leave tomorrow morning instead."

"Oh."

"Did you think you were going to get rid of me that easily?"

"If I'd asked last night, if we were still on for the weekend, would you have said yes?" I asked.

"*Querida*, it will take more than a little of your meddling to chase me away."

I wasn't sure what to say to that. I was pretty sure I should be insulted about the meddling comment, but Mateo calling me "darling" was throwing me off my game. We hadn't graduated to terms of endearment yet, and I wasn't quite sure if *querida* was a word you could use for a grandmother, a niece, or someone you were about to spend the weekend with. Then again, it could be the same as a cowboy using the term "darlin'" for every woman he came across that wasn't his real sweetheart.

I decided to ignore it and test different waters. "Do you have any leads in Ava's case?"

His sigh was enough to tell me he wished I'd taken the conversation in the other direction. "Charli, this is a police investigation. Please stay out of it."

I pushed. It's what I did best. "So, my daddy's just a witness, nothing more?"

"Is there a reason I should look for him to be something more?"

"Don't be ridiculous."

"That wasn't an answer."

"That's because your question was absurd." Seriously, did he think I would narc on my own dad?

"I thought we'd gotten to a point of trusting each other."

I thought about that for a moment too long.

"I guess I was wrong," he said. His disappointment hung in the air like a typical Texas storm. Building. Darkening. Turning into something larger than it should have been. Any second as the silence grew between us it could explode into a massive storm or dissipate into nothing. I prayed for nothing. Mateo was the one to finally break the dead air.

"I'll call you later this evening."

"Okay."

My heart wanted to skip down Main Street while my brain tried to decide if I was happy or scared witless about the weekend, or if it was the case that had me tied in knots. My body chose to work through it and ignore both organs. It was for the best.

I made my way through the secret door in the second bedroom of my apartment above the Barn. It used to be my parents' room when I was a kid; now it was a guest room that my cousin used when he came in town for business or a visit. He'd developed a book app that featured our bookstore and had increased our online sales tremendously.

I made my way downstairs and unlocked the doors for a couple that stood waiting at the front door for the store to open. When I asked if they were looking for anything specific, they advised they wanted to look at our used book section and I directed them toward the loft. Then I started brewing sweet tea for the tearoom we had in the store. It wasn't anything fancy, just rustic charm with country lace draping small tables in the largest stall on the lower level of the Book Barn Princess. I normally bought treats from Franz at the bakery across the street, but today I went with peanut brittle and chocolate turtles; comfort foods I thought everyone would need.

I grabbed a turtle and took a bite, savoring the flavors of caramel-covered pecans smothered in rich milk chocolate.

I'd chosen well.

The door buzzed and I stuck my head out of the stall to greet my customer. Scarlet strolled in looking like a fresh spring day in Texas. Her auburn hair was curled and bouncy and accentuated her bare shoulders. She wore a blue peasant dress with a very short hemline. Her stilettos almost brought her up to my eye level and displayed an expanse of shapely legs.

"I love that T-shirt!" she exclaimed with her ever-present grin.

Leave it to Scarlet to compliment a stone-washed pink T-shirt screen-printed with *Lit happens at the #BookBarn* across my chest, while she looked like a million bucks.

I smiled and told her the truth. "You look gorgeous."

Scarlet's laughter carried through the Barn like a song. "Some of us have to work at it, while others can get away with murder."

"It seems murder is on everyone's mind," I mumbled over another bite.

Scarlet's mood turned somber. "As it should be. We lost a very good woman last night. That's what I came to talk to you about." Scarlet moved closer and looked around the Barn.

I nodded toward the loft. "There's a couple customers upstairs, but so far that's it."

She pulled me back into the tearoom. I wasn't sure it was necessary. For the past ten minutes, the elderly couple upstairs had been arguing over which book was a more important depiction of American history, Margaret Mitchell's *Gone with the Wind* or F. Scott Fitzgerald's *The Great Gatsby*. Each had valid points, but the one argument they were missing was the authors' lack of perspective from the African American characters in both stories. That was a true reflection on our history that would have given both of them points in their column if they'd recognized the flaw, but they hadn't. Which one would receive more points was a matter of perspective.

"Reba Sue came in to get her nails done today."

I really didn't care to hear what Reba Sue was doing. She was probably getting dolled up for a weekend with Cade Calloway. The mayor, my ex, and the man whom I decided not to wait around for despite the chemistry between us. I still wasn't quite over him, but I'd moved forward with my life and had taken Mateo up on his offer—an offer he was probably second-guessing.

"Reba Sue is in there all the time," I said.

Scarlet looked over her shoulder and lowered her voice. "Yeah, but today she started talking about Ava's murder and how Isla came into court yesterday morning."

"Isla was in court? For what?" I thought about the conversation at the Oak Grove care facility the previous day.

"Isla accused the Judge of cheating on her."

"I heard the rumors," I acknowledged. Everyone had heard the rumors.

"Yeah, but Isla threatened to cut Ava's throat if she ever caught her sneaking into her home."

The pressure on my chest threatened to push my heart out the backside of my rib cage. I had to force the air through my lungs in order to get my question out. "Is that how Ava was killed?"

Scarlet shrugged. "No one is saying a word. It's the best-kept secret in town."

Not for long. I was determined to find out the truth. "Was Ava in court?"

"Nope. Reba Sue said she was a no-show for work yesterday."

"How would Reba Sue know if Ava was a no-show, or if she was sick, or on vacation, or just took the day off?"

Scarlett shrugged, then saw the tremor in my hands as I placed napkins out next to the tray of treats. "Are you okay?"

"I'm fine." I grabbed another turtle. This was a two-turtle day if I ever had one. "Want one?" I held out the tray, but Scarlet declined. "What was Reba Sue doing in court?"

"You don't know?" Scarlet's eyes grew wide when I shook my head. She grabbed a turtle and shoved the whole thing in her mouth. I suppose her disbelief was an appropriate response since gossip spreads through Hazel Rock faster than any wildfire ever could. Her hesitation to spill everything she knew combined with her eating a sweet she never went near had me more discombobulated than ever.

I stopped mid-bite. My curiosity was exploding through the barn roof. I knew my next question put me in the category of too stupid to live, but I asked it anyway. "What'd she do, Scarlet?"

Scarlet continued to chew, her mouth so full of delicious goodness she could barely keep her lips sealed. She couldn't possibly be enjoying the rare treat in her attempt to avoid my question. I handed her a napkin and she closed her eyes like she was going to choke as she tried to get it down. After a moment, it was clear she was trying to think of a way not to answer, and my hand went on my hip. It wasn't like Scarlet to keep things from me.

She glanced up at my jutted-out hip and impatient stare. "Cade will have to tell you," she responded through her napkin.

"I'm not going to ask Cade! We're barely talking."

She swallowed hard. "It's not my story to tell. Can I get some tea?"

I retrieved a glass and filled it with ice before pouring the freshly brewed sweet tea. "It's somebody's story to tell, and if I can't ask my best friend, who can I ask?"

"You need to talk to Cade. Not me."

I huffed. I couldn't believe Scarlet was protecting Reba Sue. "Fine. I'll ask Mateo." If Reba Sue had been arrested, it was public record. Mateo might not give me the details, but he'd tell me what Reba Sue had been charged with and how Cade was involved.

"I wouldn't do that if I were you," Scarlet warned.

"Why not?"

I watched as my best friend took a drink of tea like it was liquid courage before she answered. "I don't think Mateo would appreciate your interest in what happens between Reba Sue and Cade."

My mind immediately went to the two of them being caught in a compromising position in a public place. Maybe I didn't want to know. The images popping in my head were turning my stomach.

"Forget it. I don't want to know."

Scarlet nodded and finished her tea. "I think I'll be skipping lunch today."

I rolled my eyes. "It was one turtle, it won't put an ounce of fat on you."

"It had more than enough calories to get me through to late afternoon." She glanced at the time on her phone. "I've got an appointment in five minutes. I just thought you should know about Isla. What time are you leaving tonight?" she asked as she headed toward the front door.

"We're not."

She stopped and turned around. "What? Mateo couldn't have been that upset about last night."

I shook my head. "No, he needs to stay to work the case. We're leaving tomorrow morning."

"Forget about everyone else and enjoy your weekend. You deserve it."

There was one problem with her advice. My daddy and Isla were still in the hot seat, and I wasn't about to go off gallivanting with Mateo while either one of them got branded a murderer.

Chapter Six

My daddy came in a few minutes after Scarlet left and had been at the Barn for an hour but hadn't said a word beyond "Hello." When I asked if he'd slept in, he grunted something about being up at the crack of dawn fishing down by the river and then went to work sorting boxes of books for the literacy drive. I wasn't sure if his mind was elsewhere, if he just didn't want to talk to me, or if he was afraid I'd bring up the topic of conversation he didn't want to discuss.

All morning long we received boxes of books from the local businesses that had been collecting for the literacy drive. It seemed everyone who came by wanted to do something for Ava but didn't know how. Their gifts and the work it brought took away some of the pressure between my daddy and me, but sooner or later, we were going to have to discuss how we were going to proceed with the drive. Without Ava, we would have to establish new connections with the Department of Family and Protective Services.

"Do you want me to call to find out how to proceed with the drop-off of the books?" I asked.

My dad stood up from the box he was unpacking. He winced as he stretched with his hands on his lower back. "If you wouldn't mind, I'd really appreciate it."

"Do you know who she was working with?"

"No. Ava said she'd handle it, and I knew she had a contact. I thought we would meet when we dropped off the books."

I nodded sympathetically, even though I wanted to roll my eyes. This was why the Barn had almost gone under before I'd returned to Hazel Rock. My daddy gave and gave but didn't keep records for tax time. "I'll make some calls and see what I can do."

"Aren't you supposed to leave in a couple hours?"

I paused before answering. I was probably going to end up with the man with red horns downstairs for lying, but I needed time to see what I could find out about Ava's case. Mateo wasn't talking. Daddy certainly wasn't going to open his mouth, and suddenly I wasn't sure Scarlet was going to give me all the answers I needed either.

"We're leaving a little later than we expected. Probably tomorrow morning."

Daddy nodded and turned back to his box. "I was thinking about having a candlelight vigil for Ava tonight."

"Oh." Fuzz buckets. I should have thought of that.

"I've had them before."

"You have?" I asked.

"We had one a few years ago for Marilyn Scott when she died of cancer and one about ten years ago for Kathy Buttrum when she died in a traffic accident."

My heart nearly broke for the man in front of me who had lost so much and still gave back. My voice cracked as I walked up and hugged him from behind. "That was very nice of you, Daddy. You have a heart of gold."

He patted my hands wrapped around his chest. "I know what you're thinking, Princess. You've got it all wrong." He took a deep breath, and I got the distinct impression he felt compelled to tell me everything. I let him off the hook. The last thing I wanted between us was anything forced.

"When you're ready to talk, I'll be here for you. In the meantime, I'll call the Department of Family and Protective Services and set up a contact for the book drive. Then I'll spread the word that we're going to have a vigil at eight o'clock in the courtyard."

"Sounds good."

Daddy continued sorting the books by genre and age while I called Scarlet.

Her sweet Southern twang filtered through my cell as she answered the phone at the beauty shop. "Beaus and Beauties, may I help you?"

"Hey Scarlet, it's me."

"O.M.W. Charli. You should be packing for your trip."

I smiled. Everyone thought I should be packing for my trip. What would they think if they knew I'd packed on Tuesday? "We're leaving tomorrow morning, and Daddy would like to have a candlelight vigil for Ava tonight, in the courtyard at eight. Could you help spread the word?"

"We'll do more than that. Leave the whole thing to me and the girls. We'll take care of it. You just worry about getting yourself ready for your trip."

"Thank you, Scarlet. I knew I could count on you." We hung up after a short discussion about the vigil. I told Scarlet I would contact the courts and DFPS while she made sure the rest of the town knew about the vigil.

Next, I called Sugar. She worked for us part-time, and although she normally worked at the local Tool Shed Tavern on Friday nights, I was hoping I could enlist her to help before she had to report to work later in the evening. She was more than happy to pick up a few more hours since she didn't go to work until ten o'clock.

With Sugar lined up to come into work for a couple hours, I started making plans for my afternoon. The hardest part would be notifying the Judge of the time we were planning to have the vigil. I saw how broken up he was over Ava's death. That, however, was not going to deter me from what I had to do. I needed to question the man and find out if he was a suspect or not. He was mixed up in it somehow, and I was determined to find out how.

I quickly made a list of things to do before I left town:
1. Make contact with DFPS for book drive and notify
them about the candlelight vigil
2. Tell the Judge about the vigil
3. Talk to the Judge's neighbors
4. Go see Isla and make sure she was at the nursing home
at the time of the murder
Please let me be able to wipe her off the list of potential suspects.

My list may have only had four things on it, but they were time consuming, and I wasn't sure I could accomplish all of them prior to the vigil. After that it would have to wait until after my weekend with Mateo. I grabbed my purse from under the counter, and Princess looked up from her bed. I couldn't tell if she narrowed her eyes because I woke her up, or if she thought I was being underhanded looking into Ava's murder against the wishes of Mateo and my dad. Either way, she didn't appreciate my actions.

"I'm sorry, but you know I can't take a chance of losing him again," I whispered.

Princess blinked and laid her head back down. I got the distinct impression she understood and wasn't going to stand in my way. I didn't think she was going to help me this time, though. She liked Mateo too much.

"Did you say something, Princess?"

My daddy startled me and I nearly took a swing in his direction. I think my reaction stunned him almost as much as it did me.

"Sorry. I'm a little on edge." He nodded with understanding and I didn't wait for him to say anything further. "I've got to run some errands before

I leave tomorrow. I called Sugar and she said she'd be in at two to help. Are you going to be okay here by yourself until then?" I felt guilty leaving him, knowing how much he was hurting.

His smile was a bit sad, but his voice held the strength of a man who had seen his fair share of tragedies. "I'm fine. Go. You need this weekend off."

I wasn't sure a weekend getaway was what I needed. The time to make sure my daddy didn't spend the rest of his life in jail was more pressing to me at the moment, but I didn't argue. I grabbed my keys and cell phone and kissed Daddy on the cheek before heading out.

The drive to the county building where the Department of Family and Protective Services had a floor of offices took me to neighboring Oak Grove, where most of the government buildings were located. The town was bigger than Hazel Rock by about eighteen thousand residents and held everything from the license bureau to the jail, to the biggest department store in a hundred-mile radius, which wasn't saying a whole lot. Coleman County was one of the smallest counties in the state.

As the county seat, Oak Grove had been a grand little town at one time, with a quaint downtown encircling the courthouse. Thanks to a fire in early 1950s, however, the only thing left standing was the courthouse/jail and the county building. The rest of the buildings along the square had never been rebuilt, and the road was rerouted to eliminate the square altogether.

A few years back, a new jail had been constructed across the four-lane street from both buildings. The effect set the area a bit off-kilter from the original street that had formed a square around the courthouse. It was now curved more like the shape of an *S*. The changes had forced the side of county building to become the front, and the front facade, which had more character than any another building in town, to face the driveway to the parking lot around the back of the building. It was a bit confusing, but I supposed the design, or lack thereof, marked a piece of Oak Grove's history.

I parked around back and spared a quick glance toward the jail, hoping Mateo wasn't doing some sheriffy duty inside and spot me. He'd want to know why I was at DFPS, which I had a very valid reason for, but he would then stand around and wait for me to finish and make sure I didn't press for more information.

I needed more information.

I checked in with the security desk, went through the metal detector, and made my way to the third floor in the creaky old elevator built for four to six people if everyone was under a hundred pounds.

The doors opened with a groan and a screech and I approached the receptionist, grateful to be alive.

The heavyset lady in her forties smiled. "Everyone feels that way after getting off that old contraption," she said, noting my relieved expression. "How can I help you?"

I returned her smile and got straight to it. "I'm Charli Rae Warren. I'm one of the owners of the Book Barn Princess—"

"The pink bookstore in Hazel Rock! I *love* that store," she gushed. Literally gushed with her hands clasped together next to her cheek.

I couldn't help the pride that snuck into my posture. I loved that store too. "Thank you. I'm actually here on behalf of the store."

Her penciled eyebrows rose in question and I continued, "We are in the middle of our first annual drive for a literacy campaign . . ."

She began nodding as I spoke, her smile growing with each word. I knew she was being an attentive listener, but her animation was throwing me off so much, I wasn't sure whether I should continue with my questions. When she remained silent, I carried on with my quest. "Ava James was our original contact, but with her death last night—"

Her eyes rounded and her mouth dropped open.

Uh-oh.

They didn't know. Or at least this woman in front of me, with a name plate on her desk that said *Shirley Rishard*, hadn't known prior to me wrongly entering her office and unwittingly dropping a bomb in her lap. She seemed to crumble before my very eyes. Her shoulders drooped. Her facial features sagged as the pencil she'd been unconsciously twirling, stilled and dropped to the scarred surface of her desk. Her gray eyes slipped from an expression of shock to disbelief to grief as they slowly filled with tears. It was as if I could see each tear form as they threatened to create rivers that would breach the banks at any moment.

"I'm s-sorry," I stuttered. "I thought you knew. I just thought everyone . . ." I waved toward the office of cubicles. I could hear voices traipsing through the air, but couldn't see a soul. "Would know."

When her body began to tremble, I looked down the hallway leading to more offices, hoping for a lifeline that would save me from my horrible mistake. When nothing appeared, I reached forward and squeezed her fingers, hoping to instill a bit of the comfort I had stolen.

"I wouldn't have broken the news to you so heartlessly," I whispered.

Tears finally spilled from her eyes, breaking the spell of grief I'd cast. She pulled her hand away and patted her eyes with the back of her sleeve at her wrist. "What happened . . . to Ava?"

"I'm not really sure," I lied, but saying she was murdered seemed pretty cruel after what I'd already done.

"Was it her boyfriend?" Shirley dabbed at her eyes again as her back stiffened. "Did he finally beat her to death?"

It was my turn to be caught off guard. Did Shirley know about my daddy's relationship with Ava? Or was she talking about the Judge? "Her boyfriend?" I asked.

"I warned her to be careful. She was going to leave him, but a man in his position . . . he would never let her go." Shirley struggled to keep her eyes dry as spots of mascara began to riddle her sleeves and she slowly shook her head. "I tried to warn her."

I waited for her to fill in the blanks. Answer the questions I needed answers to.

She didn't.

Instead, she dug in her desk drawer and pulled out a napkin. I saw a box of Kleenex sitting on the table to my left and grabbed it. Shirley nodded her thanks and began to blow her nose. A delicate noise that didn't carry back to the voices in the cubicles. It seemed they were still completely oblivious to the torment I'd put Shirley through.

I knew I shouldn't question her further. It was wrong. I should say I was sorry and get back on that death trap of an elevator and call Mateo to interview her.

But I still didn't know what boyfriend she was referring to, and I hadn't talked about the literacy drive . . . plus there were two people I cared about who weren't above suspicion in the eyes of the law at that moment.

I needed answers. I asked the questions I shouldn't.

"Who was her boyfriend?"

"You don't know?"

I was pretty sure I knew who one of them was, but I wasn't sure if I knew who all of them were. I lied and shook my head while trying to keep my face as blank as possible. "No. She never said a word."

Shirley gave another delicate blow of her nose before continuing. "She's been living with John Luke for the past year. He's a real piece of work. He started beating her on a regular basis about a month after he moved into her place."

John Luke. I recognized the name from the letter Ava had written the Judge and let out the air I was holding in a gentle sigh of relief. My daddy wasn't the type to raise his hand to anyone, but he was the type to take a woman under his arm and protect her from that type of man. I was also surprised to realize that I was relieved Shirley hadn't pointed the finger in the direction of the Judge. "Did you see her with injuries?" I asked.

Guilt covered Shirley's face. "We work with this stuff, ya know? I should have seen the signs." New tears spilled down her face, and I felt awful for being the one to make her verbalize her errors. Errors anyone would have made if they'd worn her shoes.

"A few months back Ava started favoring her ribs. I asked her about it, but she said John Luke put his motorcycle down while they were out at the park and she got a couple broken ribs out of it. She said she was lucky to be alive. I should have noticed that she didn't say *they* were lucky to be alive. Then she came in with a terrible headache, when I started to massage her head to ease the pain, I felt the bump. I tried to take her to the doctor, but she said John Luke had already taken her the night before, after she fell from a ladder while hanging a picture. Then two months ago, she had a busted lip. When she started to lie to me, I just said, 'Don't.' I marched her out the front door and took her to my car. Then I drove to the park and dialed the hotline from my cell phone in case he monitored her call history. I sat there and listened while she told everything to a complete stranger on the other end of the phone. Everything she should have been telling her best friend months ago."

"I'm sorry, Shirley. I didn't know Ava had any real friends. She was always friendly, but never overly friendly toward me. I had no idea you were that close. I wouldn't have come in today if I'd known you were best friends."

Shirley nodded and added to the growing pile of dirty tissues on her desk. "Chances are I would have found out from my boss around noon. He wouldn't have been a very compassionate person to hear it from. At least with you, I feel like you cared."

I did care; I just wasn't sure if I'd cared enough to be let off the hook like that. My overall need from the moment I found out that Ava was dead was to make sure I never lost my daddy again. That's where every bit of my concern had been. And I wasn't very proud of it.

Chapter Seven

I left Shirley after having learned a few more details before she turned the conversation back to the literacy drive. She needed to talk to her boss and would be in contact with me that night at the vigil, or Monday at the latest. She also said she would send out an email to county employees about the vigil, as it was the least she could do after sitting back and letting the abuse occur for so long.

I thought about my relationship with my own best friend, Scarlet. Would she try to protect the man she loved from the law? If stuck in an abusive relationship, would she value herself so little he could make her believe she caused the abuse? Would I recognize the signs of domestic violence, or would I let denial wash away my vision with lame lies she'd invent to cover up her unwarranted shame? Would I be a helpless witness, waiting for her to make the move that she would never take to protect herself? From what I understood, it would take more strength to leave an abuser than it would to stay.

To make the scenario even worse, how would I feel if someone waltzed into the Book Barn Princess and casually told me Scarlet was dead? It was an unforgivable sin—no matter what the reasoning behind it was.

"What are you doing here?"

I jumped at the low baritone voice of the man approaching me from the side. His voice pierced my thoughts the same time his shadow hit me as I walked toward my daddy's truck.

"Cade, you scared me."

Cade Calloway had a way of towering over people, even me. He was the tallest man I knew, other than my cousin Jamal. But unlike my cousin, Cade had a powerful muscular frame to match his height. Yet he'd never *scared* me scared me—other than that time he'd gotten himself knocked unconscious during his senior year of football. He'd put the fear of God in me that day.

He smiled, that warm smile I'd always craved. His face lit and made me believe in tomorrow being brighter than today. Even on a good day. "I didn't think anything scared my fearless Princess," he said.

I returned his grin. I thought about asking why Reba Sue was in court. It somehow seemed important for me to ask, but I chickened out and teased him about his job instead.

"What are you doing? Rubbing elbows with other politicians?" As mayor of Hazel Rock, Cade shined, but we were a very small town and I knew he had aspirations for something much bigger.

"Ah, you know me too well."

I didn't know grown-up Cade that well at all, but I smiled anyway.

"What were you doing in the county building?" he asked.

Guilt captured my tongue and made me stutter once more. "I . . . I w-was there to make a contact for the literacy drive."

The teasing light washed from his eyes and he glanced back at the building. "You didn't tell Shirley—"

"You knew Shirley and Ava were friends?"

Cade closed his eyes, hiding his disappointment . . . in me. "I was coming here to tell her. I didn't want her to hear it on the midday news or through the rumor mill."

Jeez, I was the lowest of the low. "Why didn't you come earlier?" I demanded. It came out more like an accusation than I intended. "I'm sorry . . . I just delivered the news to her in such a horrible way."

Cade engulfed me in a hug meant to comfort. It did anything but. "You wouldn't have done it if you'd known they were friends."

"I should have recognized Ava had close ties there," I insisted. "She's been collecting books for the foster care program since I was a kid."

"That doesn't mean anything. I've been coming to the county courthouse my entire adult life, yet Judge Sperry is hardly one of my favorite people in the world, nor do I know him that well."

I could have sworn he mumbled something about not wanting to know the man, but when I looked up for confirmation, Cade said, "You didn't know, Princess. Cut yourself some slack."

I pushed away from his embrace knowing that part of me wanted to revel in it. The other part remembered how he'd cringed when he learned I'd delivered the bad news to Shirley. I was always disappointing him, and I wasn't able to be the person he thought I should be. "Thanks."

Something flashed through his eyes that looked dangerously like regret before he cleared his throat and asked, "How are the Judge and your dad doing? Are they talking?"

If anything would make me forget about that look, it was a discussion involving my dad and the Judge talking like two human beings. If recent rumors were to be believed, the two of them had a lot in common. I just wasn't sure I wanted to put both of them in the category of Ava's lovers.

Then I remembered the awkward pat on the back my dad had given the Judge the night before. "What's going on with those two?" I asked. "My daddy has never said a kind word about that old coot in his life."

Cade searched my face, then turned away. I could feel frustration rising off him in waves like the heat from blacktop. He turned back toward me, his jaw taut and strained. "You don't know, do you?" he asked.

"Know what?" My certainty that Cade Callaway couldn't scare me dissipated. By the look on his face, he knew something I should know. Something very important.

I was witnessing the same type of guilt I'd felt about breaking the news of Ava's death to Shirley sinking into Cade's hazel eyes. Then he put on that expression I hated so much. The one he wore in high school when he broke up with me. The one he wore when I'd confronted him about not taking me out to dinner like he'd promised. The one he wore *every* time he was hiding something from me that would have a dramatic effect on my life. "Nothing," he said.

But it was a lie. He knew something. Something that would change me and the little world I'd grown to love so much over the past year.

"What is it, Cade?" He wasn't escaping before I learned that tidbit of information that would haunt me to my dying days.

The sun was high in the sky, beating down relentlessly for March. Sweat began to bead on Cade's forehead. He ignored his discomfort as he searched my face for what I knew, or should have known. His lips pursed with his decision.

"That's something for you to discuss with your dad," he insisted. "It's not my story to tell."

"Cade, if you know something about Ava's murder—"

My response threw Cade off guard. "Ava's murder? That's not what I'm talking about."

"Then what is it?"

Cade ran his hand through the thick waves of deep brown hair. "I thought he would have told you by now," he said. "I guess I was wrong. But I can't tell you, Princess. I'm sorry. It's not my story to tell. If you need anything after he does tell you, know that I'm here for you. No matter what time of day. Call me, and I'll be there."

That was twice now someone had told me it wasn't their story to tell. Twice I was being told to chase my tail in circles. I swallowed my pride and asked the question that had been burning a hole in my chest since he'd approached me.

"Why was Reba Sue in court the other day?"

Cade squirmed. Literally squirmed like the skin he was wearing was suddenly more uncomfortable than he could stand. I would have never thought his reaction was possible.

"She was arrested for indecent exposure."

"You're kidding." I laughed. I couldn't help it. Then I thought about the reasons why Reba Sue would expose herself in public, or who she would have been with—both scenarios came back to the man in front of me.

My laughter died. "Oh."

Cade was shaking his head before the word left my mouth. "It's not what you think—"

I raised my hand to stop him. "We may have tap-danced around the attraction between us over the past year, but I made it clear that I was moving on a couple months back. You're free and clear to see anyone you want."

His hand went to his hair again. I had a habit of ruining that perfect hairdo without even touching the man. He circled in place with his nose scrunched up like he had the taste of something nasty in his mouth. Then he bent down to my level, looked over his shoulder to make sure no one could hear, and an angry whisper escaped through his lips. "She was arrested for skinny-dipping in my pool."

That was more information than I wanted to know. I started to turn around but he grabbed both of my shoulders and forced me to listen. "She was drunk and alone and trespassing. I was out of town."

I searched his eyes for the truth, and it was right there in front of me. "Oh." He didn't want her there. I couldn't help the relief that washed over me.

He released my shoulders and straightened to his full height. "My security company signed the complaint. I was trying to make it go away . . ."

"Oh." I was wrong. He didn't mind her being there.

"I've never known anyone who could say one word with three different meanings in thirty seconds."

His exasperation stirred my ire. "What do you want from me?" I demanded.

"The same thing you want from me."

We stared at each other for a moment, and the years slipped away. Growing up, he'd always been the one person I could say anything to . . . and vice versa. The whole story spilled from his lips like the years of pain didn't exist between us. "She came over and broke into my pool house uninvited. Then she got drunk on a bottle of hundred-year-old scotch and stripped down to her birthday suit and went swimming." He shook his head in disbelief. "The woman's lucky she didn't drown. If I'd been home, I would have stopped her and sent her home before she got drunk. But I was in Austin, on business."

I remembered his trip to Austin. It was in support of a health care initiative for the poor.

His lips pursed like the next part of the story was hard to repeat. "The security company came, had her arrested for burglary and indecent exposure, and gave the video to the police."

"Holy schnikes," I snorted. Reba Sue had moved to town during my years of absence, but it was obvious she did not like me one bit, and despite my choked laughter, I wouldn't wish that fate on anyone. "That's horrible."

"When I found out, I was able to keep it hushed up, but the charges were already filed and the Judge insisted that I show up in court and have them formally dismissed."

I cringed. I knew exactly what judge would do that.

Cade nodded. "Yeah. Judge Sperry, but then Isla burst into court accusing the Judge of cheating on her with Ava."

"Oh my God." I was beginning to see just how ugly a scene that day in court had been.

"So now everything I'd tried so hard to keep quiet is becoming the center of attention again."

"Did you get the charges dismissed?"

Cade nodded to a man and woman who were walking toward the courthouse and waited for them to pass before answering.

"Yes. After I got Isla calmed down, the Judge dismissed the case. But the damage has been done."

"What do you mean?"

"Liza Twaine got a hold of it. She called my office and asked for an interview."

Liza Twaine was a pit bull on crack when it came to a news story. Our local reporter would do anything for a story . . . anything.

"This is my career, Princess."

And there was the true thing that always came between us. His career. It wasn't Reba Sue or anyone else, but his political career. I needed to remember that.

"I'm sorry. I suggest you be honest. You're a victim in all this."

"Who will look like a womanizer. Sometimes secrets are for the best."

"Is that why you won't tell me what my daddy is keeping from me about the Judge? Because secrets are for the best?" I asked.

"That's different. I told you, it's not my story to tell."

I could tell he was sorry, but that didn't make me feel any better.

"If you need a friend to talk to, just call." Cade leaned over and kissed my cheek before turning away. He walked toward the entrance of the county building without another word and I couldn't help but think his parting line sounded dangerously like a song. It wasn't a song I could place off the top of my head, but maybe it was the combination of a couple different songs and that was what was throwing me off, or maybe it was just the words of a man who cared.

About me. About my daddy. And a teeny bit about the Judge.

That alone could turn my world upside down.

Chapter Eight

There was no way I was going to complete my list in time for the vigil, and I wasn't sure if I wanted to. I'd found out the secret Scarlet wouldn't tell, and I understood why she hadn't told me what she knew through the beauty shop gossip mill. The version she'd heard was undoubtedly dirty laundry no one would want repeated, and Scarlet considered Cade a friend. She wouldn't have repeated that story to her mother, let alone her best friend.

Even though I had one mystery solved, I was bothered by another. One that was much more important than a woman skinny-dipping in Cade's pool. I was missing something between my daddy, Isla, the Judge, and Ava. What it was, I had no idea. Ava couldn't tell me. Isla was a bit unreliable. Daddy wasn't talking, and the Judge . . . well . . . I shuddered just thinking about talking to the man. I tried to think of the Bible verses he would throw in my direction, but to be honest, not one was coming to mind.

I should probably add that to the list of sins I needed to confess the next time I went for the sacrament of reconciliation. My list of sins was growing, and the whole church might have to wait a day before I finished with my unending list. I wasn't sure a priest could survive that long in a little enclosed closet with no food or water at his disposal. Then again, maybe they sat there munching on bread and drinking wine.

I should probably add that thought to my list of sins as well.

I shrugged. At least the Judge couldn't lecture me about the length of time between my visits to church. He was Baptist and not likely to believe in the whole process anyway. I parked my daddy's old beat-up pickup truck along Tenth Street where Scarlet had parked her car the previous night. This time, however, I was legally parked with the truck facing the same direction as the traffic. By the time I got out of the truck, Daisy and Jessie were on their front lawn.

"You owe me a dollar," Jessie said to his wife.

Daisy shook her head and smiled. "That's my husband."

"What do you owe him a dollar for?"

"He's a big gambler. He insisted you'd be here today snooping around."

"I'm not snooping around!" I protested. I was investigating. There was a big difference—from my point of view.

Jessie pulled up his jeans a notch closer to his chest. If he wore them on his hips, he wouldn't have any trouble keeping them up, but his championship rodeo belt buckle made them want to slip down to where most men wore their jeans. Jessie wasn't a tall man; if he reached five-eight it was because of the heels on his cowboy boots. "Young lady, you made me snap a picture of a farewell letter to the Judge and then lie to the sheriff. You're here to snoop."

Daisy sighed. "That's my husband, trying to put his own sins on someone else."

Jessie scowled in our direction before he turned around and marched back toward the house. "I'm keeping my nose out of it, where it belongs."

Daisy rolled her eyes. "Can I help you with something?"

"I don't want to cause you any problems." The screen door slammed on their front porch and I jumped.

"I thought betting the dollar would give him some satisfaction when you showed up today. I was wrong. He's just as cantankerous today as he was when he couldn't stay on that stupid bull for eight seconds."

We laughed for a moment and then Daisy turned us back to the conversation we needed to have. "What can I do you for?"

"I was wondering if you could tell me which neighbors could have seen something last night. I'd like to approach the ones you know will talk."

"Most of them are at work right now. But Betty Walker lives cattycorner on the other side. Mike Thompson should be home. He lives with his mom on the other side of the Judge."

My stomach dropped, churned, and did an ugly roll. "Mike Thompson?"

"You know Mike. He sang the national anthem on opening day of the rodeo."

"Oh, I know Mike." Mike and I went all the way back to grade school. We pretty much hated each other from third grade on. Since I'd returned to Hazel Rock we'd had a couple run-ins. Like when he broke into the Barn and tried to steal a valuable book. And when he caused me to owe Cade money because Mike insisted I pay my daddy's debt when my dad was missing. Cade had paid Mike to shut him up. I wasn't sure there was enough money in Cade's vast bank account to buy Mike off now.

"I think I'll wait to talk to Mike a little later. Is the Judge home?" From the looks of the front of the house, he didn't appear to be, and my trip was looking like a bust.

"I'm pretty sure he's home. He didn't go into work today. I brought him a pan of cinnamon rolls around ten o'clock, but I don't think he touched them."

I gulped down my apprehension and smiled at Daisy. "I guess that means he has something to offer guests when they arrive to give condolences."

Daisy shook her head the same way she did with her husband. "That's our Princess." She turned and walked back into her house, leaving me alone to get up the gumption and walk over to the Judge's house.

I walked through the arbor and realized my path would lead me straight through Ava's place of death. I paused to say a prayer for her, not sure if it was my idea or the influence of being in the Judge's front yard. The silence of the neighborhood was broken by the sound of a lawn mower humming to life on the next block and a motorcycle rumbling through the stop sign at the corner. A clicking noise I couldn't immediately identify drew my attention away from the place Ava took her last breath as I searched for some type of prayer. *Now I lay me down to sleep* was the only thing I could think of. I quickly modified it in my head, but that one noise kept tapping at my thoughts until I began to focus more on it than the prayer.

My head whipped up as I recognized the quick snicks of a camera shutter. At the sidewalk where the white picket fence kept people from walking across the lawn stood TV reporter Liza Twaine. Why she had a digital camera in her hand instead of her phone or a TV camera, I had no idea. But I was pretty certain I didn't like my photograph being taken at the site of a murder.

I stomped up to the fence. "What are you doing?"

"I could ask you the same thing."

I glared at her, dressed in a sexy-as-sin skirt with her signature high heels. "Do you ever mind your own business?"

She smiled and her perfect teeth gleamed. It was enough to make me want to mess up her smile—permanently.

"Princess," I hated the way she said my nickname like it was a dirty word, "I get paid to ask questions. You, on the other hand, are just being nosy."

"I'm here to pay my respects." Sorta.

"You're here for the same reason I am," Liza confessed. "The Judge's wife was in court yesterday morning accusing him of having an affair with the same woman who was murdered on his front lawn. From what I hear, you and the Judge don't get along, yet you're here. Wouldn't you find that odd enough to take photos, if you were in my shoes?"

I scowled at the truth. I wouldn't be caught dead in her shoes.

"Yet you've visited Isla Sperry several times in the nursing home." Liza pushed her way through the spring-hinged gate and let it slam closed behind her.

Somewhere deep down inside me a protective streak emerged, and I immediately blocked her path to the front door. "You can't seriously mean to question the Judge after what happened?" It was a rhetorical question, no answer required since I meant it as a Southern dressing-down for her bad manners.

"He's a witness, isn't he?" Liza's voice held innocence she hadn't owned since she was two.

"Ava worked for him for years! You can't barge up to the man's house and demand answers to your stupid questions!" Was I talking to Liza or myself?

Liza attempted to walk past me, but I stepped in front of her.

"Get out of my way, Charli Rae."

"I'm not going to let you go up there."

"You touch me and I'll press charges."

I got up in her face. "Who do you think Mateo is going to believe?"

A wicked gleam showed in her eyes as she leaned forward. "Are you saying the sheriff's corrupt?"

"I'm saying he knows better than to believe the likes of you."

Cold water smacked my cheek like a wet fish. Liza was struck immediately after. We both scooted back at the same time, which meant my reflexes were slower, or she reacted to the assault on me before her own. She screamed and I grunted as water sprayed us from three different directions from a sprinkler system that had impeccable timing. Liza tried to run up the sidewalk toward the house, but the man standing on the front porch still dressed in his robe, stopped her in her tracks.

It was the way he held his body. Stiff, rigid, and full of authority with his head held high as he looked down his nose at the two of us. "May God have mercy on your souls, because I won't. Now get off my property before I call the police."

I was the first to turn tail and run. The man had always put the fear of God in my soul, and the fact that he mentioned those two entities together was enough to make me hit the road and let Liza Twaine fend for herself. Except she beat me to the gate despite her high heels. Her skirt had lost some of its appeal, her white blouse clung to her, and her perfectly coiffed hair would need a day at the salon. She held her camera high above her head to protect it from the rotating heads on the Judge's sprinkler system, and I couldn't help but laugh. I had no doubt that I looked as bad as Liza, and when I glanced back to see what the Judge thought of the whole thing, I caught a sad smile crossing his face before he turned around to go back inside his house.

"We're having a candlelight vigil for Ava at the Book Barn tonight at eight," I said to his back.

He paused a moment with his front door open. Then he turned back toward me, nodded in acknowledgment, and went into the house and closed the door.

I wasn't sure what I had expected from him in response, and I sure as shootin' wasn't sure how I felt about the little nod he gave me or the grin I'd witnessed. It had to have been my imagination playing tricks on me. The Judge never smiled. Never held an ounce of humor in his entire adult life. He was fire and brimstone personified. Yet for a brief moment, I could have sworn I'd glimpsed a hint of amusement cross his face, and I couldn't help but wonder about the man under all the stoicism. In the past twenty-four hours, I'd seen more emotion out of the Judge than I'd seen in my entire life.

What exactly that meant, I had no idea.

Chapter Nine

My T-shirt and jeans were soaked, but both could hide the drowned rat look better than Liza's outfit. The woman was a mess. Since I didn't have time to go home and change if I wanted to talk to Isla before the vigil, I grabbed a towel I kept under the seat for those hundred degree days that could melt the skin off your legs when you sat down and tried to minimize the damage.

I didn't want to leave a puddle in the seat at Oak Grove Manor when I met with Isla in the TV room. I got busy drying my face and arms. Then I scrunched my curls and patted the rest of my body before folding the towel underneath me. I turned the vent on and angled it toward my chest. The truck didn't have air-conditioning, which was fine until May. Then I'd be slip sliding away in sweat if I didn't have my towel.

I looked in the rearview mirror to survey the damage to my hair.

Fuzz buckets. I called Scarlet and before she could say hello, I asked, "Is there any way you could do my hair really early tomorrow morning?"

"How early?"

"Like seven?"

"That's not really early, Charli."

"It is for me."

"What happened to your hair? It looked good this morning."

"I got attacked by a sprinkler system."

I could hear the laughter in her voice. "Did you wage war on a sprinkler system?"

"No, I actually think it was trying to protect me . . . maybe."

Scarlet chuckled. "What?"

"It's a long story. Suffice to say, if the sprinklers hadn't gone off, I'd probably be calling you to bail me out of jail." I thought about that for a moment. Had the Judge set off the sprinklers to protect me? Or had he just wished to see both of us leave posthaste?

"Charli?"

I'd missed what she said while wondering about the Judge. "What? I'm sorry, our connection must have dropped for a minute."

"Where are you?"

"I'm on my way to see Isla."

"I'll meet you there." Scarlet hung up before I could tell her it wasn't necessary. I glanced down at my phone and looked at the gas gauge. I needed to stop before I returned to Oak Grove. It would have made sense to stay in Oak Grove and talk to Isla first before heading back to Hazel Rock, but I'd wanted to talk to the Judge before Isla.

Since that didn't work out, I needed to talk to her before it got too late. I pulled into the Git N' Gone and filled up the truck. My jeans were clinging to me uncomfortably as a police car pulled into the lot. I recognized the unmarked navy-blue Charger immediately.

Fuzz buckets.

The tinted window rolled down and Mateo's handsome face appeared. "From the look of your hair, I'd say you were with Liza at the Judge's house."

His delicious chocolate eyes were hidden from my view behind his sunglasses, and I couldn't tell if it was a touch of humor in his tone or if it was frustration. My answer could have two polar opposite responses.

I walked up to his car and leaned in. "I went over to tell the Judge we're having a candlelight vigil tonight for Ava."

Mateo reached up and put one of my curls back in place. I could have told him it wouldn't help, but I was enjoying the attention. "Was that your idea?" he asked.

I licked my lips and wished I could see if my action had the desired effect on him, but all I could see was the reflection of a woman with really bad hair in his sunglasses. Drat the man.

"It was Daddy's idea."

"And you volunteered to tell the Judge out of the kindness of your heart?" His voice sounded skeptical.

My dander stirred. "Why wouldn't I?"

"No reason. We still on for tomorrow morning?"

"Do you still *want* to be on for tomorrow morning?"

"Absolutely."

I grinned at his unwavering response. "Then it's a date, Sheriff."

"How about a run in the morning before we take off?"

"I've got to get my hair done, remember?" I pointed to the frizzy curls he couldn't miss.

"One of these days, you won't have an excuse to go running."

"Other than the fact that I hate to run?"

"I'll never give up, you know."

I was pretty sure he was talking about more than just running, but I decided to let it go. I had more important things I needed to focus on and I wanted answers before we left town. Answers I wouldn't get anywhere else.

"How did she die?" I asked.

Mateo's lips pursed. He didn't want to run his mouth. "That's not public record."

"Yet."

"I plan to keep that out of media."

"Mateo, Ava was working with us. How did she die?"

"If this gets out, so help me, Charli . . ."

"You know I won't tell a soul."

Mateo rubbed his forehead. I knew I didn't have any right to the information. I just needed to know.

His voice was low, and I could barely hear it over the traffic passing by on the street. "Someone cut her throat," he said.

My hand involuntarily traveled to my neck.

He nodded in agreement. "Yeah. It was brutal."

"Thank you for trusting me with the information."

Mateo lifted his sunglasses and looked me in the eye. "I trust you with more than that."

For a moment, I got lost in the meaning of those words I never expected to hear from Mateo. I really wanted to spend my Saturday night at the Tony Bennett concert with him. We'd only had one official date, which had been cut short because duty had called. Since then, Mateo had been struggling with having enough deputies to cover the county. The man had been working nonstop. We still had lunch together and some dinners, but they were normally take out or at the Hazel Rock Diner. This weekend was going to be a first—on many levels.

I changed the subject. "Scarlet made room to do my hair first thing in the morning, but after that, you won't need your handcuffs to get me to Dallas, Sheriff."

He tapped my nose and said, "I think I'll bring them just in case. See you at nine?"

My smile wobbled a bit with his comment, but then I winked and said, "It's a date."

Mateo drove off and I was glad the conversation went the direction it had. It broke the ice from our little spat at his crime scene the previous night and opened the path for a pleasant drive in the morning. I finished pumping the gas and hopped into the truck feeling better about my trip to Oak Grove Manor.

Scarlet pulled into the lot directly behind me and got out of her car, still looking like a million bucks. She took one look at me and said, "O.M.W. No one has seen your hair like that, have they?"

"Just Mateo."

"Did he cancel your weekend?"

"No!" I'm not sure who I was more offended for, me or Mateo. "He's not that type of guy," I insisted. Then I looked in the side mirror on my truck. If my curls were red, I could challenge that Scottish Disney princess with the bow and arrow for worst curly hairdo. Mateo definitely wasn't that type of guy.

Scarlet reached in her purse and pulled out a large clip. Then she proceeded to do her magic on my hair right there in the parking lot of Oak Grove Manor.

"Now take a look."

I leaned over to look in the mirror again.

"It would look better with a pair of dangling earrings. Do you have any in your purse?"

I patted my hair, amazed that she'd managed to tame the untamable. "Scarlet, you're a miracle worker. I'm fine without earrings. Come on, let's go."

We walked into the facility, and Joan was sitting at the front desk like she had been last time. Today, however, she didn't have any residents to keep her entertained.

She looked up and immediately recognized the two of us. "Charli, you made it after all! Isla will be so happy. This is the best kind of birthday present she could have asked for." She grinned and addressed Scarlet. "I didn't know the two of you knew each other. Are you here to do Isla's hair for her special day?"

Fuzz buckets. I'd completely forgotten Isla's birthday. Luckily, I'd ordered an edible arrangement of her favorite chocolate-covered strawberries to be delivered as soon as I'd left her side the previous day. Scarlet began talking to Joan like the two of them went back a long time, and I supposed they did, since Scarlet made it a habit to follow her customers all the way to their grave.

"Did Isla get the delivery?" I asked.

Joan's smile was genuine. "She did. That's all she's talked about all day."

"Good. I'm glad. It's been a rough day for the Judge. Has he made it in yet?"

Something changed in Joan's expression. Her smile slipped with what looked a lot like fear, before she recovered and sniffed. "He came by this morning. The first thing he asked was if Isla had walked away from the facility last night."

By her reaction, I was glad it hadn't been my first question. But still, I needed the same answer. "Oh?"

"I told him we were watching her closely, but Isla can be pretty slippery when she wants to be."

It was a response without a real answer. Did it mean Isla got away from her caretakers a second time on Thursday? Or was Joan responding defensively because of an accusation of neglect from the first incident? I couldn't tell, and Joan wasn't about to let me ask any more questions.

"Come on. I'll take you to Isla."

Joan took us down the same hall Isla and I had taken toward the garden. I tried to broach the subject of Isla leaving the night of the murder several different times, but it seemed like fate decided to thwart my investigation. We ran into Frank, who I'd met on my last visit. The man's Jimmy Durante nose was painted red, and I couldn't help but ask, "Why is your nose red?"

His grin was so full of joy. "It's Red Nose Day," he said.

"Shouldn't it be a clown nose?"

"Bert always said we didn't need clown noses; God had already gifted us with them. We just needed to rely on a little red lipstick to do the trick and our ability to tell a joke." He held out a Mason jar that had a red circular piece of paper taped to it. It read:

Jokes

Residents $1, Visitors $5

I reached into my purse and pulled out my wallet. The smallest denomination I had was a twenty-dollar bill.

Frank held out his jar and pouted like a sad clown with his head tilted to the side. I stuffed the twenty inside and he asked, "What do you call an alligator that wears a vest?"

I grew up in Texas. I knew this joke inside and out, but his enthusiasm was infectious. He pulled on the bottom of his T-shirt like he was adjusting a fancy vest, and the way he took on the role of the ancient reptile with his arms out in front of him was pretty comical. He held his arms together at the elbows as he slapped his palms together inches from my face. He was an alligator ready to feast on me for dinner, and I couldn't help but laugh.

"I don't know. What do you call an alligator that wears a vest?" I asked.

Frank leaned in to share his punch line. "An investigator!" he snapped. Then he winked and sauntered down the hall with a giddy-up in his step.

I looked to Scarlet and Joan, and the three of us burst out in laughter. It was the best laugh I'd had all week.

"It won't even be Red Nose Day for a couple months," I said.

As she turned to proceed down the hall, Joan looked over her shoulder, put her hand up to her mouth, and whispered, "The love of his life was British. The two of them loved Red Nose Day." She began walking toward the last doorway on the right of the hallway, and I suddenly knew this story wasn't going to have a funny ending.

"They celebrated the British and the American charity drives equally. His husband died last year, so I'm glad Frank is able to enjoy the day by bringing a smile to people's faces and reminding them to give, while he honors the man who made him whole."

"O.M.W."

I looked at Scarlet, who was wiping her eyes. I didn't think she said it for me to hear. It was just something that slipped out with her emotions. I gulped the knot threatening to bubble to the surface of my throat as we turned off into a library and found several people seated in comfortable chairs reading books, magazines, and newspapers. Off to our right was a glass-enclosed room with a few tables and chairs and a long shelf containing neatly stacked board games against one wall.

Isla and Mason Andrews were hunkered over a board game, both of them staring down at the pieces in front of them. Joan turned and held a finger up to her lips, indicating that Scarlet and I should be quiet as we weaved our way through the seating areas in the room and entered the glass enclosure.

Isla picked up two small white tile pieces from the long wooden tray in front of her and laid them down on the game board. A smile lifted her sagging cheeks and a sparkle lit up her face as Mason tried to discern the meaning of the word she spelled during her turn of Scrabble.

"You went for laughter, but I changed it into something entirely different," she said and spelled out the transformation she'd done to the word *snicker*. "S-N-I-C-K-E-R-S-E-E. Snickersee."

Mason looked at her, completely stumped by the word.

"Would you like to challenge me?" Isla asked as she rubbed her hands together.

That lump in my throat surfaced. I coughed and gagged. Scarlet began patting my back. Isla and Mason turned in my direction, but all I could think about was the word she had spelled out across the Scrabble board. I didn't need to challenge Isla. My daddy had used the word since I was a kid. A snickersee was a knife, but not just any knife. A snickersee was a knife used as a weapon.

The type of weapon that killed Ava James.

Chapter Ten

I'd heard people claim that Alzheimer's attacked the core of a person's humanity. That an abusive individual could become docile, and a kind-hearted soul could become brutal. I just never imagined I would witness it in someone I cared about. Certainly, my visit to the Oak Grove Manor had disturbed me. My questions remained long after I'd recovered and Scarlet and I wished Isla happy birthday. Scarlet did a quick set of Isla's hair while doting over her. I smiled and listened to their conversation, too disturbed to add much to it. Mason stayed and joined in on the conversation with ease. His true caring nature and concern for Isla's well-being was obvious. Yet the whole scene just seemed to add to the tragedy of tonight's memorial . . . and I needed answers.

"Did you like your chocolate-covered fruit, Isla?" I asked.

"Oh, Princess, it's divine, but there's entirely too much for me to eat. Would you like a chocolate-covered strawberry?"

I grinned, because at that moment, Isla was the woman I remembered from my childhood. The woman who brought in chocolate-covered strawberries for me and my mom—we devoured them. After my mom was gone, she brought them every year on my mother's birthday. "We celebrate life," she said. "Always, but especially on the day of our loved one's birth." It had turned the day into a joyous occasion for me, instead of another day to dread as it approached.

"I would love one."

"Then git yourself down to my room and grab a few for all of us."

I stood up, patted her hand, and smiled, but my insides were pulling apart as I made my way to room 123. This was my opportunity to get a better look at Isla's room and find out if she had a snickersee stashed somewhere. I prayed I didn't find one, but the coincidences were mounting up. Isla had threatened to cut Ava's throat. A fact I was pretty sure Mateo would know by now. And there was a possibility that Isla had somehow escaped from the facility again last night. Granted, she would need a ride, but it was possible.

I looked over my shoulder as I pushed open the door to the hallway. There was only an elderly man hunched over a walker making his way along the wall. I closed the door behind me, leaned against it, and closed my eyes to catch my breath, which had become erratic, as if I'd just run a mile at full speed. I hadn't gone running in over a year. I was pretty sure it could kill me at this point. And that was something Mateo had been harping about.

"You need to start running again, Charli. Did you go running this morning? Want to go for a run along the river?"

My eyes shot open.

I was not going to think of Mateo. That would lead to more guilt for deceiving him as well. I let my gaze fall across the room filled with Isla's grandmotherly scent. It was furnished with a wine-colored love seat and a gliding rocking chair with roses flourishing the tan cushions. A small television sat on top of an antique radio console. I'd visited Isla on a few occasions and found her reading a book in her glider while listening to the radio, which still worked. Its sound wasn't as clear as a modern-day stereo, but that didn't seem to bother Isla in the least. Off to my right was the bathroom, and beyond that, her bedroom set, which consisted of a hospital bed that was neatly made with frilly pillows and a dresser from the same era as her radio.

Scenic paintings created by Isla's own hands decorated the walls. My favorite was one she called *Grinter House*. It was of an old red farmhouse with split-rail fencing and snow covering the landscape. The house was real, located somewhere in the Midwest. Isla and the Judge had visited it during their marriage. The only person in the painting was a young boy about eight, who was frolicking in the snow with a little black terrier. The boy and the dog seemed to be having the time of their lives.

I steeled my resolve and began searching the room. I had to find out the truth, to protect my dad and this woman I loved more than I had known. The fruit basket was on her dresser, looking gorgeous and adding to the welcoming scent of the room. I ignored it and began opening the drawers of the dresser. My hands trembled with my deceit as I moved her panties and bras, socks and T-shirts, shorts and pants. Nothing.

I moved to the small nightstand next to her bed. It only contained one drawer that held the latest thriller by Lisa Jackson, a bottle of eye drops, and a pad of paper and pen. I glanced at the writing on the pad and noticed an address had been jotted down on the page with a shaky hand. I quickly took my phone out of my purse and was about to snap a photo when my phone rang. I jumped as if caught in the act and answered before the caller ID appeared.

"Hello?"

"You have company." That's all Scarlet said before she hung up and the door to Isla's room opened.

I turned around to find Mason Andrews in the doorway watching me. His eyes moved to the open drawer of the nightstand. I smiled and shifted my phone to my shoulder.

"I would love to stop by and pick up your donation. Can you give me the address?" I asked the dead air on the other end of my phone as I grabbed Isla's pen and pad of paper. I shifted my body so the director couldn't see that the address I wrote was actually already written on the pad of paper.

"Twelve-fifty-seven Armadillo Drive, River Oaks. Got it. Thank you. I'll stop by in about forty-five minutes, if that's okay?" I paused, waiting for my imaginary answer. My heart was pounding in my chest as I tore the piece of paper from the pad and folded it in half. "Thank you. See you then."

I clicked my phone off and shoved the piece of paper into my purse. Before I turned back around, I placed the pen and paper back in the drawer and closed it. "Sorry. The literacy drive has got me busy. Losing Ava didn't just hurt emotionally. It's caused some major issues with the drive. She was the force behind the charity. It's going to be hard to manage without her."

Mason was the true picture of grace, his forehead wrinkled with concern and his eyes full of sorrow. He held his hands in front of him with his fingers laced together. "I'm sorry for your loss. I can't imagine how hard something like that is to deal with. Losing a loved one is hard enough. Losing a loved one to murder is unimaginable."

My heart began to slow its roll and I decided there was no better time than now to ask some question about Isla's whereabouts the previous night.

"I know Isla wasn't very fond of Ava."

Mason shook his head. "No, she wasn't, but in her mind her dislike is justified."

"So . . . you think Isla is making it up about the Judge having an affair?"

"It's hard to say. Isla has been here since I arrived. She reminds me a lot of my own mother. She's a very kind and giving person."

I pushed for the answer I needed, then held my breath. "Was she here last night around seven to eight o'clock?"

"If you're asking if Isla signed out last night and went out? Then no, she didn't. She was here."

I exhaled and smiled as I grabbed a few chocolate-covered strawberries. "Well, we better get back there with these strawberries. We don't want to keep the ladies waiting for their chocolate." I turned for the door, but Mason hesitated.

"You weren't thinking that Isla could have hurt Ava, were you?"

"No, I . . . I was just worried about her."

I started to walk past him, but Mason touch my shoulder. It was a light, gentle touch meant to put me at ease, yet at the same time, prevent me from leaving the room. "Isla isn't capable of hurting anyone," he said and I could see the conviction in his eyes. "The Judge, on the other hand, is a dangerous man."

Mason got my attention with that statement. "What do you mean?"

"I've already said more than I should, and I have no evidence of abuse or I'd have reported it long ago, but there are some things that come up in my conversations with Isla that are very disturbing."

"Do you think the Judge is capable of murder?" I asked.

"I think there are many things in the Judge's past that we don't fully know, or understand, and I'm not sure Isla would be able to help guide us through those events. She's just not that coherent these days."

I wanted to disagree. Yell and scream that the disease had not gotten the best of her. Isla didn't deserve this, but who did? I should accept that Isla's mind was trapped in a convoluted web of truth, mysteries, and lies—except I couldn't. Unlocking her memories would be next to impossible for an expert. For me it was downright improbable.

But I was determined to get it done.

Chapter Eleven

Scarlet and I left Oak Grove Manner in our own vehicles. She was going to make a stop to pick up the candles and I was going to find out whose address was on Isla's notepad. I wasn't that familiar with the town of River Oaks. Not because it was far away—it was only five miles southeast of Hazel Rock—but the town wasn't really a town. It was a few trailer parks and a couple dead-end streets with small houses. There was no town center, and I didn't think it held one business. It was also known to be the wrong side of the tracks of the wrong side of the track. That was saying something.

The inhabitants were hardened by bad luck and known for making bad choices. Whenever Mateo had a bruise or a cut, it came from making an arrest in River Oaks. I wasn't heading out there lightly. Luckily for me, I didn't drive a fancy car, and my daddy's old beat-up pickup would fit in well with the socioeconomic stratum of the town.

At least that's what I was hoping.

I let the GPS on my phone guide me to a trailer park, where it decided to send me in circles. It was during one of those circles that I noticed a little white BMW Isetta following me.

I immediately picked up my phone. "You're supposed to be picking up the candles for the vigil."

"I called Joellen. She's got it covered."

"I'll pull over and you can hop in the truck."

"No can do, Charli. I'm not abandoning my vehicle on these streets."

"When did you become street smart?"

"When you came back to town and gave me a new type of education."

I wanted to argue that it was her ability to solve puzzles that gave her the education, except before my return, the most violence Scarlet had witnessed was a bar fight over a football game. And even those weren't really fights; the people engaging in them were normally too drunk to land a punch.

"Fine, but stay close."

We hung up and continued down the road, but my GPS kept telling me to make one U-turn after another. With Scarlet on my tail in her adorable little car and her perfect hair and perfect skin, we stuck out like a mini caravan from the homecoming parade that took a wrong turn and ended up in the trailer parks of River Oaks.

The name of the town was a bit deceiving. It didn't exactly fit the landscape. There was no river, and no oaks. There was nothing appealing to the town at all. It wasn't homecoming parade material. I'm not sure I'd call it livable, either.

The street signs were missing from the barren poles, and the trailers didn't have house numbers that were visible from the street. To make matters worse, the neighborhood we were driving through looked like it belonged at the dump on the moon. There wasn't a speck of green in sight. Not a weed. Not a shrub. Not a tree. Just dirt and rock and trash everywhere. We drove by broken toys, a toilet sitting along the pitted roadway, and furniture tattered and rotted from the weather and stray critters.

The trailers didn't fare any better. Blankets and sheets draped across the windows of the upscale units. Black paint and foil covered the windows of the rest. I felt my mood slip into darkness just driving through, especially when I saw two kids no older than three and five sitting on a crumbling stone wall wearing nothing but their underwear. The young girl's hair was snarled and matted—worse than mine had been. And that was saying a lot. Her younger brother sported a buzz cut. I didn't want to speculate as to the reason behind it, but the way the little girl was scratching her head, my bet was on lice. Initially I thought they were tanned from the recent heat wave we'd had in Texas, but as I got closer, I realized the smudges of dirt covering their bodies weren't created by the sun. But the worst part was their eyes. They held a sadness no young child should experience, and I was compelled to lift it.

I shouldn't stop. It was all wrong. I knew better than to approach children in front of their home, but they had so little, and the ex-kindergarten teacher in me was dying to rear her head and offer something to these two kids who had nothing. I pulled past them and waved Scarlet in front of me. Then I grabbed four books I thought they might like from a box on the passenger seat. I made my way out of the truck and the girl pulled her feet up underneath her bottom, ready to run away at any moment. Her little brother glanced at her and followed suit, but not nearly as quickly. Nor was the expression on his face as wary, but he mimicked the movements of his big sister, and I had no doubt within the year he'd also exercise due caution when approached by a stranger. It was a good instinct to have in any neighborhood, let alone this one.

"Hi. I'm Princess," I said, figuring my nickname would sound friendlier to the kids.

The little girl turned and was ready to run; her brother followed.

"I've got some extra books that I was going to bring to a friend of mine, but I thought you might like them."

The little girl whispered something to her brother, and he took off at a dead run to their house, his pudgy little legs moving faster than I'd thought possible.

I smiled and encouraged her protective nature. "That's what you should do when a stranger approaches you. I'll leave a couple books for you and your brother on the wall," I said. "They're for kids your age."

The girl backed away without saying a word. I laid the books down and turned toward the truck about the time a barefoot and pregnant woman younger than me yelled from the iron steps of her trailer. "Git yourself away from my kids before I call the cops!"

"I'm sorry. I'm the owner of the Book Barn Princess in Hazel Rock. I was driving through the neighborhood and saw your children. I thought they might like a few books I had in my truck."

I waited for her response. The last thing I wanted her to think was that I was afraid of the police even if I didn't want to answer any questions about what I was doing in River Oaks. If a deputy came and ran my identification, Mateo would know . . . and he wouldn't be happy.

"Lily, git yourself in the house," the woman instructed, and the little girl turned tail and ran toward the trailer. "Are you Princess?" her mother asked as she made her way across the dirt yard.

"I am," I responded with a smile. "But my real name is Charli Rae Warren."

"You're the Princess who was working with Ava on the book drive?"

Her question caught me off guard. "You know—" I winced. "You knew Ava?"

I noticed the caution in her voice. I also saw a yellowing bruise on her cheek that I guessed to be about a week old as she got closer. "She lived behind us with her boyfriend."

That was the last thing I'd expected her to say. For a moment, I'd thought that maybe her house was the address I was searching for, but it couldn't be a coincidence that Ava lived in the same area as the address Isla had written down on a pad of paper in her nightstand.

I nodded, thankful I'd stopped to give the kids a couple books, but at the same time wishing I hadn't. What did it mean that Isla had written down an address in Ava's neighborhood?

The woman continued to walk toward me, and by the time she was ten feet away, I'd recovered enough to reach out to shake her hand. She stared at my palm as if it was a completely foreign gesture in her world, then she tentatively took it. Her grip was soft, limp and timid. It lacked confidence, the same way her posture did when she wasn't protecting her kids. She introduced herself with her eyes on the ground.

"I'm Naomi."

Scarlet's car door shut and we both jumped, but it was Naomi's expression that I found more disturbing. The noise hadn't startled her, it'd scared her half to death.

"It's nice to meet you. I was just going by Ava's place to see if I could pick up some books she'd collected for our literacy drive," I lied.

As Scarlet got closer, Naomi became more guarded and her eyes darted around the yard, looking for an escape she couldn't find. Her fear was gone, hidden just below the surface of what appeared to be a severe case of embarrassment.

"Naomi?" Scarlet's voice was full of shock. Her approach was full of anger.

"Scarlet . . ." Naomi breathed. She grimaced as her hand went up to her dull brown hair and pulled it over her bruised cheek.

"What happened—" I elbowed Scarlet before her shock could outweigh her manners. She cleared her throat and got control. "When did you come back? I thought you were off to college in California on a full scholarship?"

"Jimmy and I had a baby. We're expecting our third."

"Jimmy Shoemaker?"

Naomi nodded but didn't meet Scarlet's gaze. Instead she looked to me like I could save her from Scarlet's questions. I wasn't sure anyone could.

"But what about your scholarship?"

"My kids are more important."

No one was denying that. The problem lay with how her kids looked. I didn't want to judge, but little Lily and her brother didn't appear to be anyone's priority.

Chapter Twelve

It turned out Naomi was from Oak Grove and had been a customer of Scarlet's when Naomi was still in high school. She'd received a full-ride scholarship to East Texas University for basketball. She was going to be their "itty-bitty" point guard, like Morgan William of Mississippi State, and bring the NCAA championship home to East Texas. Unlike Morgan, however, Naomi made the mistake of having unprotected sex with the wrong guy on prom night. It had been the first of a string of bad decisions by the young athlete. The worst one had been letting that no-good lily-livered piece of trash know she was pregnant in the first place. Unfortunately, Naomi knew that better than anyone. She just couldn't get out of that bad relationship. Yet.

From the way Scarlet seemed determined to take her under her wing, I was betting Naomi would be free, if she wanted to be, within a couple months. Scarlet had already made plans to stop by and cut Naomi's hair and treat them for lice on Monday when Jimmy was at work.

Naomi was the one to turn the conversation back to the reason we had ventured into her neighborhood. "I don't know what I'll do without Ava." Naomi's voice turned breathy, like the admission cost her more than I could possibly know. The confession hadn't come easy to her.

"That makes two of us," I admitted. "I'm kinda lost on this book drive."

Her gaze skimmed my face before traveling up the street. "There ain't no one there," she said.

"At Ava's?" I clarified.

She nodded in affirmation. "John Luke left the night—" Her sentence hung in the air between us. Naomi changed the subject. "I've got a key to her house, if you'd like to git the books. I know Ava would want the kids to have 'em."

It was more than I expected, and I think Naomi was surprised by her own forwardness as well. If Scarlet hadn't been there to fill a necessary void in Naomi's world, I'm not sure she would have ever said a word about Ava. In fact, she looked like she wanted to take back what she'd already said, but I wasn't going to give her the chance.

"Thank you. That means so much to me. We're going forward with the literacy drive because we know Ava wouldn't want anything to stop it from happening." I added a little bit of my history with Ava. "She's been coming to the Barn since I was a little kid to get books for the kids in the foster care system."

A smidgeon of trust crept into her expression, and I took advantage. "I'll drive around the block and meet you there, okay?" It wasn't really a question since I'd turned toward the truck and opened the door.

"Yeah," she said. "Sure."

Scarlet rested her hand on Naomi's shoulder and said something that brought a faint smile to the woman's face that I swore held a glimmer of hope as Scarlet turned toward her car as well.

I hopped in the truck and was leading Scarlet around the corner before Naomi could change her mind and tell us no. It wasn't going to be hard to locate the right address now. There were no fences between the yards, and I could see Naomi's trailer during the entire drive around the block.

I parked the truck and we met Naomi on the sidewalk leading up to the nicest trailer in the neighborhood. The yard was still plantless, yet it looked surprisingly quaint, adorned with several rock gardens of different shapes and sizes. The driveway was made of pea gravel, which was more than any of Ava's neighbors had—they had nothing to differentiate the yard from the driveway at all. The trailer itself was gray with bright pink shutters and a matching front door. The color looked a lot like the shade of fuchsia the Book Barn had been before I'd had it whitewashed the year before. There were two empty window boxes hanging underneath with a large picture window that was bordered with real curtains on the inside. The most notable feature, however, was the plaque next to the front door with the address imprinted on it: 1257 Armadillo Drive.

The address I was searching for.

Naomi clutched a key chain with a pink puff ball that held one key. She looked a little uncertain with her two kids hanging onto the back of her dingy white T-shirt that didn't quite cover her pregnant belly. I immediately sought to put her at ease.

"I can't tell you how much this will mean to the literacy drive. We're actually thinking about changing the name to the Ava James Drive for Literacy."

Scarlet chimed in. "Would you like to come to the vigil tonight? You can ride with Charli and the kids can ride with me."

"No." Naomi's response was fast and definite, catching Scarlet and me off guard, until she explained. "Jimmy will be home in an hour. I have to have dinner ready."

There was a moment of silence as if we were mourning her fate.

Lily broke it. "Miss Ava treated us good. Her boyfriend threw a rock at my brother."

"Hush, Lily. They don't want to hear about that."

I actually did want to hear all about Ava's boyfriend. I wanted to know what he was like, but I didn't want to disagree with Naomi or make her change her mind entirely. Naomi knocked on the door and waited a moment before inserting the key and turning the handle.

Naomi called out as she opened the door. "John Luke, it's Naomi. I just stopped by to feed Tweetle Dee and Tweetle Dum."

Her announcement was met with silence and Naomi walked into the trailer with her kids on her heels, and me and Scarlet close behind them. The first thing I noticed was how nicely kept the trailer was. The second thing I observed was the broken chair that had been set to the side of the kitchen table with the broken armrest lying across the seat. Naomi and the kids ignored it and walked toward a birdcage that contained two small finches. They tweeted and flapped their wings as the kids approached.

In the living room, the couch and chair were older but in good condition. A horizontal crease in the shape of the letter Y marred the off-white lampshade on the floor lamp as if it had been knocked over. Its repair had been less than perfect. The picture on the table below it, however, caught my eye.

I picked up the silver-framed photo of Ava flanked by a man and woman. It wasn't just any couple. It was Jacob and Isla Sperry. Each was kissing Ava's cheek as a thirty-something-year-old Ava stood between them wearing a cap and gown and a glorious grin.

The picture was missing the glass and I stood staring at the image, not sure what it meant. Like the lampshade, the framed photo hadn't escaped whatever had occurred in that room. It was the perfect symbol of how fragile the barrier between happiness and tragedy was. Violence had breached and shattered the perfect moment with a scratch across Ava's graduation gown.

I wondered if John Luke had been the person who had smashed the frame. Had he been a good man once? Or had he worn a facade to fool these three people into thinking he was the perfect step in Ava's road to happiness?

"I think she keeps the books in the spare bedroom," Naomi said.

I set the photo down and said, "Thank you," before I made my way toward the hallway, hoping to look in both bedrooms. Naomi saw me turn toward the master bedroom and immediately corrected me.

"It's the door on the left."

I smiled and turned toward the door on the opposite side of the hallway. "Thanks."

Inside I found so many boxes of books, I stopped in my tracks.

"O.M.W. that's enough books to fill three stalls at the Book Barn," Scarlet said behind me.

I had to agree. It would take us well over an hour to load all those boxes. I glanced at my watch. I only had an hour before the vigil started.

Naomi entered the room and caught my mouth hanging open.

"I had no idea she had this many books," I confessed.

"She collects all year round and hands out books for Christmas and at the beginning of summer. Every kid who enters the foster care system gets a new book to take with them to their first home. From then on, they can sign out from the library and their case worker will bring a book with them on their home visits."

I had to clear the lump in my throat. "Ava did all that?"

"She was a saint," Naomi said with conviction.

I had trouble reconciling the woman I knew who collected books year-round for the underprivileged with the woman who lived in this trailer. "Who lives with a man who throws rocks at babies?" I asked.

Naomi's back stiffened. "We all have our flaws."

I nodded in agreement even though I wasn't sure who she was talking about, Ava or John Luke. I hoped it was Ava, 'cause John Luke was beyond flawed. He sounded like a depraved junkyard dog with no ability to turn off his savage nature.

"I won't be able to load all of the books tonight," I said. "The candlelight vigil at the Book Barn starts in an hour. Do you think I could come back with help on Monday to get the rest?"

"I can't guarantee that I'll be able to let you in. If John Luke comes back . . ."

A desperate voice spoke up behind us. "He'll kill Tweetle Dee and Tweetle Dum without Ava here to protect them."

We turned to find Lily standing in the doorway holding her brother's hand, the birds in question sitting on the boy's head.

Naomi looked crestfallen. "We can't take them home, Lily."

I knew it was a conversation she'd already had with her daughter. Naomi already had her hands full with what I believed to be an abusive husband and two and a half children to take care of. The last thing she needed was two birds to care of when she couldn't even protect herself.

"I can take them." The words popped out before I even realized I'd said them.

Fuzz buckets.

Scarlet grinned.

The kids looked at me with more hope in their eyes than they'd probably had in the past year. Even Naomi's eyes sparked with glimpse of a light at the end of a tunnel. I would be helping Ava and Naomi and letting the kids know there were good people out there in the world at the same time.

"Ava loved those two birds. She would love for her babies to go to a good home."

I wasn't sure I was the right home for the birds. I believed Tweetle Dee and Tweetle Dum would be better off with me than they would be with John Luke, but still . . . I didn't particularly want a bird.

Except now, I had two.

Chapter Thirteen

By the time we made it back to Hazel Rock, people were beginning to gather in the courtyard. The crowd had taken every last parking spot around the Book Barn and forced me to park down the block in the parking lot of the Tool Shed Tavern. I made my way through the crowd with the birdcage in tow while Tweetle Dee and Tweetle Dum sang to their hearts' content. We'd cleaned the cage prior to loading it in the truck, and Naomi had packed up the birds' food before we locked up the house and left.

"An armadillo isn't enough for you?" Betty Walker, the owner of the Bluebonnet Quilt Shop across the street from the Barn, crossed the street and joined me. Her helmet hair looked particularly hard with hair spray this evening. Instead of her usual overly potent perfume, however, tonight she wore bug spray as a fragrance.

"Tweetle Dee and Tweetle Dum belonged to Ava. I thought it was fitting for them to be here."

Betty accepted my answer like it made sense. Maybe it did.

"I guess everyone is feeling a bit overwhelmed. The Judge was just in the store and asked me to make a photo quilt using a collection of photos he had of Isla with Ava."

"Really? I had no idea they were that close."

"At one time, they were inseparable."

This was a piece of the town's history I didn't know. A lot had happened during the twelve years I'd lived in Colorado, well beyond the sheriff becoming a judge and a new sheriff being elected. I was slowly learning about the things I'd missed through the little snippets like what Betty had just told me. It was almost as if everyone in Hazel Rock felt the need to educate me about the past. Right now, that education would come in handy.

"What happened?"

Betty leaned in. "According to Isla, the Judge had an affair with Ava."

"Do you believe that?"

Betty shrugged. "Who's to say what the truth is? The Judge denied it, and Ava kept her lips sealed. It was like she didn't want to take sides in a public argument between two people she looked up to as parents."

"Did you see anything the night Ava was murdered?" I asked.

Betty shook her head. "Franz and I were watching a movie on television. We didn't hear a thing until well after the police arrived."

Before I could ask any more questions, we were interrupted as we made our way through a group of women I didn't know. Then I saw Shirley Rishard, wearing a floral dress and flats, and recognized some of the faces around her as county employees I'd seen earlier that day. Shirley immediately homed in on the birds and rushed forward.

"Lordy, I forgot about these poor little dears. Are they okay?"

"A neighbor was taking care of them."

Both birds chirped in confirmation.

"What are you going to do with them?" Shirley asked as she stuck her finger in the cage and wiggled it up and down. I hoped the birds wouldn't think it was a worm and bite it. "They can't stay with *him*."

Since that seemed to be a consensus of all the women in Ava's life, it had to be true. "I'm not quite sure. Right now, I'm taking them home."

Shirley's eyes rimmed with unshed tears. "I'd take them in a heartbeat, but I'm afraid my cat wouldn't see them as roommate material. He'd make sweet little Tweetle Dee and Tweetle Dum into dinner."

I didn't want the birds, but leaving defenseless animals in the hands of anyone with a cat . . . There had to be someone who would like to listen to the beautiful music they created.

"They'll be fine at the Book Barn Princess. You can come visit them anytime," I assured her.

Shirley's brow wrinkled, and she hugged me, long and hard. "Thank you." Then she told me I could bring the books by on the following Wednesday and Thursday, DFPS would have space cleared out of the storage room by then.

I lost Betty in the crush and worked my way through to the Barn with several "pardon mes" and "excuse mes." The doors to the Barn opened with a swish and a ding that the birds seemed to like. They sang at the top of their lungs.

Princess was the first to react. She'd been eating up the attention of many people milling about in front of the register, and her head shot in my direction at the sound. She dropped her front legs down from the expensive pant leg they'd been resting on, snorted, and waddled to the back room with her tail sticking straight in the air.

Up until that moment, I didn't know her tail was capable of standing up like that. It was as if she flipped me the bird as she walked away.

"Someone's not happy with your new additions," Cade said from his relaxed position leaning against the front counter. His legs were crossed at the ankles but his expensive suit looked like it'd just come from the dry cleaners. Considering he was the richest man in the county, it seemed fitting that he would be the one wearing the designer attire.

"Have you come for the vigil?" I asked as I looked around for a place to set the cage. There might have been a place to put the cage before I left that afternoon, but it seemed in the hours I was gone, we'd collected more books than I could count. They were stacked everywhere.

Cade took the cage from me and held it up. He looked at the cute little finches who quit singing to contemplate the man in front of them as if to wonder if he was friend or foe. No one should live like that.

Cade put them at ease instantaneously with a coo that made me want to roll over so he could rub *my* belly. Tweetle Dee and Tweetle Dum played it cool and sidestepped on their perch to his side of the cage. When Cade's finger wouldn't fit through the rungs, Tweetle Dee improvised and pushed her body against the metal rungs so he could stroke her feathers.

"Want a couple birds? They'd make a great shtick for your next election."

Cade didn't seem offended, but he declined my offer. "I don't need a shtick; my agenda will speak for itself. What's their names?"

"Sorry, should have introduced you. Mayor Calloway, this is Tweetle Dee, the one soaking up all your attention, and Tweetle Dum is the one who seems as jealous as all get-out."

Tweetle Dum lifted his leg and stuck it through the bars.

"Holy schnikes. I never thought I'd see a parakeet shake a finger. I think he wants you to take them home."

Cade's grin told me he was on to my ploy. "I think it means they've been trained. Where did you get them if you weren't looking for a couple of birds?"

"They were Ava's."

He got that look in his eyes that brought me back to our teenage years. "You really are a Princess."

"Does that mean you want a couple birds?"

Cade chucked me under the chin. "I think they'll be better off at the Barn."

I wasn't sure I agreed. My pet armadillo didn't take too kindly to me bringing more pets into her home. It was almost as if she thought I'd been unfaithful to her.

I thought of Isla. Could her mind have rebelled at the thought of another woman coming between her and the Judge when it was something so simple as him being Ava's mentor?

My dad approached from the back room where Princess had disappeared. "Now I know why Princess is in such a huff."

"She's in a huff?"

"She's downright ticked off because Tweetle Dee and Tweetle Dum are in the Barn."

That one sentence said so much. Daddy recognized the birds on sight, and he knew the finches' names.

I lowered my voice and proceeded with caution. "When did you meet them?"

"When Ava got them. Who brought them tonight?"

"I did."

His brows raised in question, but I didn't take it any further. He wasn't the only one who could remain mute.

Scarlet's little sister Joellen arrived and handed us each a candle. "I'm not sure we're going to have enough. I picked up three hundred but I'm down to about thirty."

"Really?" I was struck dumb for a moment.

Cade came to the rescue, as always. "We'll tell those who don't have a candle to use their cellphone flashlights. We'll just ask everyone to hold it above their heads so they don't blind anyone."

We all agreed and headed out to the courtyard. Scarlet appeared in the crowd carrying some floating candles. She and Joellen began lighting them and placing them in the old rectangular fountain in the middle of the courtyard. The gentle flickering of the candles reflected off the water basin, formed from hand-cut stone pavers that had been laid sometime in the 1800s, created a somber yet romantic atmosphere for us to gather around.

Depending on what version of the story you believed, the old hospital next door used the fountain as a baptismal fountain for the sick and dying. The other version of the story claimed that the hospital wasn't really a hospital, but a place of "healing" for the cowboys who'd been on the trail too long without female companionship. In the latter version, the fountain was more of a historical hot tub for cowboys gone wild. I liked that version best.

It looked like the entire town had gathered to pay their respects, along with half the county as well. There were young kids, middle-aged adults, and elderly people. The group that surprised me the most was the young adults in their twenties. It turned out a lot of them owed Ava for taking an interest in their lives. Yes, some had fallen through the cracks, but how would Ava have felt if she'd known she'd touched so many lives with the gift of a book or two?

I watched Betty and Franz, the only baker in Hazel Rock, add to the stacks of books outside the store, along with the manager from the Hazel Rock Diner. Cade's parents slipped a check to my dad on the sly, but I knew it was for big bucks. The Calloways only knew how to do it large. Mary and Aubrey Buchanan were there from Beaus and Beauties, along with Leila and Joe Buck, the owners of the Tool Shed Tavern. The face I didn't want to see, Mike Thompson, was talking to Mateo.

Fuzz buckets.

Daddy started the vigil by saying a few words about Ava's love of literature. Then countless people, young and old, talked about the books she gave them. A few even read the inscriptions Ava wrote to them with inspirational quotes about literacy.

Daddy finally introduced the man in town who'd known Ava the longest and the best—Judge Sperry. The Judge looked older and frailer than he had that morning. On his arm was his wife, Isla, who seemed to be the stronger of the two, at least in body and spirit. She also seemed to understand the proceedings and the reason behind them. Joan from Oak Grove Manor stood off to their right in the second row. Her disdain for the Judge was evident by the curl of her lip until she saw me looking in her direction. Then she smiled and nodded in acknowledgment. I returned the gesture, then gave my attention to the Judge while sneaking peeks in the direction of Mike and Mateo.

Mateo's notebook was in his hand. It hadn't been a few minutes ago.

"I met Ava my first year as sheriff in Coleman County," the Judge told the crowd. "She was just a teenager with a chip on her shoulder and no family to watch over her." A sad smile crossed his face. "Like so many kids, the system had failed her. She was a biracial kid in a predominantly white county. Too old to be considered 'cute and adorable,' and no one wanted a mouthy teenager . . . no one knew that better than Ava. Her mama had died of a brain aneurysm and she never knew her daddy. She was abused in her second foster home, and nobody believed her. At that point, Ava lost faith."

Sniffles could be heard throughout the crowd. Some of them were my own. Several of them came from Isla and I saw my daddy move in her direction while Mateo watched—everything.

Judge Sperry cleared his throat. "But given a chance, Ava flourished. She came to work at the sheriff's office at just eighteen. She worked harder, longer, and more diligently than anyone else, and she became part of our family . . ." The Judge's voice cracked. "The daughter we never had."

Isla's tears were flowing down her checks, and my daddy had his arm around her shoulder while she tried to stop the tracks of grief with his hankie. I wanted to make the Judge shut up. Everything he said was beautiful but also gut-wrenchingly sad. I wasn't sure if I could watch all the grief around me much longer.

"Even though Ava meant the world to Isla and me, I wouldn't have asked her to be my clerk when I made judge if she wasn't such a good person and a hard worker. She dedicated her life to helping others within the foster care system. She truly had the biggest heart I've ever known, and I will miss her dearly." He reached for Isla's hand and pulled her to him.

I wasn't sure if it was a political move, a reconciliation, or if he truly did need to give comfort to his wife.

"We will miss her desperately," he choked out. Isla buried her head in his shoulder and cried as the Judge led a prayer for Ava. Every head was bowed, but as much as I wanted to, I couldn't. My eyes were on Mateo, who made his way behind my father. His gaze caught mine and held. Disappointment and dedication to duty shone through the dying light of the candles.

It was the last thing I wanted to see.

Chapter Fourteen

I wanted to mill about with the people who came to the vigil and thank them for attending. I needed to show our appreciation for the books and cash that had been donated to the literacy drive, but the drive to protect my daddy left me fighting against the push of the crowd to get to the entrance to the Barn where Mateo had disappeared with my dad. He'd whispered something in Daddy's ear that changed everything. My dad had kissed Isla on the cheek before turning to the Judge to shake his hand. The whole thing seemed surreal, and I began to wonder if I'd fallen asleep. In that setting, my fight against the crush of the crowd made sense—a never-ending struggle to protect my father.

Except I was wide awake, and Daddy's need of protection was real. I decided my best bet was the side door to the tearoom near the gate to the alley. I didn't think Mateo would try to talk to him in front of the main doors. They'd make their way toward the back of the store, or if I was lucky, they'd be sitting down with a glass of sweet tea and talking, man to man, about our trip in the morning.

Funny how I'd rather Mateo talk to my daddy about a weekend of fornication between the two of us over the alternative. I shoved my key in the lock and pushed the door open while scanning the room. Neither was insight.

Fuzz buckets.

I quickly closed the door and heard low voices talking just outside the tearoom. Tweetle Dee and Tweetle Dum added a few chirps into the conversation from up near the register as if they had two cents to offer.

"A witness said he saw Ava leaving your house with blood on her shirt yesterday morning."

I slapped my hand over my mouth to prevent myself from crying out and continued to listen through the stall wall. Every bone in my body wanted to confront the lie, but my daddy wasn't talking to me, and in order to defend him, I needed to know what we were up against.

"That's true."

Wait . . . what? I hadn't seen any blood marring Ava's clothing. I pressed my ear to the wall trying to hear over the birds who'd decided to sing a few bars in harmony.

"Is that all you're going to say?"

"Mateo, I told you the night Ava was killed. She had been beaten badly when she showed up at my house. She never came out and admitted it was John Luke who beat her, but we talked about her going to a shelter where she would be safe."

"You did. You just failed to mention Ava was at your house at six thirty in the morning."

"If I did, it was purely by accident."

One of them released a heavy sigh. I was betting it was Mateo, but my heart was pounding so hard in my chest, I couldn't tell.

"Do you carry a knife?" Mateo asked.

"I think you know the answer to your question. I'm pretty sure you borrowed it the last time we went fishing together." My daddy's voice held a hint of amusement, but I'd had enough. I was not going to stand by idly eavesdropping on the opposite side of a thin wall and let this travesty of justice occur. Daddy deserved better, and Ava certainly deserved a more thorough investigation than the word of Mike Thompson. Pleasure weekend be damned.

Mateo knew I wouldn't stand by and let it happen either. "I know your temper's brewing in the tearoom. Come out and save us all the trouble."

I stepped out of the stall and planted my hands on my hips. "My temper is more than brewing, it's about to flare."

"I figured it was." Mateo's voice held no emotion, and I couldn't begin to read the expression on his face—because there was none.

"Mateo Espinosa, if you think for one minute that my daddy—"

My dad interrupted my rant. "He's just doing his job, Princess."

"Accusing you of murder is not doing his job," I insisted.

Mateo stood his ground. One of his best qualities could be his worst. "I have to eliminate all possibilities, Charli."

"This is my daddy! How can you possibly think that I will go away with you for a weekend after a stunt like this?"

"Princess—"

"Don't." I couldn't hold the hurt in. Both men had let me down. One by not opening up to me, the other by not protecting the one who wouldn't open up. Which was ironic since Daddy had told Mateo more than he'd confided in me from the very beginning.

I glared at my daddy, and a tear had the audacity to spill onto my cheek. I swiped it away. "You may not trust me, but I believe in you, and he should too."

A flicker of pain flashed in his eyes before he silently reached into the front pocket of his jeans, pulled out his knife, and handed it over to Mateo.

"We'll talk later. Right now, you need to understand that Mateo is doing his job for Ava. I want him to make sure no stone is left unturned. She deserves that." He rubbed his jaw, then turned away. "I'm going out back and round up Princess. I'm sure it will take me a while."

It was his way of saying we would have the Barn to ourselves. We could have a knock-down drag-out argument, or a kiss-fest to make up. Either way, it was up to Mateo and me.

The door closed and I looked at Mateo. He was gazing down at my daddy's knife with his jaw clenched. I looked down at the blade he had exposed and saw what he saw. Except I saw it in a different light.

The dark stains weren't there from a killing. They were there from cleaning . . . a fish. Daddy had gone fishing that morning, not hunting for someone to kill. Granted, it wasn't like him to put a dirty knife away in his pocket, but I was betting he didn't even realize he'd done it.

I moved closer to Mateo and looked him straight in the eye. "You know better than to think what you're thinking."

"What am I thinking, Charli?"

"You know darn well what you're thinking. You're thinking that's Ava's blood on his knife." My hand went to my hip and my lips pursed. "Well, it's not."

"I had hoped you knew me better."

I hesitated. "What do you mean?"

Mateo closed the blade. He pulled a plastic glove out of his back pocket, slipped the knife inside, and put it in his shirt pocket. It wasn't his normal evidence collection. Not by a long shot.

"I mean . . ." It was Mateo's turn to advance on me.

Unlike him, however, I didn't hold my ground. I backed up until he had me against the stall wall to the tearoom. The same wall I'd listened through.

"I am trying to clear your dad's name of any suspicion. I was upset to see the blade was dirty because it means it will take longer for the lab to say not only is Bobby Ray's knife not the weapon that was used to kill Ava, because the blade doesn't match up with the cut marks on Ava's skin . . ."

His body met mine. With anyone else, it would have been intimidating. With Mateo, it made me forget everything but how good he would be at dirty dancing. His full body press was making my mind wander to more pleasant activities. He smelled beyond good.

"And the blood found on the knife is not human. That's what I mean." His breath tickled my lips.

"Oh." My voice sounded like it belonged in a Lifetime movie. Breathless with anticipation. It was beyond ridiculous, yet that was all my fuzzy brain could muster.

His lips came into contact with mine the same time a trash can crashed to the ground out back. If it had stopped there, that dreamy scene would have heated up between us, but Daddy yelled right before a dull thud hit the Barn wall, and our lips never completed the tango. My thoughts immediately shot outside.

"Daddy!"

I would have pushed Mateo away, but he was off me before my exclamation hit the rafters. He ran through the bookstore with me hot on his heels, neither one of us slowing down at the back door as we entered the pitch darkness behind the store. Mateo quickly moved me out of the light from the doorway and shoved me back against the wall. I tried pushing him away, but he was an immovable wall of hard muscle.

"Daddy!" I called.

"I'm over here."

I looked to my left and saw the trash can tipped over, wobbling back and forth in a rocking motion on its side. A pair of boots stuck out from behind it as if someone was sitting on the ground and leaning against the Barn. Daddy struggled to gain purchase on the concrete patio, failing twice before Mateo reached him. I was as close as the shirt on his back and Mateo immediately let me take over as he scanned the area with his flashlight for whoever Daddy had been fighting.

"Are you okay?" I asked as he gained his footing. Princess was tucked into his left arm, trying to snuffle his neck while Daddy held his right bicep. Through the narrow beam of light from the back door, I could see blood seeping through his sleeve and fingers.

"I think I've been stabbed."

"What? What do you mean you *think* you've been stabbed?"

Mateo was talking into the mic on his shoulder asking for an ambulance and for officers to assist in the search.

"Who attacked you?" Mateo asked as he looked over his shoulder at my daddy.

"I don't know. He caught me totally off guard."

"Which way did he go?"

"I don't know."

"Can you describe the person who did this?"

"I think he was about my height."

"Did you see any skin or hair color? Any clothing?"

Each time my daddy shook his head. "I'm sorry. I was worried about Princess. She jumped from my arms right before I got cut. I tried to catch her and that's when a saw a flash of silver and felt the pain in my right arm. I never heard or saw a thing before that."

"Think about it. Did you hear anything that would tell us where the suspect went after he attacked you?"

Daddy shook his head. He looked disgusted and ticked off. "Just like now, I heard a bunch of noise from people getting in their cars from the vigil and leaving. I swung at him and made contact with his jaw, but not hard enough. He shoved me into the trash can and we tussled a bit and ended up on the ground. I think Princess was using her head like a battering ram and hitting him. By the time I got the trash can away from me, he was gone and Princess was by my side. Then you opened the back door."

"Did he say anything?"

"No."

Mateo looked at Daddy. "A man about your height. That's all you can tell me?"

Daddy shook his head again. "I can't say it was a man for certain, no."

"I'm going to take a look around. You two go inside and wait for the ambulance."

Daddy didn't argue as I took Princess from his arms and led him inside to the tearoom. Once there, I got some clean towels and had him apply pressure while I cut the sleeve off his shirt. When he lifted the towel, I got my first real glimpsed of his injury, a five-inch gash traveling diagonally across his bicep. The wound was deep and made my stomach turn sideways.

The paramedics arrived and told us he would need stitches, but Daddy refused treatment and they were gone before Mateo returned.

"How bad is it?" he asked.

"It's not good," I told him. "He refused to be transported to the hospital, but he needs stitches."

"I can drive myself."

"You're not driving yourself, Daddy. I'll take you."

"You've got a weekend trip to pack for."

"I'm not leaving you!"

"You are leaving me. I'm fine."

"You're not fine."

"I am a grown man who can take care of himself."

"Daddy—"

"No buts, Princess. You haven't had a vacation since you came home."

"It's not a vacation. It's one night," I argued.

"Exactly. One night. Go. Sugar works at the store tomorrow and I work Sunday. There's no reason for you to stay."

"He's right," Mateo added.

My daddy smiled at Mateo. I glared.

"But under the circumstances, I think it'd be better if you asked Scarlet to go with you."

Daddy scoffed. "Don't be ridiculous. Now you sound like Princess."

Mateo wasn't daunted. "Did he demand your wallet? Your watch? Anything?"

"No, I was walking back to the Barn carrying Princess when all of a sudden she freaked out and jumped from my arms. I tried to grab her before she hit the ground, but that's when he cut me."

"So he didn't want anything from you. He just attacked you. And if Princess hadn't lunged from your arms, his knife would have been right about . . . here." Mateo's arm was at the height of my daddy's neck. He looked at my daddy and made sure his message got across. When he saw my face, however, he cleared his throat and dropped his arm. We were all on the same page. Ava may not have been the only one the killer had in his sights.

"Something's going on in this town, and it's my job to find out. I'm sorry, Charli, but I can't afford to leave right now."

"Mateo—"

It was Daddy's turn to be shut down by the sheriff as Mateo ignored his attempt to argue. Mateo was too busy trying to talk me into keeping the tickets to the concert. "I'll take him to the hospital and see to that he gets stitches. You call Scarlet and the two of you go. Have a girls' weekend getaway."

I stomped my foot, frustrated that both men thought I should turn tail and run out of town while they stayed to face the boogeyman or whoever was out there sharpening his knife on the residents of Hazel Rock. "I'm not leaving."

Scarlet interrupted. "Of course you are." I turned to see her standing at the entrance to the tearoom with the female deputy from the crime scene the night before. "It's high time we had a girls' weekend in the Big D. It's an offer you can't refuse." Tweetle Dee and Tweetle Dum began singing again, and it almost seemed as if they thought I should go as well.

But it wasn't the prospect of a girls' getaway with Scarlet that made me change my mind. It was the wink that accompanied her proposal. Scarlet knew something, and if the Big D was where she thought we needed to go, then look out, Dallas.

Chapter Fifteen

Daddy texted me after Mateo dropped him off at home. He had twenty-three stitches to close the gaping wound in his arm with ten stitches underneath to repair a small tear in the muscle. He said he was lucky; nothing was permanently damaged. I didn't think that was lucky: I thought he was blessed. Blessed that he'd been holding Princess. Blessed that the knife hadn't come in contact with his neck. Blessed to be alive. Stitches wouldn't have helped if his attacker had been able to finish what he'd tried to do—if a startled Princess hadn't jumped from his arms.

I looked down at her, in awe of what I owed the little four-legged beast who was so ugly she was cute. "Will you protect him while I'm gone?"

She blinked her beady eyes and I could have sworn she smiled before she rubbed up against my shin.

"She's got you wrapped around that freaky pink shell of hers," Scarlet teased.

I bent and scratched Princess behind the ears. "I for one am very happy you have that adorably freaky shell. Without it, my daddy wouldn't be here."

Princess snuffled my hand and followed us to the door. I grabbed my suitcase and all three of us left my apartment. I let Princess in the store since it was a couple hours before it opened. I uncovered the birdcage, then fed and watered Tweetle Dee and Tweetle Dum. They seemed fairly content. Princess, however, protested when I headed for the door, but once the door was locked, we watched her go behind the register where we kept a daytime bed just for her.

"Tell me again why we're leaving at the crack of dawn before I even get to see my dad and make sure he's doing okay."

Scarlet looked around like someone might be eavesdropping. I couldn't help it, I did the same, but downtown Hazel Rock was its normally quiet self. The bakery across the street was the only business in town that was open, and we could see Franz loading his display case with fresh pastries.

"We don't have time," Scarlet said before I could even take a step in his direction.

"We have to eat," I argued.

"I have food in the car."

I shuddered at the thought of what Scarlet brought us to eat. Between the two of us, she had the hourglass figure men craved and I had the shape of a stick woman. She ate health food and I wanted real food—like donuts for breakfast.

She opened the one door to her two-seater Isetta and crawled in first. How she made it look graceful in four-inch heels and a snug-tight dress was beyond me. I had on a gray vanity T-shirt with *I'm just a Poe Book Barn Princess* imprinted in pink on the front, jean cut-offs, and my black combat boots, and I still had trouble maneuvering into the little car that seemed like more of a death trap than a vehicle.

"Could you try to make it look like a girls' weekend getaway?" Scarlet asked as I closed the door.

"I got the distinct impression this wasn't about living it up on the town in Dallas but more about finding out what the heck is going on."

"True, but appearances are everything."

"And this is what everyone would expect me to wear when I'm going to be in an itty-bitty car for several hours eating," I cringed as I looked inside the bag of health food I had to move onto my lap, "tasteless cardboard."

"That tasteless cardboard keeps my figure in check."

"I don't have a figure," I argued. "Where are we going?"

"Fort Worth."

"What? But you said—"

Scarlet whipped her car out of the parking spot and we were on the freeway in no time flat. "I said we were going for a girls' weekend in the Big D to put the men in your life at ease."

I was pretty sure my daddy was the only man who qualified as being in my life at this point, but didn't argue.

"I happen to have heard from a reliable source that the police are looking for John Luke."

"Everyone knows that."

Scarlet rolled her eyes. "Would you let me finish?"

"Okay, sorry. The lack of breakfast is going to make me crabby."

Scarlet reached in the bag and pulled out two breakfast bars. "I brought one for each of us."

I read the ingredients: grains I'd never heard of, nuts I would bypass for walnuts or peanuts any day, and dates. Yuck. The only time I'd seen anyone eat a date was in that old movie my daddy loved, *Raiders of the Lost Ark*, where the monkey died after eating a date. From the look of the bar I unwrapped, I seriously doubted that monkey's date was poisoned. It was just nasty.

Scarlet continued with her story while I sniffed and nibbled on the bar of sawdust made gooey from the date. "It just so happens that Mary saw John Luke driving Ava's car the day of the murder."

"Didn't he always drive her car?"

"That's the point. He was always driving it. Everyone saw him driving it."

She looked at me like I should be able to figure out what she was talking about. I couldn't. I shrugged. "And?"

"Annnd," Scarlet dragged the word out like she was slowing down her conversation for a particularly slow audience, "he hasn't been seen since . . . Neither has the car."

"Oh . . . but what does that have to do with going to Fort Worth?" I asked.

"I had Joellen do some checking yesterday on Instagram."

I grabbed the cooler she had in the back, grateful she'd thought of packing water for me to wash down the grain a cow would hate. "What does having your sister check your social media account have to do with Ava's death?"

"Focus, Charli. Joellen checked John Luke's Instagram page."

I stopped mid-swallow and nearly choked. "What did she find?"

A glorious smile spread across Scarlet's face. "The girlfriend that John Luke always goes running back to when his relationships bite the dust."

I thought of Cade. Was that what I was doing with him?

"Did you hear me?" Scarlet asked.

"Sorry, yes, but what does that have to do with . . . ohhh! So we're going to look for John Luke at his old girlfriend's house in Fort Worth." I thought about the implication of that. This was information Mateo would want to pursue, and he wouldn't be happy that we were horning in on his investigation.

"Why didn't you tell Mateo last night? This would help him catch Ava's killer."

"We can't do that until after we talk to John Luke."

Obviously, Scarlet had been smelling too many perm solutions. "I don't want to talk to John Luke. I want the cops to talk to John Luke. That's their job. My job is to run my family bookstore. Your job is to make people beautiful. That's it. I don't want a side job of apprehending fugitives wanted for murder. I just want to point Mateo in the right direction. That's it."

"But John Luke's not wanted for murder."

"He will be once Mateo gets a confession out of him."

"That's the problem. John Luke has been around the block so many times on domestic violence charges, he knows better than to say a word. He won't confess. He waits for his victims to recant. Then John Luke skates."

"How do you know that?"

"I told you. I do Sally Ferguson's hair, she tells us what men to avoid. John Luke has been on that list since he came to town."

I thought about that for a moment. Sally Ferguson was a good friend to have in a small town with very few single men to choose from. Not that I needed to worry about it, but who knew what the future held.

"So how do you know his ex-girlfriend—what's her name?"

Scarlet's grin lit up her face once more. "You'll love this." She glanced in my direction to make sure she had my full attention. "Abbey Norma Parson."

I repeated the name, wondering if I should recognize it from high school, but couldn't come up with a face.

Scarlet's smile along with her shoulders dropped with disappointment. "Everyone on Instagram calls her Ab. Think about her name. Ab Norma Parson—abnormal person."

A laugh sputtered from my lips before I could cover it. "It can't be real. It's a joke, right?"

"Nope. No joke."

I tried to hold the giggle, but Scarlet's grin didn't help. "That's just cruel. What parent would make a kid go through school with that name?"

Scarlet shrugged. "The same kind of parent that would give a girl the name Femall Watson and spell it F-e-m-a-l-e."

It was impossible to stop giggling. "What? You're lying."

Scarlet laughed. "Maybe, maybe not. Anyhoo, Abbey lives in Fort Worth."

I took a bite of my bar and washed it down with water before the taste killed me. "She actually lists her address on her account? That's stupid."

"No, it's not listed."

"Then how do you know she lives in Fort Worth?"

"I had Joellen check the longitude and latitude from a picture John Luke posted of the two of them last year."

"Last year! We're chasing an address from last year?"

"No. She verified it with a recent photograph Abbey posted on her page of lasagna she was cooking last week."

"How can you check the longitude and latitude of a photo?"

"It's actually really easy. Unless you disable the location services on the camera on your phone, every photo has the longitude and latitude embedded into the photo. You download the photo and extract the GPS coordinates from the properties of the photo. What you should watch for is that it extracts the coordinates from the location of when the photo was uploaded to Instagram. Then you run the coordinates online and boom! You got their location."

"That's freaking crazy. How did you know that?" I pulled my phone out of my pocket and began scrolling through my settings.

"I saw it on an episode of *48 Hours*."

I pulled up my location services on my photo app. Fuzz buckets. Every photo I'd ever posted had listed my location to every Tom, Dick, and Scary out there. I immediately changed my setting from WHILE USING THE APP over to NEVER. Then I texted my dad for the gazillionth time since I'd rolled out of bed.

Are you doing okay?

Yes, I'm fine. Sugar says the store is fine. Princess is fine. Hazel Rock is fine. Have fun.

How could I have fun? I was worried sick something would happen to him.

I texted back. *I love you.*

I got a string of heart emojis back from him and laughed. My daddy was using emojis.

Scarlet reined me back in. "There's just one problem."

Of course there was. I clicked my phone closed and listened.

"She lives in an apartment complex. We have the building location, but not the apartment number."

I nearly gagged on my last bite of breakfast bar. Tree bark would have gone down easier than that thing. "How do you propose we find the apartment? Knock on every door until John Luke answers the door?"

"But that's the best part." Scarlet looked like she was going to jump out of the car with excitement. "We're going to conduct a stakeout."

My best friend had lost her ever-loving mind. "A stakeout?"

"Yes, ma'am. I checked it out on Google Maps and Google Earth. We can park around the corner and watch for Ava's car. It'll be a piece of cake."

I thought about my favorite cop show. Steve McGarrett and Danno were great at stakeouts and Kono Kalakaua kicked butt. Charli and Scarlet—we didn't quite have their skill set. And I was talking about the actors, not the characters. But still, this could be fun. My lips turned up at the corners as I warmed up to the idea.

Scarlet's eyes sparkled. "I see your mind working. You know you're just as excited to be on a stakeout as I am."

I reeled in my emotions. "What do we do when we find him? How do we approach him?"

"We'll have to play that by ear."

"By ear? We're going to go in without a plan?"

Scarlet took her hands off the wheel as if to say, *what's wrong with that?*

Everything was wrong with that, but when I was going seventy-five miles an hour down Interstate 20 toward Fort Worth with my best friend on my side, it sounded like an adventure I couldn't pass up. Especially if it kept my daddy safe and put a killer behind bars.

Besides, what could go wrong?

Chapter Sixteen

"I'm dying over here."

"O.M.W. You're not dying."

"I feel like I'm dying. It's a hundred and twenty degrees in this car, there's not a breeze to be found, and my stomach is killing me."

"You're probably backed up from all that toxic food you eat." Scarlet's voice didn't hold the excitement it had earlier. Now she sounded tired of listening to me.

"I'm probably going to explode from all the fiber you've put into my body. We've been here all day and Ava's car hasn't moved an inch. How do we know John Luke is even here? He could have dumped the car and headed for Colorado. That's what I would do." I grabbed my stomach as it rolled for the umpteenth time.

"Because Abbey Norma Parson posted that her man has returned."

"There's a picture of him?"

Scarlet held up her phone with Abbey's page filling the screen. "She posted it on one of those pink hearts backgrounds."

Sure enough, I was staring at a screen of pink hearts and white lettering that announced, *My man is finally home for good!* The post had two Likes, one crying emoji, and one comment that said *WTH, Ab?* Obviously, not all of Abbey's friends were on board the welcome-home wagon train.

My stomach rolled once more as I wiped the sweat off my brow. "I need to find a restroom."

"What? We can't leave now. We'll miss him leaving."

"The only one who's moved in this parking lot was an elderly couple and a bunch of homies slinging dope."

Scarlet's lips pursed. "We can't leave." Then she pushed a button she knew would make me stay. "Kono wouldn't leave."

Except my stomach rolled again and I knew it was only a matter of time. "Kono is on a stakeout for five to ten minutes tops during filming. Not ten hours!"

Scarlet stuck to her guns. "She wouldn't leave."

"She gets fed real food, while I've been eating the worst food known to man."

By the look on Scarlet's face, I'd overstepped a boundary, but my stomach had had enough. "Scarlet, I have to use a restroom."

"Fine, but don't blame me if he leaves in the meantime." She started the car and I immediately went for the air-conditioning. Thank God someone had convinced her to have it installed in her little Suzy Homemaker Oven that had been baking me all afternoon.

On our journey to Fort Worth, I'd told Scarlet everything I knew about the case, including the bit about the blood on Ava's shirt the morning she died. Nothing put a fire in Scarlet's spirit like the thought of any woman being abused. I felt it too, but Scarlet had an anger burning in her gut that was dying to be released. I had something else lighting a fire in my stomach.

Scarlet zipped out of the parking spot we'd occupied for most of the day and headed toward the one exit in the entire complex. I wasn't sure what the place had looked like when it was first built, but currently the apartment complex named Holy Temple was the exact opposite of anything holy, and there wasn't a temple within a ten-mile radius.

We headed east out of the neighborhood and stopped at the first store in sight. Scorpion Liquors was the only store within a couple miles of our location. The windows had bars on them, but I could still see a few spiderweb cracks reaching out from two bullet holes in the glass. Nice.

I hopped out of the car before she came to a complete stop and dashed inside. "Where's your restroom?" I asked the guy with the long stringy hair standing behind a slab of bulletproof glass. He looked up from the hot rod magazine he was reading and mouthed the word, "What?" before flipping a switch to turn on the round silver mic positioned at eye level.

I tried to maintain my composure as I asked a second time, "Where's your restroom?"

"It's not for public use."

"You've got to be kidding me." I wouldn't make it to the next store— wherever that was.

"Sorry." He flipped the mic off and went back to his magazine.

I tapped on the glass and watched him exhale as his eyes slowly reached my face. He flipped the switch again. "Listen, lady, we don't allow no tricks in our bathroom."

"Tricks? Wait—what? You aren't suggesting I'm a prostitute, are you?"

He shrugged as if to say, *if the shoes fits . . .*

The only thing that kept me from pulling him through the little silver grate covering his mic was the roll my stomach decided to take. I needed that restroom. "Please. I'm not a prostitute. I'm here with my friend, Scarlet . . ." My best friend had decided to step out of her car and stretch her legs. I grabbed the first lie that popped into my head. "Scarlett Johansson." I was definitely going to visit the man downstairs when I died. "We got lost while looking for a friend's house. I just need to use a restroom." My voice sounded about as pleasant as a feral cat, so I waved toward Scarlet, who was pacing back and forth.

Her shape had all the right parts. Her alabaster skin glowed, and her red hair fell in glorious waves across her shoulders.

He tossed a set of keys into the money tray at the counter and slid it to my side of the glass. "Go through the door and turn right."

I didn't hesitate as he stood up and leaned over the counter to get a better look at Scarlett. The hallway was full of boxes of merchandise that should have been out on the shelves for customers to browse through. Then again, by the looks of the security setup, maybe they kept a minimal supply within reach of their customers' pockets. I opened the door on my right and thought I'd die.

It was beyond filthy. The white pedestal sink hadn't been white in twenty years and the toilet was no different. The tile around the toilet was a color I didn't even want to think about, and there was no toilet paper on the roll, just an empty cardboard spool sitting on the back of the toilet tank.

I could *not* use this bathroom.

My stomach rolled. I looked around for cleaning supplies and found none. I looked in the hallway. Nothing. I went back out to the bulletproof glass, tapped on the glass, and interrupted the peep show Scarlet was unwittingly providing for the cashier.

"Do you have some cleaning supplies?"

The guy pointed to the second aisle.

"You want me to take something off the shelf?"

"No. You can buy some off the shelf."

"You're kidding."

"I'm not the one who feels the need to clean the john."

I turned away before I growled and stalked to the cleaning supplies. The first thing I grabbed was a pair of rubber gloves—$5.99. The spray cleaner only came in a value pack for $6.99. I grabbed it and shoved it under my arm. The paper towels were $9.99 for a six-pack of a generic brand. I didn't need six. I needed one. Then again, by the weight of them, I'd probably use the entire half dozen on the toilet alone.

"Do you have toilet paper stored in back?" I yelled toward the front of the store.

The guy pointed one aisle over without taking his eyes from the camera on his phone that was directed at Scarlet.

"Unbelievable," I muttered as I made my way to the next aisle.

Luckily the toilet paper came in packs of four, not twelve or twenty, and was the cheapest necessity of the day at $4.99.

I reached the register about the time Scarlet decided to come into the store to see what was taking me so long. She wiggled her fingertips at the cashier, who grinned back at her. It caused a shiver to shimmy up my spine. I put the items on the counter, grabbed a couple candy bars, and pulled my credit card out of my wallet.

"We don't have room for all that," Scarlet said.

"We'll make room."

"Couldn't you wait until we got home to do your shopping?"

I barely got the words passed my clenched teeth. "The bathroom needs cleaned. They don't have any supplies, so I have to *buy* them. If there's anything left over after I fumigate that hole back there, we're taking them with us."

"But—"

The look I shot Scarlet made her shut her mouth, although I was pretty sure part of her was laughing at my predicament. Wait until she noticed the drool falling on the counter by Mr. Smooth.

He rang me up and I swiped my card through the machine.

"It was declined," he informed me, all the while smiling at Scarlet.

"Run it again." The gruffness of my tone got his attention and he looked to see if I was being disrespectful to his fine self. I formed a grin and struggled to spit out, "Please."

"Hell's fire, woman. You got the temper of that mean drunk that came in last night."

"I'm not drunk and I don't have a temper." My expression said otherwise.

"That's what he said. Said if the glass wasn't between us . . ." He held his hand up to his mouth like he was passing along a secret to the movie star on my left—through the intercom—for the entire empty store to hear.

"He actually used the F word, if you know what I mean. Said he'd put me in my place faster than I could spit on the sidewalk." He shoved a couple bags through the little money slot. I snatched them, but he was too caught up in trying to impress Scarlet to notice my anger.

"Well, duh." His mouth hung open and his eyes drooped like a Saint Bernard's. "The sidewalk is outside. I'm in here. Ab told him to behave, and then she paid for his beer. I wouldn't have paid for his beer."

I stopped bagging and exchanged a look with Scarlet. "Was this last night that Ab came in here with her boyfriend?"

He nodded. "I ain't never seen him before. But from the way they were acting, I'd say they were good for a night or two."

Yuk. His implication made me want to use the bleach spray on my ears. "What time were they in?"

"Right after I started at eight o'clock."

That meant John Luke couldn't have been the one who attacked Daddy. There was no way he could get from Hazel Rock to Fort Worth before one in the morning. If, of course, that was him with Ab last night.

"Was he about my height, skinny, receding hairline with a goatee and big blue eyes?" I asked.

"Yeah, brah. He's got these freaky eyes that look like one of those dolls you squeeze and the eyes pop out. I told Ab she could do better at Billy Bob's."

"Billy Bob's? Do you mean the bar?" Scarlet asked.

"Yeah, she works there on weekends. She's a bartender."

A bartender. The perfect girlfriend for an alcoholic. My stomach signaled I was done; I needed to clean the bathroom so I could use the facilities. "Excuse me." I pulled Scarlet off to the side. "He thinks you're Scarlett Johansson. See if he can identify John Luke from his picture on Instagram. I've gotta use the restroom. Now."

I heard Scarlet talking to the clerk as I made my way into the stockroom. I tore open the pack of paper towels and made a path to the toilet and then to the sink. I wasn't going to clean the floors, but I also wasn't going to walk on them. My next priority was the toilet. I sprayed it with a perfunctory layer of bleach and I worked on the sink while the cleaner worked on the toilet bowl. Ten minutes later, the trash can was full and the bathroom was the cleanest it'd been in twenty years. Not that it was clean, but it was slightly inhabitable. I disposed of my rubber gloves, never wanting to see them again, and took my remaining supplies with me.

The clerk was talking to another customer when I came out. I caught the tail end of his story about his prowess with "Scarlett" and smirked. In his dreams. His shirt was signed *Scarlet* across the front in red ink.

Scarlet was already in the car, raring to go by the time I made it outside. "You got a hot date later tonight?" I asked as I crammed my new cleaning supplies into the back of the car. They took up half of the rear window.

"A hot date with you—trying to catch a killer," she said. "Why?"

"Nothing. Did he come out of his little box for you to sign his shirt, or did you go into his inner sanctuary?"

"Neither. He took it off and shoved it through the little hole. I may need to use that bathroom cleaner on my eyeballs."

"If you're going to let someone think you're Scarlett Johansson, you might want to sign your name with two *t*'s."

"That could count as forgery."

She had a point. Scarlet headed back to the apartment complex so we could continue our stakeout that wasn't half as fun as it had sounded earlier that day. A least I had real food to snack on if I got hungry. She drove through the entrance of Holy Temple, and I was pretty sure a drug deal was going down between a kid on a bicycle with his pants down to his knees and a guy sitting so low in his car I couldn't see his chin. Scarlet was observing the two of them as if they were a mathematical equation she was having difficulty figuring out.

"Don't stare," I warned.

"Why?"

"Staring at dope dealers will get us shot."

"He's fifteen," she argued.

"Have you ever watched the news?" As beautiful and intelligent as Scarlet was, she lacked the needed skills to stay alive in the city.

"How do you know that's a dope deal?"

"You forget, I traveled from Hazel Rock to Denver on my own. I saw a lot in a few short days. You learn to leave everyone alone when you're on your own."

We drove to the back of the complex, and I got the distinct impression Scarlet's opinion of me had just been twisted ever so slightly. Whether it was for the better or not, I wasn't sure. She rounded the corner, and our biggest fear was staring us right in the face.

"He's gone," Scarlet said.

"I guess we're going to need those Black Widow skills you're famous for after all."

Chapter Seventeen

The expletive that came out of Scarlet's mouth was so out of character, I wasn't sure what to think as the palms of her hands hit the steering wheel.

"We've been sitting in this car all day, and all we have to show for it is a bunch of cleaning supplies and a clerk who says John Luke was in his store last night. All because you had to use the restroom." Scarlet closed her eyes; otherwise, they would have been shooting fifty-caliber bullets in my direction. "I've had listened to you complain about the food I brought for us all day long, my dress is a wrinkled mess, and my hair looks terrible." She leaned her forehead against the backs of her hands resting on the steering wheel.

If her hair looked terrible, my hair looked like a tornado had set down in the middle of it and stayed for five hours. But that wasn't the important part. I'd been a lousy friend to Scarlet and had literally driven her to cuss, which I'd never heard her do. Scarlet had given up her weekend to help me out, and all I'd done was complain and cause us more trouble.

"I'm sorry," I said. I looked at the time on my phone—eight-forty-five. About the same time John Luke and Abbey were buying liquor the night before. How had we missed them going through the neighborhood tonight? "Were you watching the street in front of the liquor store the entire time we were inside?"

Scarlet sighed and sat up. "No. It's not entirely your fault. While you were in the restroom, I went over to the wine display and chose a bottle of wine for later at the hotel tonight." She pulled a bottle of wine out from behind my seat.

Fuzz buckets.

"Do you know you are the best friend a woman could have?" I asked.

"If I was the best, I could tell you where John Luke was at this very moment."

"I think we know the answer to that."

Scarlet's brow wrinkled and then her eyes widened as it dawned on her. We said "Billy Bob's" in unison and smiled. I'd never been to Billy Bob's. I was too young before I left Hazel Rock and too busy since I'd returned. It only seemed fitting if I was going to miss Tony Bennett crooning with Mateo sitting next to me that I got to enjoy Billy Bob's with my best friend.

"Let's see if any of the neighbors have seen John Luke and know when he got into town before we head for the bar."

"Deal," agreed Scarlet.

"But let me do the talking."

That was going to be difficult for Scarlet. She loved to talk.

We started with the eight apartments the car had been parked in front of. The building was all beige brick from the 1960s and had two exterior hallways with four sets of stairs leading to the second level. All of the mailboxes were located at the entrance of the complex, so there was no way to check who lived in what apartment. We started with apartment 621. We could hear a television on the inside, but no one came to the door. Apartment 622 directly across the hall wasn't much better. The old woman who came to the door wouldn't open it and yelled through the wooden barrier, "Go away. I'm not buying nothing."

The door to apartment 623, at the back end of the hall behind 621, was answered by a teenager. He took one look at Scarlet and said, "Yo, I heard you was in the hood. You punkin' me?"

I don't think Scarlet understood a word out of his mouth, so of course she couldn't leave it up to me. "Excuse me?"

I stepped in front of her. "Actually, we're here to punk Abbey Parson. Do you know her?"

"I ain't talkin' to nobody but the Black Widow." He grinned and rubbed his chest.

Scarlet poked her head around me. "Want me to sign your shirt?"

"Baby girl, I got somethin' better." His shirt was over his head before I could say "Ms. Johansson doesn't do that," and he had a Sharpie in his hand as he pushed out a tattooed chest that was more defined than I would have expected. Still, he couldn't have been more than eighteen, and it creeped me out.

Scarlet hesitated but then grabbed the marker and began signing his chest. The kid began to pull out his cell phone, but I immediately put a halt to that. "No pictures. Ms. Johansson doesn't allow any photos to be taken."

Scarlet distracted him with questions about Abbey. "Do you know Abbey Parson?"

"I know some babe upstairs named Ab. She's a bartender."

"Does she live alone?" Scarlet asked.

"She's got a man who comes and goes. You need a man?"

I didn't think he qualified for manhood yet but didn't comment. Scarlet was tongue tied for the first time in her life. I held up my phone with the photo from John Luke's Instagram page. "Is this him?"

"Yah."

"Which apartment does she live in?" I asked before Scarlet could. I was getting the distinct impression my lie about Scarlett Johansson was going to come back and bite us on the backside.

"Directly above me in 627. Can I get a kiss?" He leaned toward Scarlet.

She smiled and blew him a kiss as I pulled her away and pushed her up the exterior set of stairs, completely ignoring apartment 624.

"Stay sweet!" she yelled at him.

I looked back to see the kid videoing Scarlet from behind. "Cover your face," I whispered to Scarlet, who obliged but couldn't help but add her two cents' worth.

"We're not doing anything illegal."

"You're signing Scarlett Johansson's name, surely there's some kind of law about impersonating a celebrity."

"I'm signing 'Scarlet.' It's not my fault these people think I look like her." The smile on her face, however, said she was flattered by the confusion. Who wouldn't be?

Since we had no idea what we would say to Ab or John Luke, I skipped her apartment and knocked on the one across the hall while Scarlet kept an eye on Abbey's door. A little girl about eight years old with braids and a Disney nightgown answered.

"Hi there, is your mommy home?" I asked.

She nodded.

"Can I talk to her?"

She nodded a second time.

"Could you get her for me?"

A third nod and the door closed in my face.

I looked at Scarlet, who shrugged. The door opened and a twenty-something woman who looked like an older version of her daughter opened the door, looked at Scarlet and squealed.

"Oh my God! It is you! Can I get a picture?" Her cell phone was already recording, but my hand blocked her view.

"I'm sorry, no photos."

Her expression looked like she wanted to smack my hand away, but she didn't. She had something else in mind. "Can I get you to sign my baby girl's arm?"

"Ms. Johansson doesn't sign children," I interjected.

Scarlet shook her head in agreement and smiled to soften the blow.

"Would you sign my shoulder?" she asked as she turned and bared her shoulder to Scarlet.

"This is getting downright scary," I muttered.

Scarlet smiled. "Of course."

"Do you know Abbey Parson?" I asked as Scarlet signed away.

"Sure. She makes a mean whiskey sour. Blends it with ice. It is one fine drink."

I could have used three whiskey sours. "Does she have a boyfriend?"

"What's it to you?"

"We're trying to set up a reality television show, and we need information on her so we can punk her." Where I came up with that lie, I had no idea.

Scarlet was grinning from ear to ear. She was thoroughly enjoying herself.

"Can I be part of the show?" the woman asked.

"Of course," I lied. Again. It was becoming too easy.

She squealed again and hugged Scarlet.

I pushed for more answers. "Does Abbey have a boyfriend?"

"She's got a piece of crap that comes by when he's in trouble."

Finally, we were getting somewhere. "Do you know his name?"

"John Luke."

She tried to take a video of Scarlet on the sly, but I moved in between them. About that time, I heard voices on the lower level. I glanced down the steps but couldn't see anyone. "Is he here now?"

"I saw the two of them leave about thirty minutes ago."

I let out a disgusted sigh for the woman's benefit. "I had hoped to get this filmed tonight." I turned to Scarlet. "I'm sorry, we're going to have to postpone the filming."

Scarlet was totally ready to play her role. "It's okay. I got to meet—" She waited for the woman to fill in her name.

"Shonda, and this is my baby, Kendra." The little girl peeked out from behind her mother, and Scarlet gave her the biggest smile possible.

"I got to meet Shonda and Kendra. Two beautiful and intelligent women."

I looked at Shonda, who was experiencing a moment of pride in herself and her daughter. "Will they be back tonight?" I asked.

She was more than happy to oblige. "Ab was on her way to work. John Luke goes to mooch liquor. They'll be home around three since Billy Bob's closes at two a.m."

I heard several people ascending the steps at once but wanted to get one more question in. "Do you know when John Luke got in town?"

"I'd say last night, but I don't know for sure. That's when he started parking in my spot and ticked off my baby's daddy."

Five people, three guys and two women, reached the second floor, took one look at Scarlet, and began heading our direction.

"Thank you!" I said as I pushed Scarlet toward the set of steps at the front of the building.

"Ms. Johansson, can we have your autograph?" asked one of the women as they began to run toward us.

"Run!" I told Scarlet.

She took off with me hot on her heels and her fans closing the distance. We made it to the car, got in, and slammed the door closed just before they reached the car. By then three more people joined and phones were recording us from every direction. Scarlet carefully backed up and we drove toward the exit of the complex at a walking pace with camera phones recording every step of the way.

I pulled the first thing I could from the back and tried to hand it to Scarlet to block the cameras from her side of the car.

"I'm not taking that! Besides, I might hit someone if I can't see what they're doing."

I held up the package to block the passenger window and saw that I'd grabbed the four-pack of toilet paper that was now three and I was holding it up in front of my window.

Fuzz buckets. If that made it to the media, we'd never live it down.

"If we get out of this without going to jail, I swear I will never impersonate a celebrity again," I said.

Scarlet laughed and blew a kiss to her fans.

Chapter Eighteen

We made it out of Holy Temple without killing, maiming, or otherwise hitting any of the residents and headed for downtown Fort Worth.

"We've got several people who've verified John Luke was here last night when my daddy was attacked, but not one of them cleared John Luke for Ava's murder. Where do we go from here?" I asked.

"Billy Bob's," Scarlet said as she swayed to the music on the radio. She was happy and in her element, thriving on the attention of her adoring fans—who weren't hers.

"What's the plan when we get to Billy Bob's?" I asked.

"The ladies at the beauty shop say John Luke is a talker when he's drunk. We'll blend in with the crowd and listen to what John Luke has to say."

I couldn't hide my skepticism. "He's not just going to just blurt out that he murdered his girlfriend."

"No, but he may say he was with her when she died. The only person who was with Ava was her killer. That, along with him beating her earlier that morning, is a start to a conviction."

I looked at my shirt. It was fine while sitting in the car, but John Luke would recognize the Book Barn Princess reference immediately if he saw me in the bar, and Scarlet couldn't blend in at a convention of gingers, let alone in a bar.

"I need to change before we go into Billy Bob's."

Scarlet slipped a glance in my direction. "I tried to tell you it wasn't appropriate."

"Are we near the hotel?"

"The hotel is in Dallas. We're in Fort Worth. It's too far to go there and come back."

I began looking at the stores on each side of the highway. Anything would do, but it was too late for any of the malls. "My dress won't go with my boots, and the heels I packed for the concert won't work at Billy Bob's. There!" I pointed to the next exit, which had a Target bull's-eye glowing in the night sky.

Scarlet took the ramp and we were entering the store a few minutes later.

"We need hats."

"Hats?" I asked.

"The last thing we need is for John Luke to recognize us."

"True, but I'm not sure a hat will go with your dress." If anyone could pull it off, it'd be Scarlet, but I still had my doubts.

"A pair of boots and a hat will look perfect. You go find yourself something to wear and I'll pick out a pair of boots and two hats."

We separated to find our purchases. I immediately spied a jean skirt with a cute pink cold-shoulder tee with oversized white and pink peacock feathers printed across the front of the material. It was adorable, not something I'd usually wear, and inexpensive. I tried them on and was shocked how good the outfit looked. I approached the fitting room attendant.

"Is it possible for you to cut the tags off these and let me wear them out of the store?"

She looked at me like I was nuts.

"I didn't know my boyfriend was taking me to Billy Bob's tonight. I don't have anything appropriate to wear, and since we're from out of town, I don't really have anywhere to change." Geez Louise, I was going to burn.

The clerk smiled. "You'll love Billy Bob's. Come here, I'll cut them off and notify the cashiers that you're coming their way."

A few minutes later I met Scarlet at the front of the store wearing my new outfit. Scarlet had a pair of adorable cowgirl boots that would look incredible with her dress despite their inexpensive price tag, and she was carrying two cowgirl hats—one black to match her outfit, and a pink one that matched the feathers on my shirt amazingly well.

"How did you know I'd pick pink?"

"What other color would you choose?"

She had a good point. We headed toward the register and I insisted on paying for her boots and the hats. Fifteen minutes later we were in line to pay at Billy Bob's. I'd never heard of the headliner performing that night, but that wasn't unusual when it came to the country music scene. The crowd seemed excited and the beat of the opening act was getting everyone in the mood for a little bit of boot scootin' across the floor. Scarlet was still attracting attention from every male in the area, but she handled it with class, and we were soon inside the bar scoping out the bartenders. With nine bars to check and a crowd of about 3,000 people, we decided to split up and meet in the middle. But just as Scarlet started to walk the other way, I spied Abbey and grabbed Scarlet's arm.

"Isn't that Abbey at the bar near the pool tables?"

Scarlet squinted, then grinned. "And that's John Luke playing a game of pool." She nodded toward the far side of the building where John Luke was playing a game with a big guy who was an inch taller than he was round. He looked more like a biker than a cowboy. The two of them did not fit in the Billy Bob's crowd, and both appeared to be well into the sauce. I spied a bouncer off to the side keeping an eye on two of them. Obviously, I wasn't the only one who thought they looked like trouble. If we were lucky, we'd get what we needed and wouldn't get caught in the middle of it.

Scarlet and I approached the bar station Abbey was working and waited our turn to order drinks. She was in her late thirties with brown hair and a cute face. She had a confidence behind the bar that I suspected she lacked in relationships. Otherwise, she wouldn't be with John Luke. Beyond the ring to his name, John Luke had no redeeming qualities whatsoever.

When Abbey finally looked up to take our order, she saw Scarlet first and her eyes widened. Scarlet winked and held her finger up to her lips to silence Abbey's question.

Good grief.

Scarlet ordered an amaretto sour for me and a soda with a twist of lemon for herself. When I tried to pay, Abbey declined.

"It's on the house," she said and winked at Scarlet.

I put a twenty-dollar bill in her tip jar and whispered to Scarlet, "That must be fraud, identity theft or something. Quit!"

Scarlet shrugged. "This town is fun."

"I would imagine every town is fun for Scarlett Johansson."

"Gimme another round, Abs." The voice behind us was familiar. Not a friend's voice, but one I'd heard in Hazel Rock's Tool Shed Tavern a time or two. Garbled by alcohol, it had the ability to send goose bumps up my arms. Scarlet and I froze.

"You've had enough. You've been drinking all day," Abbey replied and took a drink order from the guy next to John Luke.

"Ab, I said, give me another round." His anger was palpable. If the bar hadn't been between them, I wasn't sure what John Luke would have done.

Abbey slammed a beer on the bar, and John Luke reached between Scarlet and me as we turned our backs to him.

"Scarlett, Princess, what brings you to Fort Worth?" he asked.

Fuzz buckets. John Luke had recognized us even with our hats on.

We turned around slowly and I decided to play nice, especially since Scarlet was ready to snap his head off like an alligator going for a piece of rotten chicken. "John Luke? What are you doing here? You're not spying on our girls' weekend out, are you?"

John Luke grinned, and I joined the ranks with Scarlet. I wanted to smack that grin right off his face. Ava was sitting in the morgue while the man who supposedly loved her was playing pool, drinking free beer another woman was undoubtedly paying for, and he didn't feel a bit of remorse. Luckily, John Luke was too deep in his cups to notice my anger.

He took a swig of his beer and put his arms around our shoulders. His beer spilled on my new shirt.

"Oops, my bad, Princess. Want to go someplace and take it off?"

I was inches from taking something off—like his head. Somehow in the few minutes we'd been in his company, John Luke had decided he liked hanging out with Scarlet and me. Which worked for us, even if we wanted to put him down like a mad dog.

"Who are you playing pool with?" I asked.

"That's Boone. He's from Cut and Shoot."

Scarlet and I immediately looked for weapons on his buddy. The town of Cut and Shoot, Texas, had been one we'd feared as teenagers in Hazel Rock. We didn't dare go there after learning the town history of a brawl breaking out over a church service and the whole town being involved in cutting and shooting each other. That lesson was enough to keep us close to home.

As an adult, I learned Cut and Shoot may have embraced the name, but the violence never occurred. The stories of the dead and dying, however, still messed with my psyche, and from the look on Scarlet's face, she was feeling the same apprehension.

I looked at John Luke's eyes to gauge his level of intoxication. His pupils were dilated and his eyes were glassy. He stumbled as we walked toward the pool table, and Scarlet and I exchanged a look. It was time to get him to talk before we got in too deep.

"Did you find us some competition?" Boone asked as he rubbed his scraggly beard and eyed first me then Scarlet up and down.

"Princess and I are going to play you and Scarlet," John Luke informed us all.

Any other night I would have laid him out flat. Tonight I welcomed John Luke's arrogance. Boone racked the balls and handed his stick to Scarlet. I couldn't hear what he said to her, but I got the impression he wasn't as safe as John Luke was at the moment.

Scarlet positioned the cue ball and leaned over the table to take her shot. Boone decided to lean over her back and place his hand on her rear end. I closed my eyes and prayed Scarlet didn't get us killed. When I opened them, she was standing up and her face was up-turned toward Boone's. This time, I couldn't hear what Scarlet was saying, but Boone turned white and backed up with his hand covering his manhood.

I grinned. That woman, barely pushing five feet, was my hero.

Scarlet turned and took her shot, sinking the green six ball. Her next shot sank the three ball in the left corner pocket, and I knew it was time for me to question John Luke while she cleared the table.

"What brought you to Fort Worth, John Luke?"

"Ava and I had a falling-out."

"Really? I hope it wasn't too serious?"

He smirked. "Nothing a little cooling off time won't cure her of."

My breath hitched. How could he talk so casually about her lying in a refrigerator?

"What happened?" I asked as Scarlet sank her third ball.

"She's got a thing for the Judge. Been working overtime."

"The Judge?"

"Yeah, that old geezer, Sperry." His words were slurring, and I wondered how far gone he really was.

"Do you really think she was cheating on you with the Judge?"

John Luke shrugged like he didn't care, but I could tell his anger was building as his words slurred. He was ticked.

"Judge's wife seemed to think so. She called the house and wanted to know if the Judge was there. That man isn't welcome in my home. He may be her boss and tell her what to do with every speck of her life, but I'm the boss at home. I tell her what to do, not him."

"I'll bet," I muttered. Too bad he didn't have a home. That trailer belonged to Ava.

"What?" John Luke was having trouble focusing on me.

"I said, I'd be upset too."

That seemed to pacify him and inspire him to tell me more. "She mouthed off at breakfast and I popped her in the nose." He bumped my nose with his fist. It wasn't hard, but I could imagine how it felt when he put his anger behind it instead of showing me how he'd delivered the blow. I took a step backward.

"What'd she do?"

"Ran from the house and got in her car."

"Did you follow her?"

"Nah. She was bleeding pretty good, so I figured she learned her lesson."

"Did she run to the Judge?"

"Nah, man. I told her she needed to choose between me and him."

"What about her job?"

"She can get another job."

"Hadn't she worked for the Judge for over twenty years?"

John Luke shrugged. "She chose me." He took a swig of his beer as he swayed and Scarlet dropped another ball in the side pocket. Boone was grinning from ear to ear. He'd picked a ringer for a partner.

It was time to ask the most important question. "Why did you kill her?"

John Luke stared at me. His head jutted out toward me as if he was trying to rehear the question I'd asked. Then he pulled his chin back and chuckled. Chuckled.

My fist clenched. The music disappeared. All I saw was the ugly mouth of an abuser who had killed his girlfriend because he thought she had the audacity to cheat on him with her boss.

"What are you talking about? I didn't kill Ava. She's at home, stewing over a broken nose."

His words sank through my thoughts of violence. "You didn't kill her?" I asked.

John Luke's face lost all signs of humor and he seemed to sober up a bit. "What do you mean? Are you telling me Ava's dead?"

I nodded. Suddenly I was very sure that he didn't kill Ava, and I'd once again just delivered the news of her death in a completely inappropriate way. I felt ashamed of my behavior. Not that he deserved the curtesy of the news being delivered in a different manner, but still, my behavior was wrong. From the crinkle in his brow, I wasn't sure if he was going to cry, cuss, or turn violent. I couldn't read him.

"What did she do? Did she jump off the bridge? That stupid . . ." John Luke was no longer talking to me, he was gazing over the pool table without seeing any of the balls in play. But I was listening to every word he said.

"She was always threatening to end it all. Put me out of my misery. I guess she gone and done it after all. Good riddance."

I'm not sure how it happened. We were standing face-to-face. Close enough to touch each other. I was staring into his eyes and the next thing I knew, John Luke was on the floor holding his nose. Blood was dribbling through his fingers and onto the floor . . . and my hand hurt more than all get-out.

Fuzz buckets.

Chapter Nineteen

Boone was the first one to grab me. I wouldn't have fought back if he'd just tried to keep me from going after John Luke, but he spun me around and tried to put some kind of choke hold around my neck. The pressure felt like he was crushing my throat and stealing my breath. I scratched his arm and stomped on his feet. I heard a loud crack and saw the end of a cue stick clatter to the floor next to John Luke. Boone grunted in my ear and his arm loosened a tad, allowing me to breathe. The next noise he made was a bit higher than a grunt, and his arm fell away. I rushed forward as a group of cowboys descended upon us. I turned to see Boone legitimately cupping his jewels this time. Scarlet was grinning like a pet raccoon, and I got the distinct impression she'd delivered on her earlier threat—from behind Boone.

As the men quickly surrounded us, I immediately recognized the bouncer who'd been keeping an eye on Boone and John Luke, but it was the other faces—the ones I knew—that threw me for a loop. Faces from Hazel Rock—in Fort Worth, a hundred and eighty miles from my hometown.

They were bull riders. The cowboys who rode into my hometown once a year for our Cowboy Invitational and stole the show. Leading the pack was the rodeo star Dalton Hibbs, who had captured Scarlet's heart with his dangerous good looks, blond hair, and blue eyes. Boone didn't stand a chance. Dalton threw one punch with his overbuilt riding hand that normally kept him from falling off a bull, and Boone was on the floor next to John Luke.

Cowboys everywhere were looking for the next face to punch as more bouncers rushed through the crowd and formed a protective circle around the two men on the floor, making sure no one else got involved.

Scarlet squealed and jumped into the arms of her boyfriend, and as her hat fell off her head, I heard several bystanders ask, "Is that Scarlett Johansson?"

"No!" I answered before the rumor could spread. "That's Dalton Hibbs and his girlfriend."

A little awe sparkled in the eyes of some of the crowd. Everyone in Billy Bob's knew Dalton Hibbs. He was as big as it got in the rodeo circuit.

"I want to press charges," John Luke said through his hand as one of the bouncers helped him up to his feet. He staggered but pointed a bloody finger in my direction. "She broke my nose."

Scarlet stopped kissing Dalton for a moment to say, "He punched her first."

I thought about the moment John Luke's fist had encounter my nose. It wasn't really a punch, and I couldn't say he assaulted me, but I could tell the bouncers he was wanted in Hazel Rock.

"This is John Luke. He's wanted in Hazel Rock, Texas, for domestic violence assault, and I believe the police want to question him in regard to a homicide."

"I didn't kill Ava, I just punched her in the nose!" John Luke insisted.

Several men turned angry eyes toward John Luke, and he seemed to recognize that his words wouldn't win hearts, but they did influence the crowd in Billy Bob's. He closed his mouth as two cowboys I knew had to be stopped by the bouncers. Dusty Lamb and Travis Sinclair were full of testosterone that was demanding to be released, and that seemed to egg on the entire crowd.

A couple of off-duty cops working at the bar immediately calmed the vigilante atmosphere I'd created. My heart sank as Abbey pulled one aside. He nodded several times and then turned to look in my direction. I tried to smile, but failed miserably.

He and Abbey approached the circle, where Boone was starting to gain his legs with the help of two bouncers. John Luke was flanked by a couple of bouncers who plopped him in a chair and gave him a towel and a bag of ice to stop the bleeding.

"That's him," Abbey said.

"He's the one who hit you?"

"Yes, sir. This afternoon at my house when I wouldn't get him a beer. He backhanded me across the face."

In the full light from the pool tables I could see an abrasion running across Abbey's face that I hadn't seen while she'd been behind the bar. My guilt disappeared. I was wrong for what I'd done, but John Luke was

a monster who needed to be stopped. He might not have been a murderer
. . . yet, but he'd hit two women in three days, and his days of creating
domestic violence statistics had come to an end. This time, he was going
to be held accountable.

The officer put John Luke in cuffs and then turned toward the bouncer.
After that, I didn't see what happened to John Luke. Travis took one look
at me, grabbed my hand, and hauled me outside. We were three blocks
away before he finally said something.

"You've got a knack for finding trouble."

"You've got a talent for arriving at the right time to rescue me."

During the last rodeo, I'd ended up in a stock pen with one of the meanest
bulls I'd ever seen. Turned out, he'd been drugged, and Travis was the first
to arrive to help me. At the time, I thought he'd been the one who threw
me over the top of the stall. Now I knew he was more the type to throw a
woman over his shoulder.

"Princess, from the punch I saw you throw, I'd say you're the last
woman in town who needs rescued." He grabbed my hand and looked at
my knuckles. "Although you could use a doctor for that hand."

The knuckles on my left hand told a story I was glad the cops hadn't
seen—three were bleeding and the middle two were swollen and turning
a nasty black and blue.

"Huh. The last time I punched someone, you were in Hazel Rock.
Maybe trouble follows you."

Travis flashed that million-dollar grin all the rodeo fans adored. "Darlin',
that's a given." He put two of his fingers in the palm of my hand. "Can
you squeeze my fingers?"

I squeezed them and winced. "Yeah, but it doesn't feel very good."

"No crunching or grating sensation?"

I shook my head.

"Then I'd say we need to get it cleaned up and get some ice on it. Where
are you staying?"

"In Dallas."

He looked up at me through long lashes. "We could go to my hotel. It's
right down the street."

I knew what Travis was implying. We'd had a double date with Scarlet
and Dalton the last time he'd been in Hazel Rock. It had ended poorly when
Dalton was arrested for a murder he didn't commit, but before Travis had
left town, he'd kissed me and said he'd be in contact. We'd texted a few
times, but there was no commitment between us. I wasn't a fool. A guy
in his position wasn't a one-woman man.

"I think that would compound the list of bad decisions I've made on this trip."

Travis grinned. "I think that's the first time a woman has said I was a bad decision. If I wasn't married to the rodeo, I might have to sweep you off your feet and marry you."

It was my turn to grin. Travis was a nice guy, and someday, when he was ready, the right woman would let him do just that. Unfortunately, I wasn't that woman. "A man like you can stand to be knocked down a peg or two."

"True, but let's not publicize it. Okay?"

"Deal."

My phone beeped and saved both of us from the moment becoming uncomfortable. I looked at the text and saw a picture of Cade at the diner with my daddy. They were having dinner and a beer together. Cade had texted: *Your dad's in good hands.* I smiled. Daddy must have told him I'd been worried sick, and Cade decided to send the photo to put me at ease.

I texted back: *Thank you!*

Anytime, Princess.

Travis looked over my shoulder. "Ah. So the mayor has finally made his move?"

"What? No, it's not like that."

Travis smiled. "I think it is."

My phone rang before I could respond, and the caller ID showed Scarlet's name. "Are the cops looking for me?" I asked as I answered the phone.

"No. Where are you?"

"I'm down the street with Travis."

"Really?"

"It's not like that." I smiled at Travis, who leaned in for Scarlet to hear.

"She shot me down. I'm heartbroken." Travis grabbed his chest, and I pushed him away with my good hand.

His chivalry, however, didn't disappear. "Have a seat. I'll go into the restaurant and get some ice for your hand."

I took a seat on the cement planter outside the barbecue place we'd stopped in front of, mouthed *thank you*, and waited for him to return.

"Why aren't the cops looking for me?" I asked Scarlet.

"Because I told them it was self-defense."

"There were too many witnesses who saw that it wasn't."

"Abbey and the bouncer said that it was."

"Get out." I couldn't believe the two lied for me.

"I'm not kidding."

"Did you know the guys were in Fort Worth?" I asked.

"No. Dalton was supposed to arrive sometime tomorrow for the rodeo this week, but when I told him we were heading to Fort Worth, a few of them headed this direction early."

"How did they know we were at Billy Bob's?"

"I texted him while we were at Target and told him it wouldn't be the same without him there."

"Oh."

I could hear the grin in her voice. "It was a heck of a surprise. Listen, the officers wanted to know if you wanted to press charges on Boone, but when they ran him through the computer, he had a felony parole violation, so they took him into custody on that."

"A parole violation?" Geez, I knew how to pick 'em.

"Yeah. He was on parole for armed robbery. They said if you wanted to press charges, to stop by the police station. Dalton was none too happy with us."

I'd hate to hear what Mateo would have said if he'd arrived with Dalton. Luckily, he didn't have to know—unless John Luke said something to Mateo's detectives when they questioned him regarding Ava's murder.

I'd cross that bridge when I had to.

"Is that you, sitting in front of Riscky's?" Scarlet asked.

I looked back toward Billy Bob's and saw Scarlet and Dalton walking hand in hand. I waved and we hung up.

Dalton still looked ticked off, but he hugged me and said he was glad I was okay.

"Sweetie, can you give me a few minutes with Charli?" Scarlet asked.

It was obvious Dalton didn't want to leave us alone, but he walked over to the fountain and gave us some space.

"Charli, you know I wouldn't normally ask this . . ." Scarlet hesitated, and I knew exactly where this conversation was headed.

"Of course you can stay with Dalton," I said. "You never get to see him, and I live right across the street."

"I know, but this was supposed to be a girls' weekend."

"We both know that's not true. We set out to get a confession from John Luke, and we did it with witnesses to boot. John Luke is finally going to pay for what he did to Ava and Abbey. Our mission is accomplished. If I could use your car, I can drive to the hotel and pick you up in the morning."

"Are you sure you can drive?"

I sucked it up and flexed my hand, not letting her see any sign of pain. "It looks worse than what it is. Please go. You deserve this after the day we've had."

"What about you?"

"I have a king-size bed waiting for me. Nothing sounds better than that."

Scarlet hugged me around the neck, and I realized how tender my throat was but kept it to myself. "You really are a princess," she said.

"I think John Luke might disagree."

Scarlet laughed, and Dalton and Travis returned with my ice. After a few minutes of gentle but painful administrations from Travis, we all walked to Scarlet's car where Scarlet grabbed her bag and her health food and transferred it to Dalton's rental. Travis kissed me on the cheek and told me he was just a text away if I changed my mind.

We both knew I wouldn't, and I hit the road feeling very alone.

An hour and a half later, I was in my hotel room feeling worse than ever. I'd showered and was standing in a dark room wearing a T-shirt and underwear, looking at the view of Reunion Tower glowing in the Dallas skyline. The bed looked too big for one person, and the quiet I thought I'd enjoy was deafening. When my phone buzzed, I welcomed the interruption.

"Hello?"

The smooth baritone on the other end warmed me from the inside out. His question, however, made me feel as low as armadillo droppings.

"How was the concert?" Mateo asked.

"I . . . ah . . ." I decided to come clean. "We didn't go."

"Was Billy Bob's everything you thought it would be?"

"You knew? I'm struggling here not to upset you, and you already knew?" I wasn't sure if I was relieved or ticked that he'd tested me.

"I wanted you to know that you didn't want to lie to me."

That was the last thing I'd expected him to say. "What? That doesn't make sense."

"You miss me." His voice held enough confidence for ten men.

I rolled my eyes. "That's not true. Scarlet and I are having the time of our lives."

"I have no doubt Scarlet is having the time of her life . . . with Dalton in Fort Worth. How's your hand?"

"You know about my hand?" How did he know about my hand? "Then you probably know that Travis took care of it," I said.

"Travis is at Billy Bob's." His confidence wasn't shaken in the least.

Unbelievable. "Do you have spies watching me?"

"I have a buddy on Fort Worth PD who happens to work off-duty at Billy Bob's. I got an interesting call from him about an hour ago."

"So why didn't you call and chew me out earlier?"

"Why would I chew you out?"

"For interfering in your case."

"You helped the case."

"You admit it?" I smiled.

"I admit it. I don't like it. You could have been seriously hurt going after John Luke like that."

"He's not the killer."

"I know."

"Because your buddy called and told you he was beating Abbey Parson while Ava was being killed?"

"Because I have gas station video of him in Fort Worth at the time of Ava's murder."

"How did you get that?"

"My detectives are the real thing, Charli."

I cringed. I'd just insulted him without meaning to. "I'm sorry. I know they are. Did you hear that John Luke confessed to hitting Ava in the nose the morning she died?"

"I did. Thank you for that. We'd already planned on filing charges on him with your dad's testimony, but that adds to our case."

"My dad?"

"Yeah, after John Luke beat her, Ava went to your dad for help."

Of course she did. Because that's the kind of man my daddy was. "They weren't . . ."

"Dating? No, they've been friends for years. Your dad was the first to recognize she was in trouble with John Luke. He told her he'd be there for her if she ever needed help, and he was."

My eyes filled with tears. "I should have seen that."

"Probably, but I also think you want him to be happy and you saw Ava as someone who could potentially make him happy."

He was right. I did want my daddy to fall in love again—to feel the companionship he'd had with my mom. I sniffed and grabbed a tissue off the desk before I started blubbering.

"Tell me about our room."

I couldn't help but laugh. "*Our* room? You mean the one I'm standing in all alone with an oversized king bed and a balcony overlooking the Dallas Skyline with Reunion Tower glowing in shades of pink?"

"Is it pretty?"

"It's gorgeous." I watched the tower turn from dark pink to light pink and I thought of home and the Book Barn Princess. "Wait. I've never seen the tower pink before. Did you—"

"It pays to know people."

"You had them turn the lights pink?"

"It's computer generated. It only involves a few clicks of a mouse."

"But still . . ." My voice cracked. "You did that for me?"

"I did that for you."

Mateo had not only bought tickets to the concert I'd always wanted to see, he'd booked the perfect hotel room and created the perfect atmosphere for a romantic weekend—that I was spending alone.

"I've got something else for you."

I couldn't help but tease him. "You do realize that you'll never be able to compete with the weekend you created for me. The weekend you didn't even bother to attend."

Mateo laughed, but then his voice became soft and seductive. "I would give anything to be there with you."

I believed him. Completely.

"Are you lying on the bed?"

It was my turn to laugh. "You're not going to turn this phone call into something naughty, are you?"

"Lie down on the bed, Charli."

I did as he said without arguing in the least. Then I heard a piano in the background, and I recognized the tune immediately. A bass took over where the keyboard left off and the slightly gravelly baritone of Mateo's voice began singing "Steppin' Out with My Baby." I'd never heard him sing or hum anything, but the man had a voice that could make men jealous and women swoon.

I smiled because despite everything, this was turning out to be the most romantic date I'd ever had.

Chapter Twenty

I was up bright and early, feeling better than I had expected to when I'd arrived at the hotel the night before. I went for a swim, took my time getting ready, and texted my daddy to make sure he was okay. He told me to stop nagging him, he was working and everything was fine. I checked out of the hotel and did some shopping in the Fort Worth Stockyards before I met Scarlet and Dalton for lunch at the Cattlemen's Steak House. A tasty lunch and a few uncomfortable moments while Scarlet and Dalton said goodbye and we were back on the road to Hazel Rock.

"You're not mad at me for ditching you last night?" Scarlet asked.

"Not at all. I had a very good night."

Scarlet's eyes left the road to look at me. "What made it so good?"

I held up a picture of Reunion Tower lit up in pink.

"O.M.W. that man's got it bad."

I was hoping I wasn't the only one who thought that but didn't want to discuss it any further. "Before we get back to town, would it be all right if we stopped to see Isla?"

"Of course. Is this personal or investigative?"

"Both."

"I'm all in." Scarlet stepped on the gas and I held on to the dash. Some things never changed.

A few hours later, we pulled up in front of Oak Grove Manor, and the three amigos were sitting out front in rocking chairs. Frank threw an elbow to one of his buddies and they all looked in our direction. By the time we got out of the car, all three of them were asleep with their chins on their chests.

"Aren't they cute?" Scarlet said.

"Adorable."

As we passed, I saw Frank's left eye peek open, and his two buddies were checking out Scarlet's backside. I laughed and their eyes immediately closed as Scarlet turned around.

"What?" she asked.

"Nothing. I'm just getting an eyeful."

Scarlet looked at me like I was losing my mind, but I just kept walking. On the way out, I'd have to introduce her to Frank and his friends.

Joan was sitting at the front desk reading a book that looked like one of the mysteries I'd brought for Isla. Her hair was pulled back off her face, and the style made her look even older than she had on my previous visit. She looked up from her reading and immediately stashed the book out of sight. I couldn't tell if she didn't want us to know she was reading or if she was hiding that particular book.

"Charli, another surprise visit. How nice." Her tone didn't sound like she thought it was nice.

"Is Isla in?" I asked.

"She hasn't left her room, but Mr. Andrews is playing Scrabble with her."

"The director's here on the weekend?" I asked.

"Mr. Andrews comes in *every* day." Her tone made me feel like a chastised little kid. "These people are his family. If you'll wait just a minute, I'll call Isla and see if she's up for visitors."

I had to respect a man who devoted so much time to his clients, but it also made me feel a bit like a heel that a complete stranger would come to work on his day off to play Scrabble with Isla and I was stopping by because I wanted information about the Judge. Where was the Judge? It was Sunday. Shouldn't he be spending it with Isla?

Joan got on the phone and dialed Isla. "Isla? This is Joan. You have a visitor." Joan looked at me. "No, honey. It's Charli from the Book Barn Princess in Hazel Rock." She paused another moment as she listened to Isla. "Of course. I'll send her back."

Joan hung up the phone. "Do you know where her room is?" Her tone still held judgement that I didn't particularly care for.

"Of course." I repeated her words so she understood just how routine my path to Isla's room was.

Scarlet and I walked toward the west wing.

"O.M.W. what did you do to Joan?" she whispered as she gazed back down the hall. "She's watching us."

"I'm beginning to think she's a bit creepy."

"Really? I'm not sure what gave you that idea." Scarlet smiled and waved behind us.

"Humph," echoed down the hall.

"Remind me not to visit Isla with you anymore. I'm in good standing with these people."

"I thought I was too, but apparently not."

We passed by a nurse's station, but the two women standing at the counter were busy discussing their lunch and never looked up. When we reached Isla's room, the door was open and Isla was sitting at her table with a Scrabble board in front of her and Mason Andrews sitting directly across from her.

"Ha!" she said as she laid down several tiles on the board. "T-R-A-D-U-C-E. Traduce."

I leaned over to Scarlet. "Is that a word?"

"It means to speak maliciously and falsely of; slander; defame."

"Oh." Fuzz buckets. That's twice Isla had spelled words that made me wonder what she was trying to say. Was it a confession, or was it the only way she could express her grief over the whole ordeal?

I knocked on the door and the two of them looked up. Isla immediately got up and limped over with her cane to give me a hug. "Eve! It's been so long since I've seen you." I closed my eyes and returned the hug Isla thought she was giving my mom . . . who'd been dead for twenty years.

Isla released me and turned toward Scarlet. A moment of confusion passed her face, and Scarlet filled in the blank. "It's Scarlet, ma'am. Remember, I do your hair?"

Isla looked back and forth between the two of us and then grabbed my arm. "You mustn't let me make mistakes like that, Charli."

"It's a common mistake, or so I've been told."

"It is true; you are the spitting image of your mother. But your mom? Well, she was a quiet woman, and you haven't been quiet since you came out of the womb."

"Are you sure you're not thinking of Scarlet?" I teased.

Scarlet put her hands on her hips with a feigned look of offense. "I think I resemble that comment very much, thank you." Then she hugged Isla.

"I'm going to go check on Mrs. Bigalou. You have a nice visit with Charli and Scarlet." Mason Andrews tipped his head and left the room.

"He seems like a very nice man," I told Isla as she offered a seat to us and took her place in front of the Scrabble board.

"He is. Mason came to Oak Grove after his mother passed away. Guilt can change a person's life."

"What do you mean?"

Isla shrugged. "Mason was an office manager for a major hospital out west. He made really good money, but when his mother fell and broke her hip, no one was there to help her. She died in her own home."

"O.M.W. That's horrible!"

I could think of stronger words than *oh my word*, but it was nice to see Scarlet reverting back to her pre-Charli-influenced language.

"He's dedicated his life to helping the elderly?" I asked.

Isla smiled and her gaze traveled to the window. "He's like a second son."

"I didn't know you had a son," I told Isla.

She looked at me, somewhat confused, then laughed, a gentle and joyful noise. "Eve, honey, you are the funniest daughter-in-law I could have asked for."

Her words froze the blood in my veins. That was the second time Isla had called me by my mother's name in less than fifteen minutes, but this time she called me her daughter-in-law. Isla began counting her Scrabble pieces.

"Silly me, I didn't pick up two pieces to replace the letters I played," she said.

But this time it was my turn to zone out. I looked at Scarlet, who seemed too scared to move. A memory flashed through my thoughts. My mom playing Scrabble with Isla—at the Book Barn Princess—and then again in our apartment. Isla had been there when my mom had been sick. She'd taken care of her when I'd been at school, but I never remembered Isla being in the same room as my dad . . .

It couldn't be. They would have told me. My mom would have told me. My dad wouldn't have let so many years pass without me knowing I had family in Hazel Rock. This was not a secret you kept from someone.

"Evie, honey. It's your turn," Isla said.

I looked down at the letters in from of me and saw only one possibility. A word that seemed to tell me the universe was playing kickball with my psyche. I put the letters on the board and watched Isla for a reaction.

The word meant even more to her than it did to me—if that was possible. Her eyes were rimmed with tears.

"When are you going to bring that little Princess of mine by to see me?" she asked.

I'd heard enough. I couldn't handle any more. It was like poking a dead horse and waiting for it to explode. I wasn't stupid enough to shove the stick in too far. Or maybe I was too afraid of the outcome. It would be messier than I could handle.

I surveyed the damage to Scarlet's shoe and saw that she wouldn't be able to walk unassisted to her car. Nor would she be able to walk without her shoes on the oil-covered gravel.

Fuzz buckets. I needed time alone.

A vintage Camaro I recognized pulled off the road in front of us.

Just peachy. Now I'd have to face Scarlet's questions and Cade Calloway's inquiry as to why we were walking along the road when it was ninety-five stinking degrees outside. Geez Louise, I'm not sure it could get much hotter. Cade looked as fresh as ever in a pair of khaki pants rolled up at the ankles and the sleeves rolled up on his button-down shirt. Wearing deck shoes and aviator sunglasses, he looked like he should be shopping on Martha's Vineyard, not walking along a stretch of road in the middle of Texas.

"You two okay? Did Scarlet's car break down?"

"She broke off her heel," I said.

Scarlet held up the missing appendage for Cade to see.

"Then why are you walking?"

I changed the subject. "What's up with the new outfit?"

Cade's cheeks flushed. They actually turned the shade of my favorite armadillo's shell.

Scarlet butted in. "Charli was mad."

"I'm not mad." *Mad* was a simple word. My feelings were too complex for such a plain and manageable word. A more appropriate description of my mood might be mordant, irascible, or splenetical. But even those didn't begin to touch the surface of what was going on inside me.

Cade ignored my question and stayed focused on my mood. "What are you mad about?"

I threw my hands in the air.

Scarlet nodded. "She's right. She's hurt."

"I'm not hurt."

Cade's left brow rose and he took off his sunglasses, but he didn't say a word.

"I needed some exercise." More like an exorcism—something mean was dying to get out of me.

Cade volunteered to die on a stake. "I'll take her home."

"Would you?" Scarlet asked at the same time I said, "That's not necessary. I can walk."

I stepped away from Scarlet, who wobbled before Cade slipped his arm under hers.

"Have a seat in the Camaro while I get Scarlet back to her car."

I looked at the two of them retreating, and huffed. I was probably sending smoke signals out of my ears all the way across Coleman County. What had I done to deserve them?

The answer to that question was simple. Nothing. They were two good and caring people, and I really didn't deserve to have them—at all. I turned around and walked toward the Camaro and got in the passenger side.

The cool air-conditioning felt incredible, but it didn't make me feel better. Scarlet zipped by in her little two-seater and *beep-beeped* at me again with a wave. My return wave didn't have half the amount of enthusiasm.

Cade got in the car, and it felt much smaller. In high school, I loved riding in his car. Today, I felt like I had no personal space.

"Are you going to tell me what this is about?" I waved my hand up and down, indicating his attire.

"Only if you tell me about what happened at Oak Grove Manor."

I folded my arms. "Forget it." I looked out the side window. "Just drive."

He put the car in gear and pulled out onto the road. The music on the stereo was the seventies rock that he'd listened to as long as I'd known him. I'd never understood the attraction, but I could tell it'd never lost its appeal for him by the way his thumb tapped on the steering wheel. It took him two miles before he tackled the problem once more.

"Did Isla say something that upset you?"

The slight hesitation in his approach spoke volumes and reminded me of the secret Cade had said was my dad's to tell.

"You know."

Guilt washed over his face. "Know what?"

"And you didn't tell me."

He closed his eyes and submitted. "Princess, it wasn't my story to tell."

"Have you known my entire life? Has the whole town known and only little Princess was kept in the dark about the dirty little secret?"

"There's nothing dirty about it," Cade insisted. "No one knows except me."

"Scarlet knows. At least she does now. Dad knows. Isla knows . . . oh my God. He's my grandfather?" I'm not sure why I hadn't thought of Judge Sperry being a relation until that very moment. It was probably the shock of finding out I actually had a living grandparent. Or that my parents had lied to me my entire life. Thirty years of deception—how could they do that?

"How is it my ex–high school boyfriend knows, but I don't?"

"I found out by accident."

"What accident?"

Cade ran his fingers through his hair. It was his telltale act of frustration. Unhappy and just plain uncomfortable with the position he found himself in. "It wasn't really an accident . . ."

"If it wasn't an accident, than what exactly was it?"

"It was part of my job."

"What in Sam Hill does being the mayor of Hazel Rock have to do with knowing my family secrets?"

"Not mayor. Attorney. Last year I updated the Judge's and Isla's will for them. Beyond that, I can't tell you anything more. It's protected by attorney-client privilege."

"You have got to be kidding me!"

He ruffled his curls again. "Princess, I shouldn't have told you that much."

"There's no doubt in my mind that everyone in Hazel Rock knows you prepared the Judge's will."

"Probably, but that doesn't mean I could confirm it if somebody asked."

"You've known since I came back and said nothing."

Cade got off the highway and turned onto Main Street. "I found out right before the election."

"The election? You mean the election that you won? The election that I waited patiently to be over? The election that was the reason why you were too busy to have dinner with me?"

"I was having a hard time seeing you and knowing that I was part of the deception."

Finally, a confession I could believe for those weeks of avoidance after the election when we were supposed to have a date. A date that never happened and the reason I moved on.

I leaned my head against the headrest and closed my eyes as Cade parked in front of the Barn. He left the engine running, and I could tell he was looking for a reaction from me. Forgiveness for knowing what I didn't about my own stupid life. Understanding for why he'd avoided going out on a date with me.

He'd been put between a rock and a hard place with only a pair of deck shoes to kick his way out. I understood his dilemma in my head, but my heart felt bruised. It'd taken one heck of a beatin' and I wasn't sure it was ready to heal.

I turned toward Cade and asked the question I deserved an answer to. "What's up with the new look?"

He searched my face, but I don't think he found what he was looking for. "I'm being groomed to run for the senate. The party wanted to know if I could blend in with the power players on the East Coast."

"Did you pull it off?"

"I'm not sure, but if you have to ask, probably not."

It was interesting to see Cade uncertain. There were very few times in our history that I could remember him being insecure. "I have no doubt you pulled the wool right over their eyes. You certainly did mine."

I got out of the car and walked past the front of the Barn. The Closed sign was flipped and the lights were out. Daddy was gone for the day, which was probably a good thing. I headed toward the alley and through the gate with the sign hanging above it proclaiming it to be Eve's Gate. I'd always believed it held the spirit of my mom—conking Cade on the head as he got fresh when we were teens, dropping on the head of an overly persistent reporter, and crashing into Mike Thompson's nose when he demanded money he didn't deserve. This evening as the sign groaned in the wind, I could hear a whisper of an apology: *We should have told you.*

"You're darn tootin' you should have told me." I stomped up the stairs to my apartment where I was greeted by the only innocent person I knew. "Princess!"

My little pet scurried around my feet; her toenails clicking across the floor in a happy dance. It was almost enough to wash away my feelings of betrayal. Unfortunately, almost didn't quite cut it.

Chapter Twenty-two

I rolled out of bed with puffy eyes and the smell of armadillo on my arm and chest. Princess had recognized my need for comfort and had jumped up on the bed and curled in the crook of my arm. Last night I didn't mind how her scent enveloped me. She was home. This morning, she just plain stank.

"I love you, Princess. But snuggling seems to agree a little too much with you."

Princess struggled to keep her eyes open and lost the battle as she huffed and then tucked her head back under her tail. I would have loved to join her.

I took a shower and made my way to the store in twenty-five minutes—just in time to receive the new shipment of children's books we'd ordered for the drive. It was to be the Barn's personal contribution to the event.

I fed and watered Tweetle Dee and Tweetle Dum, then began sorting the donations we'd received over the weekend by age group. Some of the books brought back memories of my own childhood of settling into an old chair in the loft and reading for hours. The only thing that would bring me out of the imaginary worlds created by Laura Ingalls Wilder or the authors who wrote as Carolyn Keene, would be a call from my mom telling me it was closing time. Then the three of us would head out the side door of the Barn, go through the gate and up the stairs to our apartment. Those were the best days of my life . . . and they were a lie.

I was still having trouble wrapping my brain around that and trying to figure out what could possibly keep my parents from telling me that the Sperrys were my paternal grandparents. They had a different last name, for Pete's sake!

The side door to the tearoom opened and closed, and I knew it was my daddy. I wasn't sure I was ready to face him.

I looked up as he walked into the main sales floor of the Barn. "Good morning, Princess."

His greeting wasn't any different than any other morning, but I could see the caution in his eyes.

"He told you."

Daddy nodded.

"Funny how everyone tells everyone else the important details of my life, but I get left out in the dark." I sounded spoiled, pouty, and about five years old.

"Let's talk."

I turned away. "It's almost time to open the store. Let's not."

"We're opening late today. This is more important. You're more important."

I might have cried, except I'd done too much of that the night before. Today the anger had taken over. "Fine." I brushed by him, got myself a glass of sweet tea, and sat down in the tearoom. Daddy walked over and started his coffee, something I normally did for him, but the five-year old in me was throwing a tantrum, so the coffee was purposely forgotten.

Before sitting down at the table, he put a box of cookies in front of me. "I thought these would be the perfect breakfast today."

No-bake chocolate-chip oatmeal cookies were my favorite, and I'm not one to look a gift horse in the mouth. The treat was too scrumptious to pass up. Forgiveness had nothing to do with my acceptance of the cookies.

I took a bite and savored the goodness.

"I'm sorry," Daddy said.

I looked at him across the table and waited.

"You're not going to make this easy on me, are you?"

"A thirty-year-old secret isn't something that comes easy to anyone."

Daddy took a deep breath and blew it out. "You're right. Where should I begin?"

"Start at the beginning. Who brought you into this world?"

"Isla Warren."

That made me pause. It explained the difference in the name and gave me hope. The Judge wasn't my grandfather. "Who's your father?"

"Jacob Sperry."

Fuzz buckets.

"They weren't married when you were born?"

Daddy shook his head. "My father wasn't in my life until I was thirteen years old."

"Thirteen?"

The coffeemaker finished, and Daddy walked over and got a cup of his coffee. He probably needed the fortitude to finish his story. When he turned around, he dove right back in. "My father never knew my mom was pregnant. He went into the military and she moved away to live with relatives. Unwed mothers weren't exactly viewed as acceptable back then."

I remembered how hard single parenthood had been on my daddy when I was ten. I couldn't imagine how hard it'd been on Isla in the early sixties. "Did you grow up in Fort Worth . . . or was that a lie as well?"

"I lived in Fort Worth my whole life, until I married your mother."

"You told me your parents died before you got married. Why?"

"Let me get to that." Daddy chose not to sit down this time. Instead he leaned against the counter and crossed his ankles, his coffee mug gripped in both of his hands. "My father showed up when I was thirteen, and I wanted no part of him. My entire life I'd watched my mom work two, sometimes three jobs to support us. I'd delivered newspapers before school and mowed lawns after school. Then one day he showed up and wanted us to be a family. Needless to say, I wasn't on board when he wanted me to take his name."

"Why wasn't he there when you were born?"

"He was on leave from the military when my mom got pregnant, but he left and my mom couldn't find him. She knew he wanted a career with the Marines, and she wasn't about to go to his commanders and tell them she was pregnant. It would have put a blemish on his record. So she disappeared. He had no idea where she went, and couldn't find her. After that, they both went on with their lives."

"How did he find out about you?"

"He went into a convenience store in Fort Worth where Isla was working and saw her."

I could understand my daddy not wanting to take the Judge's name. A man like the Judge would be the last person I would choose to have as a father, but . . . "Why did you lie to me?"

"When I met your mother, I fell in love with her before I even knew what hit me. My dad was a police officer at the time working the beat in Fort Worth. He was against me marrying your mom. He said our kids would be ostracized, unable to fit in the black or the white community, and we had no right to do that to any child. I told him where he could stick it, and your mom and I ran off to Austin."

"And Isla?" I asked. Did she feel the same way about my biracial heritage?

Daddy turned away and looked out the side window above the countertop. "Isla chose to stand by Jacob. I disowned the two of them the day we left."

I could feel his pain across the room. I wanted to comfort him, yet I didn't know how. I wasn't sure that was my role in this scenario, or if he should be comforting me.

Daddy continued talking to the window. "When your mother got sick, she called Isla. As it turned out, the two of them had remained in contact with each other throughout the years. Between the two of them, they worked up a scheme for your mother and me to buy the Barn in the very town where my father had become sheriff. I didn't know anything about it until after the sale went through."

"But I never knew they were my grandparents."

"No. Despite your mom's attempt to reunite us, I resisted it all. Denied you an extended family and denied your mother . . . peace of mind before her death."

This whole thing went deeper than I'd expected and held a heck of a lot more pain than I could even imagine for my daddy. I got up and hugged him from behind.

"I'm sure Mom understood your feelings."

"She was the best person I've ever known. How she could forgive, when I couldn't, is beyond me."

"I'll have to agree on that. Mom was something special."

"When she died, Isla tried to be part of your life, but I refused. I was angry that Eve had been taken from me. Angry that she was taken from you. No one was going to fill her shoes."

"No one could have."

Daddy laughed at that. "You're right there."

"How did you become close with Isla again?"

"When you left, she was the only one who really understood my pain. She knew what it was like to make mistakes that you couldn't take back. Cade helped bring me back to the Barn and focus on the business, but it was Isla who helped me find me."

There was still one question I had to ask. "Why didn't you tell me when I came home?"

Daddy turned around with a sad smile on his face. "I was afraid I'd lose you all over again. Can you forgive me?"

That was the question of the hour. Could I forgive him for his mistakes— again?

Chapter Twenty-three

The sound of pounding on the side door of the Barn saved me from having to answer my daddy's question. I walked to the door and found Joan from Oak Grove Manor staring me in the face. She appeared none too happy to see me. Or maybe she was irritated that the Barn hadn't opened yet.

I opened the door. "Sorry, Joan. We're opening a little late today."

"She's your grandmother!" Joan shouted in my face.

Even though I knew who she was talking about, having someone say Isla was my grandmother sounded as foreign as someone saying good morning to me in Mandarin. Neither language registered with my brain.

"Excuse me?"

"I asked you if you were related to Isla and you denied her. That sweet little old lady who needs her family more than ever right now, and you denied her!"

Daddy interrupted Joan's verbal assault. "Joan, I think you best go."

"And you! You're her son! You people make me sick. You act like you care, but you really don't. You appease your conscience by stopping by to see her irregularly while she wastes away, just wanting to be with her family during every last moment she can still remember you."

Joan was shaking with anger. I appreciated someone who cared so much about Isla that she would risk everything by coming by and giving me a piece of her mind. But she also didn't understand the delicate dynamics at play in our relationships either.

Daddy voiced our feelings perfectly. "Joan, we appreciate how much you care about Isla and the rest of the residents. But I'll kindly have to ask you to leave unless there's a book I can help you with."

Joan made a noise that was similar to a growl, but it was higher pitched and girly as she clenched her fists at her sides and stomped her right foot. When Dad and I just looked at her, she turned around and marched straight out the door I'd let her in.

"Can I go back to bed?" I asked.

Daddy grinned. "No. We're in the middle of a book drive, and we have boxes upon boxes to sort. I just wish Ava could see how much everyone loved her."

"What was your relationship to Ava, Daddy?"

His brow smoothed as he remembered the woman we had both thought so highly of. "At first, I despised her," he admitted. "We came to Hazel Rock, and I couldn't understand how Jacob could take her under his wing and turn his nose up at my wife. Then your mother told me that Jacob had watched out for Ava since she was abused in the foster care system in Fort Worth. He couldn't change the system, but he stayed in contact and made sure she was okay. She aged out of the program at about the time Jacob become sheriff in Hazel Rock, and he gave her a job. She was the daughter, or granddaughter you should have been, and I resented her. Then I got to know her through the store, and I understood Jacob helping her. She was soft spoken and lacked self-confidence. She needed a support system. He gave that to her. I couldn't resent him doing that for her after I left, especially when she was the reason he didn't want your mother and I to have children."

"Ava?"

Dad nodded and picked up his empty coffee cup. This was the longest talk we'd had about the past since I first came back to Hazel Rock. I was glad we'd had it, but it didn't really make me feel good. It made me feel like egos had gotten in the way of what was really important.

Family.

We heard someone tapping on the glass of the front door and decided we'd hashed out enough for one day. I took charge of this intrusion and let my daddy get his second cup of coffee. As I made my way to the front of the store, Princess hopped down the steps.

"You finally decided to join us, huh?"

Princess yawned and sat down in front of the register. She was the perfect store mascot. Smart, cute, and full of spunk, or least the potential for spunk once she had her breakfast.

As I approached the door, I observed two young kids I didn't know, along with three women—Scarlet, Shirley Rishard from Department of Family and Protective Services, and a pretty young woman I didn't recognize—until she turned and said something to the little girl holding her hand—Lily.

If a family could be transformed over a weekend, this family had been, and it wasn't just the clothing. Lily's hair was cut in a bob at chin length and curved around her long, angular face. She had on a pair of capris with a Disney Princess shirt and little tennis shoes that weren't new but looked adorable. Her little brother Jimmy, Jr.'s hair looked the same, but his clean face showed off a devil-may-care attitude rather than the beaten-down look he'd had the last time I'd seen him looking to his sister for guidance. He had on a plaid shirt and the littlest pair of Wranglers I'd ever seen. He wasn't sporting boots, yet I could imagine the teen he'd turn into wearing them every day. Naomi was the biggest shock of all, and I think I may have stared a bit too long. Her hair was cut into layers that blew in the wind and still looked good. She had chunky highlights weaving through her natural color that looked anything but drab. She wore a light amount of makeup that almost hid the bruising on her face, and her new mani-pedi brought out the pink flowers in her maternity dress. She was a very pretty young woman.

I unlocked the door and smiled at the group that greeted me. The kids ran past me heading straight for Princess, who waited patiently for them to slide to a stop in front of her. Tweetle Dee and Tweetle Dum began chirping behind the register as if their feelings were hurt that the children hadn't noticed them first. Lily was the first to make her way over to the birds.

"It's not dangerous, is it?" Naomi asked as Jimmy Jr. hugged my armadillo.

"Princess loves kids," I told her, even though I was pretty sure Princess only tolerated them. They tended to knock on her shell like it was a glass fish tank, pull her tail, and tweak her ears like she was some imaginary Yoda creature. Once Naomi's kids got their fill, Princess would skedaddle.

"You look . . . beautiful," I told her.

Naomi blushed and looked down at her feet. "Thanks to Scarlet and the ladies at the shop."

"Scarlet weaves magic into everyone's appearance."

I shook Shirley's hand. "Thank you for coming by. Would you like to see the books we've already sorted? I think you're going to be happy with the amount we've collected, but storage may be an issue for you." I turned to the kids, who were being surprisingly gently with Princess. "Lily? Jimmy? Would you guys like to pick out a couple of books?"

Naomi started to object. "Oh, I can't . . ."

"It's on the house, or rather the Barn," Daddy interjected as he approached us with his coffee in his hand. He didn't know Naomi or her kids, yet despite their new clothes and new hair styles, Daddy could spot a family in need.

Naomi blushed again. "But . . ."

Daddy wasn't taking no for an answer. "No buts. That's the way we develop our customer base."

I quickly introduced everyone to my Daddy, but he and Shirley already knew each other, while Naomi and her children had never been in the Barn. I wasn't sure they'd ever made it out of their trailer park with Jimmy Senior ruling the roost.

"Daddy, would you show Shirley and the kids the books?" I asked.

He nodded, and he and Shirley headed toward the back of the Barn, where we'd stored boxes upon boxes of books for foster kids.

"What'd you do to your arm?" Lily asked.

My dad wasn't daunted by her curiosity. "I got over twenty stitches in it last week."

I saw Lily look up with an expression of awe. "No lie?"

I couldn't hear his response, but from the expression on his face and the reaction of the two kids, I was pretty sure Dad's tale was growing to monster proportions.

I turned toward Scarlet and Naomi. "How do you think Jimmy is going to react to your makeover?"

Naomi stiffened. "I'm not going back."

"You're not?"

"No. I've been thinking about it for some time. I need to do this for my kids. Jimmy Junior hit Lily over the weekend, and she didn't fight back. They're turning into us, and it's my fault for not stopping it sooner. Jimmy and Lily have seen what happens between their dad and me, and they're acting the way they've been taught. I can't have my son grow up to be like his father, and I certainly can't have Lily grow up to be like me. I just can't."

"Are you ready?" I asked.

Scarlet answered for her. "I'm taking her and the kids to a shelter when we leave here, and Shirley's got them set up for an appointment with a caseworker on Wednesday. Once they're at the shelter, the staff will help her get an order of protection to keep Jimmy away from her and the kids. Since they won't be at home, Naomi wanted you to have the key to Ava's house. She figured you'd need it to get in to retrieve the books for the drive. Especially now that John Luke is in jail."

I reached out to shake Naomi's hand. "Thank you."

Naomi smiled. It wasn't a full-blown grin or anything like that. It was a slight rise to the corners of her mouth. The kind you see on the face of someone who's forgotten how to smile, like joy was so foreign to her she didn't remember how to express it anymore. "Thank you. I probably wouldn't have made this move if you hadn't come through the neighborhood with Scarlet in tow. She knows how to motivate the laziest person."

"You're not lazy. Given the right environment, I suspect you'll be back in the workforce and making a real home for you and your kids before you know it." Scarlet rested her hand on Naomi's shoulder. "Your dreams will come true."

Naomi looked like she didn't quite believe it, but she wanted to. "Was that Joan that I saw leaving a few minutes ago? She didn't look very happy." Naomi began twisting her fingers and looking up at me through her eyelashes.

Her question took me by surprise. I couldn't imagine how she knew the receptionist at Oak Grove Manor or why Joan would make her nervous. "As a matter of fact, it was. How do you know Joan?"

Naomi looked as if she wished she hadn't said a word but answered the question anyway. "She's Jimmy's mom." She hesitated, glanced toward the direction of the kids in the back of the Barn, and continued twisting her fingers. Scarlet grabbed her hand and squeezed it for support. "I was worried she saw the kids at Beaus and Beauties. She wouldn't appreciate me spending money like that."

Naomi was fishing, politely asking if Joan had mentioned her or the kids across the street, and I suspected her mother-in-law's presence at the Barn had been the real reason Naomi had Scarlet bring her over here. She was worried about the repercussions of Joan reporting back to Jimmy. It was heartbreaking to see a grown woman afraid to get a makeover because it would cause her husband to become suspicious, maybe even violent.

I tried to reassure her as much as possible, but I was honestly having trouble reconciling Joan, the woman who was ticked at me because she thought I'd neglected my grandmother, with Joan the mother-in-law who clearly didn't care enough to stop her own son from neglecting and abusing his own family. It didn't make sense. "She never said a word about seeing you or the kids. She was pretty upset with me when she left. I don't think she would have noticed a purple longhorn in front of her by then."

"What did you do?" Scarlet asked.

"It was about Oak Grove Manor."

Scarlet immediately understood that I wasn't going to bring up Isla in front of anyone, even the people who didn't have a clue about my past, or lack thereof, with my grandparents.

She nodded and changed the subject. "I was wondering if you could help take the kids to the shelter? I've only got enough room for two in my car, and I thought maybe you could follow with the kids in the truck. Mary helped me pick them up this morning, but she's got customers until this afternoon and I didn't want to take any chances of Jimmy showing up after we saw Joan."

"Of course. Let me talk to my dad and make sure he was planning to stay."

After conferring with my daddy about the store and Shirley about dropping books off on Wednesday, we gathered the kids with their selection of books in tow and headed toward our cars.

I opened the door to the truck and looked down at Lily and Jimmy. "I don't have any car seats."

Scarlet headed across Main Street. "I've got a couple on the porch in front of the beauty shop."

I looked at my best friend carrying two car seats across the street like they weren't a foreign entity in our world. When she saw the dumbfounded expression on my face, she grinned and handed one to me as she climbed into the truck and installed the first one in the middle of the bench seat. She clicked the seat belt, then tugged on the end before wobbling the seat back and forth and yanking on the end of the belt one more time.

Scarlet stepped down and took the second seat from me.

"Who are you and what have you done with Scarlet?" I whispered in her ear.

"Mystery is the key to any relationship. Lose that, and it goes down the crapper."

I laughed. I'd never get used to Scarlet using any kind of language that was remotely dirty. She followed the same procedure with the second car seat and then rechecked both of them while I stood back in awe.

"Jimmy, you get to ride in the middle." Jimmy frowned at the idea, and Scarlet immediately told him why he got to ride in such an important position. "It's your job to tell Charli if she's doing something wrong. She's new at driving."

Naomi looked as if she was going to object to me driving her kids, and I leaned over and told her the truth. "I've been driving since I was fourteen." I didn't tell her I'd stolen my daddy's truck to drive to school so I wouldn't ruin my hair and the sheriff . . . my grandfather had caught me.

Thinking back, it made me wonder if he'd actually been watching over me during my childhood. At the time, I'd thought he was harassing me. Knowing what I knew now, maybe it was something else entirely.

"Lily. It's your job to make sure she doesn't cross the solid white line on the side of the road. Deal?" Scarlet asked.

Lily gave a curt nod and helped Jimmy climb in before getting into her own seat. Once the kids were in and Naomi checked to make sure they were secure, we were on our way with Scarlet leading.

I turned on the radio and Jimmy corrected me. "That's the wrong station," he said through his thumb, which had made its way to his mouth the moment he was settled in his seat.

"What is?"

Lily answered for him. "We're only allowed to listen to Daddy's station."

"Do you like Daddy's station?"

Jimmy shrugged.

Lily was a bit more vocal. "We don't know any others."

"I'll tell you what. I'll change the station until you hear a song you like. Jimmy gets to choose first. Lily, you can choose the next one." Both kids nodded and we proceeded through the dial.

"That one!" Jimmy yelled and I stopped on the old rock station Cade listened to as "Hooked on a Feeling" by Blue Swede began playing. The two kids began giggling, and I started singing the nonsensical "oogas" throughout the chorus to entertain them. They looked at me like singing was a sin, then tentatively joined in. Before the song was over, they were bouncing to the beat. That moment of pure joy on their faces would live with me forever.

As we crossed the river, it was Lily who spotted the truck coming toward us.

"It's Daddy!" She pointed to the man driving a white truck in our direction, and in that little gesture, it was like she drew Jimmy Sr.'s attention to the occupants of my truck. He looked over at us, and the two kids waved.

I cringed and watched Jimmy Sr. do a double take. It wasn't moments later that he was doing a U-turn behind me and my phone rang.

"Don't pull over," Scarlet instructed. "I'm calling the police."

We hung up, and I tried to distract the kids by finding a new station for Lily to choose.

"It's your turn, Lily," I said as I watched my rearview mirror.

Luckily, the kids were oblivious and Lily immediately found a song she liked, one I could relate to as Meghan Trainor began rocking the airwaves from my old radio with "Woman Up." I tried to sing and sigh with the song, but I was completely distracted by the truck passing one car and then another behind us. Only a Toyota Prius stood between my truck and Jimmy's. My phone rang and I immediately clicked it on.

"It's never a dull moment with you, is it?" Mateo asked.

"Where are you?"

"Waiting for you to pass Rodeo Way."

I looked up ahead and figured we were about two miles from where he was waiting. "Did Scarlet fill you in?" Jimmy passed the Prius and nearly caused a head-on collision. I pressed harder on the gas pedal and eased closer to Scarlet's bumper. Hopefully she'd get the message and speed up.

"Are you going to pull him over?"

"That's the plan."

I glanced at Jimmy, who was gaining on me. "What if he doesn't pull over?"

"We'll deal with that if the time comes. Where are you at now?"

I saw the street sign stating Rodeo Way was one mile ahead of us. "One mile to your east." I turned my head toward the side window. "The kids don't know he's behind me."

"I won't turn on my siren unless I have to."

"Charli, keep your eyes on the road!" Jimmy yelled next to me.

"Where are your eyes?" Mateo asked.

"On the road," I said.

"Charli, you shouldn't talk on your cell phone while you're driving," Jimmy insisted.

"You're right," I told him.

"Bye, Charli." I could have sworn Mateo was laughing as he hung up. I put my cell on my lap and gripped the steering wheel with both hands as Jimmy Senior began to pull up alongside my truck. His illegal lane change over the solid no-passing line was in complete view of Mateo's patrol car sitting at the next intersection. Scarlet accelerated and I followed suit, but Jimmy was determined to overtake me. I wasn't sure what he'd do when he did, and I was extremely glad when we passed Mateo and I saw him pull out behind us. I was even happier for the semi headed in our direction that forced Jimmy to pull in behind me once again.

"It's your turn, Charli," Lily said.

I glanced over at her. "What?"

Jimmy chimed in. "It's your turn to pick a song."

I tried to smile and act like I wasn't watching the flashing lights behind me. "Of course. Sorry, I got distracted." I switched the dial and stopped at the first station as I watched Jimmy Sr. slam his hands against the steering wheel and pull over onto the shoulder.

"Really? That?"

I'd stopped the radio without even thinking about anything but the irate man in the pickup on the side of the road who had Mateo approaching his driver's side window at a snail's pace. A second patrol car pulled in behind Mateo's. I breathed a sigh of relief and focused on the song Jimmy didn't really care for.

I smiled. "Absolutely. I love the smooth sound of Tony Bennett's voice." I loved it more when Mateo sang with him, but for the moment, Tony would do just fine. Jimmy seemed to contemplate my choice and before the song was over, his legs were bouncing to the beat of the song.

We made it to the shelter without any more interruptions, and I said goodbye to the kids. I was kind of sad to take the car seats out of the truck, but then again, I was pretty happy to have the radio back all to myself.

Chapter Twenty-four

Daddy was watching the store and Scarlet was headed back to her shop. I still had questions about not only my heritage, but who killed Ava and who left my daddy wearing a bandage across most of his bicep. I'd been so sidetracked with everything else, I'd lost my focus. Although I didn't think anyone could possibly consider Daddy a suspect after he'd been attacked behind the store, I didn't think he was completely eliminated as far as the law was concerned either. Nor was Isla, or the Judge, and although I wasn't feeling particularly protective of the Judge, for Isla sake and my dad's, I was more invested in proving everyone's innocence than ever.

The problem lay with Isla. She knew more than she could tell me. I drove to Oak Grove Manor and parked the truck. Big drops of rain struck the ground around me as I exited the vehicle, and I made a run for the front door. I shook my hair out once I was under the awning and shivered with the breeze picking up. I swore the temperature dropped ten degrees from my truck to the door.

I went inside and was thankful that Joan was off-duty. Maybe she was bailing Jimmy Sr. out of jail on all the traffic tickets Mateo had piled on him.

I couldn't help but wonder if there was a connection there that I was missing—Joan's anger about my relationship with Isla—me being indirectly responsible for Naomi moving out with her kids and Jimmy Sr. being left in the cold without a wife or children. Yet I wasn't sure how that could possibly connect with Ava, other than the two women being neighbors. Maybe Ava had started to help Naomi plan her escape, and that encouragement put Ava in the crosshairs of one angry mother-in-law.

It was a stretch, and I had no proof. But it was possible . . .

I signed in with the woman named Beth that I recognized from previous visits, who called Isla and told her I was there. I made my way to her room and noticed the halls seemed unusually quiet for the dinner hour. Isla met me at her door with her cane and gave me a huge hug.

"I can finally show my love for you and not be ashamed," she said and then pulled back to look me in the face. Her eyes brimmed with unshed tears and I couldn't help but feel a bit choked up.

"Why didn't anyone tell me when I was a little girl?"

"Your grandfather and I didn't deserve to have you, but your mom welcomed me into the store and gave me the best gift of my life."

I could understand why she felt like she was given a gift, but I couldn't help but think I'd been denied one. And now Isla wouldn't remember me much longer. Maybe not tomorrow.

We moved into her room and sat down in her little seating area with her Scrabble board between us. As much as I wanted to ask about our relationship, I felt I needed to talk about Ava. Everything hinged on finding her killer.

"Isla, why did you accuse the Judge of having an affair with Ava?"

Isla fiddled with the corner of her shirt. "I was wrong. You know how I get confused sometimes . . ." She looked up at me with a haunted shadow in her eyes, and I nodded. I couldn't possibly understand how hard it was for her, but I knew she became confused. "Jacob and your father came by to see me before work, and before Jacob left, he said he was going to spend the day with Ava. When he was gone, all I could think about was him leaving me to be with her. I got angry and wasn't going to wait for him to come back to me."

A tear slid town her cheek, and I reached across the table to squeeze her hand. Isla wiped it away. "I think I may have ruined Jacob's day."

The Judge may not have been having an affair with Ava, but according to John Luke, he controlled Ava's life, and Ava's own letter to the Judge said she let him down. I needed to know if there was more to the relationship that would make Isla believe the two were having an affair.

"Isla, did the Judge control Ava?"

"What do you mean?"

"Did he dictate who she could see, what she did?"

"Don't be silly. He treated her like the daughter we never had . . . or the granddaughter we'd hoped to have." Isla leaned forward and stared me in the eye. "Jacob would never hurt Ava. From the day she was kicked out of foster care, she may as well have been our own."

I was surprised to realize that her confession was exactly what I wanted to hear, and I smiled to reassure her. "Tell me, what can I bring you the next time I visit?"

The next words that came out of Isla's mouth, however, were exactly what I didn't want to hear. "Eve, honey. I so desperately want to see that little Princess of mine. Could you bring my granddaughter to see me?"

I nodded, too afraid to say anything that would upset her and me at the same time.

"But you must be careful," she said and lowered her voice as she furtively glanced toward the door. "There is something evil going on here, and I'm afraid for her safety."

"Why would you be afraid for Princess?" I asked.

"She hasn't been by to see me in a while. They say that's a *mortal sin.*"

The way Isla said *mortal sin* literally sent shivers up my arms. It reminded me of my encounters with the Judge in my early years, and Joan that morning. Was everyone obsessed with my wicked ways?

"Who's they?" I asked.

Isla looked over her shoulder, leaned over the table and—

Frank walked in like he owned the place. "You two young ladies need to join our karaoke night," he said with a smile so big, I swore I didn't notice his nose at all.

"I think you're confused, old man. This isn't your room." Isla stood and pointed to the door.

"It's okay, Isla. Remember, this is Frank. He's a friend who lives here," I explained.

Isla looked at me and then looked back at Frank. I could see she was struggling to put the three of us in our rightful position in her life, but she couldn't quite get the square pegs to fit in the round holes.

It made me want to cry.

"Isla, remember, you told us this morning that Charli was your granddaughter. Right there in the lobby of Oak Grove Manor?" Frank continued to paint the picture for Isla. "I was sitting with Roger and Glenn in the chairs against the wall near the reception desk. Joan and Mr. Andrews were also there when you came out and told all of us the good news."

Suddenly the surprise visit from Joan at the Barn made a little bit of sense. She'd found out about my relationship to Isla, a relationship I'd denied a few short days ago, and Joan's inner knight in shining armor wanted to protect one of the residents at Oak Grove Manor. It was too bad her gallant code didn't recognize the need to protect her own grandchildren and Naomi from her abusive son.

"You told everyone that I was your granddaughter?" I asked Isla, not sure if she'd be able to switch gears and see me as Charli again.

She plopped down in her chair and paused for a moment before she smiled. "I'm pretty proud of you, Princess."

"I'm pretty proud of you too, Isla. You're one heck of a role model."

Isla blushed and made some kind of "pfff" noise as she swatted the air in my direction. "You're the role model for the younger generation, Princess. You hold your head high."

I went over and kissed her cheek. "I need to get going, but you really should join Frank and the others for karaoke."

"I'm not going to screech at all these people," Isla said, but I could tell a part of her wanted to join in. So did Frank.

"Come on, Isla. Roger, Glenn, and I need a soprano to distract everyone from our flat vocal trio."

I was guessing Roger and Glenn were Frank's counterparts of the three amigos, and I couldn't help but laugh at the thought of Isla leading that group of misfits.

Isla looked back and forth between us again, and for a moment, I thought she was lost and didn't know who either one of us was. But then a smile spread across her face and she agreed to join in on the fun.

"As long as Joan won't be there. She got mad at my Princess this morning," Isla said as she stood back up and made her way toward the restroom. "Let me freshen up and I'll be down there in a jiffy."

I looked to Frank, wondering what that was all about as the restroom door swung closed.

But Frank knew exactly what Isla had been saying. "Joan can be a bit vocal about the treatment of some of the residents. She doesn't understand family dynamics aren't always traditional."

That one word, *traditional*, spoke volumes about the limitations of Joan's views. She'd spoken fondly of the love Frank had for his dead husband, but that didn't mean she had the capacity to understand it when she was faced with it on a daily basis. "Was she mean to you and your husband?" I asked.

Frank smiled. "No. She didn't understand us, but she tried. That's all we could ask of a woman like Joan."

I thought about what Frank said and didn't like it. Joan should have been the one to make them feel comfortable, not the other way around. "Maybe I should talk to Mr. Andrews. I'm not sure I want Joan around Isla."

Frank leaned in to confide in me without Isla hearing in the other room. "No need. Mr. Andrews asked her to take a few days off, but then this afternoon, she came in and took a leave of absence."

"Seriously?"

"She had some family issues she had to deal with."

Isla came out of the restroom with her hair neatly secured in a ponytail and a slight glisten to her lips. I was glad to see her attention to her appearance.

"I'm going to go ahead and leave. Is there a treat I could bring you tomorrow? Some fresh strawberries or something from the bakery?"

Isla's face lit up. "I would kill for one of Franz's strawberry cheesecake cupcakes."

I wasn't quite comfortable with Isla's phrase choice, but I could totally get on board with a cheesecake cupcake. I kissed her on the cheek once more and headed out the door, nearly running into the Judge.

"I'm sorry," I blurted out. When he didn't say anything but continued to stare at me, I changed my response. "I-I'm sorry, sir."

The Judge's expression stayed guarded, and if I wasn't mistaken, he was a bit insecure. Join the crowd. When he finally did respond, his words were stilted and sounded as if they'd been torn from his mouth. "Ava spoke highly of you."

"She was a good person."

He nodded in agreement and the silence stretched between us.

"Well, I best be going."

"Will you be at her visitation?" he asked.

"I wasn't sure you'd want me there."

"Isla and I have always wanted you there."

"You didn't want to see me born."

"I didn't want to see my grandchild struggle the way Ava did."

"I had two parents. Ava didn't."

"She had relatives who wouldn't take her."

"Would you have turned me away if my daddy had died?"

"Of course not."

I nodded. "Neither would my aunt Violet. You should have given my parents a chance."

"I suppose my own prejudice kept me from seeing that your parents' child would have been raised differently than Ava."

"Did you love her?"

"She was a like a daughter to both of us." He hesitated and then filled in the answer to the question behind the question. "Nothing more."

I wasn't sure what else to say to him. I'd never liked the Judge. I didn't hate him. He just lived a different kind of life than I did. I supposed our moral codes were similar, but mine wasn't steeped with verses from the

Bible. I believed in it, I just didn't cram it down the throat of every wayward five-year-old I'd had in my kindergarten class. And I was pretty sure the Judge would have handled Jimmy Jr. and Lily much differently than singing "ooga ooga" with them in the truck with the radio on full blast.

"Well, I'll see you tomorrow night."

The Judge nodded and said, "Goodbye, Princess," before patting me awkwardly on the upper arm.

I left the facility without any more chance encounters other than the old guy in the wheelchair sitting under the front portico. It was the same man I'd seen last week sleeping with his chin against his chest. This evening he was fully alert and in a talkative mood.

"Is that your truck?" he asked.

I looked over at my truck parked by itself in the parking lot. It appeared to be sitting funny, almost listing to one side.

"I don't think you'll be going anywhere anytime soon," he said.

"What's wrong with it?" I asked.

"I'm not an expert, but I'd say you've got two flat tires. They don't make them like they used to." He shook his head as if disgusted with the way things were nowadays.

"Thanks," I said and approached my vehicle. The entire truck leaned to the right, and as I rounded the vehicle, I saw the problem.

The old man was wrong. I was pretty sure they *never* made tires with six-inch slits in the sidewalls.

Fuzz buckets.

Chapter Twenty-five

My wait for two new tires seemed like forever, but in actuality it was only forty-five minutes. It paid to have a friend who owned a garage. Dean MacAlister was there faster than roadside assistance and he had two used tires to replace mine, which weren't even good enough to be turned into tire swings. He changed the tires lickety-split and I was on the road home and phoning in a police report before it got too late.

Mateo called before Princess and I went to sleep, and we talked until midnight. It was nice to have someone to talk to who wasn't involved in the history of my family drama. He understood my anger, my confusion, and didn't try to tell me what I should feel. Nor did he judge me for my childishness. I wanted to start over with each of them, I just wasn't sure I could. The one person we didn't talk about was Cade. That was just a bit too weird.

He told me that he'd written Jimmy Sr. every traffic violation in the book, including driving with a suspended license, which had caused him to have to post bond. Jimmy had wanted to complain about the officer "with the giant ego" not listening when he said his kids had been kidnapped by a woman in a truck, but was later informed by the service of an order of protection that his wife had custody of the kids and he was not allowed to see them until his court date. At that time, Jimmy had more than a few choice words for that officer.

It wasn't the first, nor would it be the last time Sheriff Espinosa was accused of having an oversized ego. I tended to like it on the man. At least when we were on the same side of the law.

I'd brought Tweetle Dee and Tweetle Dum up to my apartment before I put my head on the pillow. I was growing used to the music they created and liked the way their beautiful songs tended to relax me as I drifted off to sleep. Princess chose to sleep in her bed, with a towel she'd dragged from the dirty clothes over her head. She was a bit irritated with our nighttime serenade, and I was thankful not to have to change my sheets again so soon. We each liked our space, and I was glad she was somehow able to read when I needed it and when I didn't.

Tonight I needed it, and as soon as I closed my eyes, I was asleep. My alarm went off too soon and I slapped the snooze button, desperately wanting just a few more minutes. Tweetle Dee and Tweetle Dum had another idea. They didn't sing, they chirped in an annoying cadence that sounded like my alarm.

I groaned. "All right already."

Princess snorted and rustled in her bed. She wanted no part of me, my alarm, or the birds. I packed them up and headed toward the kitchen. I made some toast, changed their paper, and gave them fresh food and water. Then I took a quick shower before heading downstairs with my tweetle stereo to start my day.

We only had one more day before the literacy drive was over. Daddy was coming into work at noon, and at that time I was going to go to Ava's and pick up the books she'd collected for the drive. It was going to be a questionable legal situation since no one knew if Ava had a will and she had no real family to speak of. She had, however, allowed Naomi to feed the birds and take care of her houseplants. As far as I was concerned, Naomi had more say over Ava's house and her possessions than anyone else. I wasn't sure how the law would view it, so I kept my mouth shut about my plans to Mateo and Daddy. The Judge wasn't even in the equation.

I was busy boxing up more donations when the front bell dinged and the doors swished open. I turned to greet our customer and saw Cade making his way into the store. He hadn't seen me yet, and I watched his moment of uncertainty as he stood in the entryway in his button-down shirt rolled up to bare his strong forearms. Today he wore jeans that were more expensive than Wranglers but looked just as good, if not better. His boots were the well-worn ones he wore when he worked on his ranch, not the ones he wore to political events. And his hair was slightly mussed. He glanced behind the register, then scanned the main sales floor and tearoom before he spotted me in the back. His smile was slow, and nothing like the political one I always saw him giving to other people in town. This was the Cade I knew and had loved.

"Hi," he said.

My response was brilliant. "Hi."

"What are you doing?"

"Boxing up books."

Yeah, this conversation was right along the lines of the first one we had after we'd recognized each other as boyfriend/girlfriend material.

"Are you still mad at me?"

"No."

"Thank you."

"There's no reason to thank me. I recognized the tough spot you were in. I wouldn't have done it the way you did, but I wouldn't have done what my mom and daddy did either."

Cade nodded and looked around the store. "It's not very busy today."

I wasn't sure this conversation could get any worse. "Nope." I started working again.

"Scarlet called me this morning."

I rolled my eyes. The best thing about having Scarlet as a best friend was having someone to confide in. The worst thing about having Scarlet for a best friend was that she tended to do what she thought was best for me, which may or may not conflict with my opinion. In this instance, the conflict was real.

"Oh, what did she have to say?"

"She said you're planning on going over to Ava's house today by yourself to pick up the books for the drive."

"That's the plan."

"Let me help, Princess."

"What? Are you going to hire some of the boys at the Tool Shed to help load the boxes?"

Cade ignored my smart tone. "No, I thought I'd go over with you. We can use my truck and load the books into the bed."

"That's not necessary. I got new tires last night."

"I heard."

"I'm sure it was just a random act of crime."

"Random acts of crime follow you."

I shrugged and closed the box I was working on. "They have to follow somebody."

"I also know you don't want to tell Bobby Ray or Mateo you're going over there. It would be a shame if it slipped out and they found out about it."

I stood up and gave Cade my best evil eye. "Are you blackmailing me?"

It was his turn to shrug. "I suppose I am."

My lips pursed together of their own accord. "Fine."

A smug grin spread across his face.

"But we're taking my truck. Not yours." The last thing I needed was for someone to see Cade driving me away from the bookstore. Everyone would think we were going out on a date. That would be the beginning of way too much drama that I didn't need. Or want.

I closed my eyes and chose to believe the lie.

The front door opened with a ding and a swish and Daddy walked in. It didn't take him a beat to find us. "Hi, Princess. Cade, what brings you here?"

"I'm taking Princess out to lunch, if that's okay?"

Daddy looked a little surprised. I stepped up and stomped on Cade's foot in the process. I heard him grunt but Daddy didn't, nor did it wipe the smile off Cade's face. It just crinkled it a bit.

"Cade volunteered to help me drop off some of these boxes at Department of Family and Protective Services. The fire department has a couple boxes as well, and I wanted to swing by to pick them up." Our volunteer fire department only had two boxes, but now was as good a time as any to retrieve them. "I thought it would be best to have our mayor be a part of the donation. If we have time, we'll go through a drive-thru," I said.

Daddy was genuinely appreciative of Cade's assistance. "Thank you, Cade. I wasn't going to be much help lifting these boxes with my bum arm."

"Not a problem. You know I'm more than happy to help."

"Yeah, it will be great for an East Coast press release." My tone held more sarcasm than my words, if that was possible.

Cade started to object, but it was Daddy's rebuke that made me feel bad. "Princess, your mama didn't raise an ungrateful, snot-nose brat."

"Sorry. I know." I turned to Cade feeling like a five-year-old again. "I'm sorry, Cade." And I was. My own feelings were causing me to treat others poorly, and I had no reason for it.

"It was no less than I deserved."

Cade taking the blame did nothing but make me feel worse. "Let me get the two-wheeler and we can take these out to the truck. We may have to make two trips since I don't think they'll all fit in one."

"Why don't we load these into my truck, and I can drop them off on my way home."

I accepted without any further discussion. Getting all of Ava's boxes in the back along with what we had and what the fire department had was going to be difficult. This way, I didn't have to worry about losing part of the load.

By the time we loaded the two-wheeler up four times and put the boxes in the back of Cade's truck, we were both visibly sweating. My shirt was stuck to my back and his was sticking in all the right places. I looked away before my mind wandered to all the wrong places.

"That's only the beginning. You realize that, right?" I asked.

"Just bring it, Princess."

I couldn't help but smile. "Good to know you're up for the challenge."

I went back into the Barn and got my purse and keys. "I'm off, Daddy."

"Don't get yourself into any more trouble," he said.

"Trouble hasn't been my middle name since high school."

Daddy looked skeptical and I blew him a kiss.

I went out and got in my truck, reached over, and unlocked the door for Cade.

"Have you ever thought about restoring this old thing?" he asked.

"Are you insulting my ride, Cade Calloway?"

Cade held his hands up in the air in surrender. "No offense intended."

"Good. None taken."

I turned over the engine and it rumbled to life the way it always did. Except it had an additional snap, crackle, and pop I could feel in the ignition. "What the Sam Hill . . . ?"

A thin trail of smoke snaked its way up through the shift housing where my hand sat on the gearshift.

"Let me take a look before this thing blows up on us."

"Ha ha. Very funny, Cade Calloway."

Cade laughed and had his door open as I said, "I'm sure it's just the clutch. I'm probably due for a new one."

He ignored me and squatted down to look under the truck as the gear housing started to sizzle.

"Get out of the truck, Princess!" Cade yelled.

"What? What for?"

The man looked like he'd seen a ghost as he reached in and pulled my arm harder than was necessary. I pulled back, but Cade wouldn't release me. Instead, he was yanking me across the seat like a crazy man.

"Get out of the truck, now!" Cade yelled in my face.

"Have you done lost your mind, Cade Calloway?"

"There's a bomb!"

"A what?"

Cade was done arguing with me. He grabbed the front of my shirt and pulled me the rest of the way across the truck and out the door. Then he pushed me into the middle of the street just as an explosion ripped through the air.

I landed on my face in the middle of Main Street with Cade on top of me.

It was the last place I wanted to get intimate with my ex-boyfriend.

Chapter Twenty-six

"Are you alive?" I yelled.

"I don't think I'm dead." His voice seemed muffled in my ear, despite the proximity of his mouth.

"Then could you get off me? I think I've eaten enough dirt for one day."

I felt Cade grunt more than I actually heard it, before he rolled off my back. I turned over and sat up. We were in the middle of the street and my truck was ablaze. I supposed it was a good thing that the spots to the left and right of it had been vacant. It gave room for parts to fly and flames to burn.

My ears were ringing, but that appeared to be the only thing damaged by the explosion. At least to me. I leaned over Cade, who was staring up at the clear blue sky marred by yellowish brown smoke from my truck. The right side of Cade's head was smoking with red embers that I immediately smacked out. "Are you hurt?"

Cade blinked. "I'm not sure. Why are you banging my head?"

I didn't want to tell him his hair was singed nearly to the scalp on one side, the curls were straightened and looked like a frightened cat's back on top of his head, and the left side looked completely normal. Then again, maybe his hairdo could pass for some type of funky Mohawk.

Could politicians get away with a Mohawk on the East Coast?

"Your hair was on fire." I left out that for the first time in his life, Cade was having a bad hair day. A *really* bad hair day. The kind of day that probably negated every single one of mine combined.

"Is anything else on fire?"

"Not that I can tell. Can you sit up and I'll check your back?"

Cade did as I asked but groaned the whole time.

There was very little left to the back of his shirt, but his skin looked fine. I rubbed it to make sure.

"Are you feeling me up?"

"I'm trying to make sure you're in one piece." If I enjoyed touching his perfectly sculpted back in the meantime, that was my business. "Nothing hurts?"

"I'm having a hard time focusing on your voice, and the back of my head feels gooey," he said.

"I think you might have a concussion." I looked at the back of his head. "And you're going to need stitches or staples on your head."

"A what?"

"A concussion!" I yelled.

Scarlet appeared out of nowhere with Mary and Joellen right behind her, and they helped me to my feet. "O.M.W. are you okay?"

"I think so," I said, but by the way their heads leaned back, I may have been yelling without even knowing it.

"Don't mind me, I'm fine."

The four of us turned to Cade, who was sitting on the ground with his legs straight out in front of him. He waved and the corner of his mouth raised.

No one moved until Joellen reached into her pocket and pulled out her cell phone. She'd snapped several pictures of our bedraggled mayor before Scarlet smacked her hand.

"Make yourself useful and call 9-1-1," Scarlet told her.

"Princess!" Daddy came running out of the Barn but couldn't immediately see us in the street since the fire was between us.

"I'm here, Daddy!" I moved so he could see me and he came running out and hit me almost as hard as Cade had tackled me to the ground. I let him hold me as long as he needed to since I needed the comfort of knowing I was alive just as much as he did.

"I'm fine," I heard Cade say and Daddy released me.

"What happened?" he asked as he approached Cade.

"Cade saved me."

"Can you stand?" Daddy asked Cade.

"I'm fine," Cade repeated.

"I think he has a concussion."

The sound of sirens blared through town as the first fire truck barreled down Main Street.

Betty Walker came out of the quilt shop and met Franz on the front porch. "Are they okay?" Franz asked.

"They're fine." Scarlet waved them off.

Customers and employees from the diner and the antique stores stuck their heads out their respective front doors, craning their necks to get a better look without risking being hurt in any further explosions. Liza Twaine, our local pushy reporter, shoved her way through the crowd and started filming what was left of my truck. The flames were licking at the sky at the height of their glory.

It wasn't every day an explosion rocked downtown Hazel Rock. I hated that I was involved in it, but I knew if one occurred, everyone knew it had to be connected to me. These people just didn't draw this kind of action. Nor did Cade. In fact, the only kind of attention he brought to town was media coverage for charity events and accolades for good deeds—not bombings.

I watched as Liza turned her phone toward Cade and started to zoom in. I immediately stepped in front of her view and bent over Cade. "If you can get up, we need to get you in the beauty shop before the media gets here."

"I'm fine," Cade repeated.

"Your hair isn't."

Cade felt his head on the left side. "It feels fine to me."

Scarlet stepped up. "Trust me, you want me to take care of it."

Daddy wasn't having any of our fussing over Cade's hair. "The man is injured. Wait until the paramedics get here."

"The media beat them." I pointed toward Liza stalking down the middle of the street.

"I'll take care of Liza."

"She's not the only one with a cell phone." I turned to Joellen, who had her phone out videotaping my truck—the truck my Daddy had owned before I was born.

The fire engine stopped in front of us with a deputy pulling up behind it. Once their sirens turned off, I could hear more sirens in the distance.

"I'd like to get out of the middle of the street," Cade said. It was his first sentence that was longer than a couple words, and we all took it as a sign that he might have a concussion, but that was probably the worst of his injuries. I grabbed an arm and Scarlet grabbed the other as my Daddy headed off Liza Twaine with a promise of a view of the action from inside the bookstore. The Barn would have the absolute best view of the burning truck of anywhere that wasn't the middle of the street.

I couldn't believe she fell for it.

Cade leaned on me, and for a moment I thought I would buckle. The man weighed more than he looked, especially when it seemed he was dead weight on my shoulders.

"Your knees are bleeding, Princess."

"That happens when a man your size tackles a woman in the middle of the street."

"I think you got the worst of it." Cade seemed upset by that.

I tried to reassure him. "I think your hair got the worst of it."

Cade lifted his head toward the mirrors inside Beaus and Beauties. He blinked. Again. Comprehension came slowly. "Holy—"

"Don't say it."

Cade stared at his reflection in the mirror as we sat him in a chair. He went down with an "oof" from me and Scarlet.

"If anytime was the time to cuss, now would be the time."

"My truck looks worse," I told him.

He stopped turning his head side to side and gazed up at me, his pupils completely dilated. "I'm sorry I couldn't save your truck."

"I'm sorry I put you through this." I waved toward his head and brought his attention back to his disastrous appearance.

Joellen popped in for a moment and snapped another picture.

"O.M.W. Joellen. Is that the way you treat a hero?"

"What?" Cade and Joellen said at once.

I filled them both in. "If it wasn't for Cade, I'd be out there . . ." I pointed to the smoldering remains of my truck—black smoke spiraling in the air as the fire hoses beat the flames into submission and exposed the charred remains. "Thank you for not letting that happen to me, Cade."

The voice from the doorway took us all by surprise. "I'd like to second that emotion," Mateo said. Then he got down to the business of his job. "Before you clean him up, Scarlet, I've got a couple paramedics that'd like to take a look at him and a couple detectives who'd like to talk to him."

"Of course." Scarlet pushed her sister and Mary into the back room as paramedics and a detective came into the shop.

I moved over toward Mateo, who looked me over from the top of my head to my toes. "*Dios mio*, Charli. Your knees are bleeding."

"My knees are fine."

He bent down to take a closer look and pushed against my left knee.

"Ow, dagnabit, Mateo, that hurts."

"I think they should look you over too." He waved at one of the paramedics.

"I'm fine." I waved him off. The poor guy looked back and forth between us, but somehow my scowl won the day, not Mateo's.

"You're frustrating."

"Likewise."

"What were you doing with Cade?" His question was nonchalant, but I could see the real question behind the act. He wanted to know if something was rekindling between Cade and me.

I went with the truth. Sorta. "Scarlet called him and he volunteered to help move boxes. We were going to the fire department to pick up some more donations. It was a political move on his part." I neglected to mention that I'd been headed to Ava's house.

Mateo nodded. "Tell me what happened with the truck?"

"It blew up."

"The gas line caught on fire?"

I shook my head. "No. I mean I started the truck. There was this popping noise at the ignition and then smoke at the gearshift. Cade got out of the truck and looked underneath it. Then he popped back up and said there was a bomb and he dragged me out of the truck."

"A bomb?"

I nodded. "A bomb."

"What kind of bomb?"

I shrugged. "Not a clue."

"How did Cade know it was a bomb?"

"That's something you'll have to ask Cade. I can tell you his answers are a little wonky right now."

"Like his hair?"

I couldn't help the smile trying to build. It was either grin or cry. I grinned. "Like his hair. Did you get a picture?" I really hoped he'd gotten a picture.

"That's an opportunity I couldn't pass up. Besides, it's evidence in the case."

Chapter Twenty-seven

"Take my truck," Cade said.

"You trust me with your truck?" Cade loved his truck.

"I trust you. I'm not sure I trust the universe around you."

"Was that a compliment or an insult?" I couldn't tell.

Cade thought about it for a moment. "I'm not sure."

Or maybe he just zoned off and then came back to us. He'd been doing that a lot, which was why we insisted he at least allow Mateo to take him to the hospital after Scarlet worked some fast magic on his hair. I didn't see the point of a new style considering the staff at the hospital would be shaving the spot around the gash anyway, but Cade and Scarlet both seemed to think it necessary.

Especially since Liza Twaine was outside on the porch interviewing Joellen about what she'd seen. Scarlet had made her little sister promise not to show the picture of Cade's hair post-blast.

Mateo got off his radio and turned toward Scarlet. "Is your camera system still down?"

"O.M.W. I forgot about it. No, I got it fixed about a month ago. Do you think there's footage of Charli's truck blowing up?"

"We'll have to see."

Scarlet finished with Cade's hair about the time Liza finished Joellen's interview. The reporter tried to follow Joellen into the beauty shop, but Mary stopped her at the door.

"Sorry," she said in a tone that sounded like *stick it where the sun don't shine*. "We're closing early today because of the parking area being blocked by these hunky firefighters." There were at least ten women in the shop; between friends and relatives, the place was packed.

Liza tried to stick a purple pump in the door to keep Mary from closing it in her face, but when she saw Mary was undaunted by the thought of hurting her, Liza pulled her foot back just in time for the glass door to slam closed—Liza's foot intact.

Scarlet and Mateo headed for the back room and I followed.

"You should stay with Cade," Mateo said to me.

"Joellen's with Cade."

Mateo started to tell me something about it being police business, but I immediately set him straight. "That was my daddy's truck that he gave to me. I have memories of moving to Hazel Rock in that truck. Memories of Daddy and me taking my mom to the hospital before she died. I learned how to drive in that truck." I could have gone on and on, but I left those particular memories hanging out there for him to contemplate. "If someone blew up my truck on purpose, I want to see who did it."

Mateo didn't like losing a battle, but with each point I made, Scarlet's head bobbed up and then down in agreement, and he knew I'd see the video right after he left, anyway.

"Fine." He held his hand up to stop my forward progress. "But what we learn from the video does not leave this store room. Deal?"

I nodded and Mateo looked at Scarlet.

"O.M.W. do you really think I would share that information?"

Mateo raised his left brow.

"Fine. You have my word."

We went to Scarlet's office off the back room. It was as spotless as the rest of the business with a modern design that was the exact opposite of her vintage Airstream trailer she lived in behind the shop. Mateo and I sat in the two chairs in front of her desk as Scarlet pulled up her security system on her computer, then turned the large computer screen in our direction. She started the viewing at noon. The view was mostly of customers coming and going in front of Beaus and Beauties, but there was a clear view of the parking in front of the Book Barn and our front door. Scarlet fast-forwarded through Cade entering the store, followed by Daddy a short time later. She put it in real time as we saw Cade and I exit the store.

I hadn't realized Cade had put his hand on the small of my back, but Scarlet noticed it and looked for a reaction from Mateo. I peeked as well, but he just watched the screen as we loaded books in Cade's truck and then got into mine. Moments later, Cade got back out of the truck and looked underneath. The near panic in his movements was obvious, and I found my heart racing just watching the events unfold.

It was scary watching our near-death experience, and as I watched, I realized the two of us had been lucky no cars had been driving down Main Street at the time of the explosion. We could have survived the bomb only to become road pizza.

Scarlet's breath hitched as the truck exploded and Cade and I went flying through the air. We watched as the side mirror flew off the truck and struck Cade in the back of the head. It explained the cut and the concussion. Mateo wanted to watch until the fire department finished to see if there was anyone hanging around watching the entire incident, but we didn't see anyone suspicious.

"Can you start at six a.m. and go backward so we can see if anyone tampered with the truck after Charli parked it last night?"

"Sure." Scarlet did as he requested, but we soon found the nighttime footage more difficult to see. At about three a.m., however, a white pickup drove by the Book Barn Princess very slowly going eastbound. A few minutes later we observed the same truck going westbound on Main Street.

"Can you slow it down to see if we can see the driver as he's going west through town?" Mateo asked.

"Sure." Scarlet rewound the video and played the part where the driver did his second pass.

"Stop!" Mateo ordered.

Scarlet did as directed, and we all stared at the image of the driver. It was a little blurry, but the truck and the scraggly hair of the driver had me convinced. "That's Jimmy Shoemaker!"

Mateo nodded, his expression tight and ticked.

"When did he post bond?" I asked.

"About an hour after I brought him in. His mom bonded him out."

I snorted. "Of course she would."

Mateo looked at me, waiting for me to explain my response.

"She came into the store yesterday morning so mad she was nearly spitting fire. She wasn't very nice."

"What was she mad about?" Mateo asked.

"About my treatment of Isla. At least that's what she said."

"Let it play in real time from the point the truck heads west. I want to see if we missed him near the truck."

Scarlet did as Mateo asked, and we all leaned in to get a better view. About ten minutes after Jimmy's truck had last been seen on the screen, I saw it. "There!"

We watched as a white male with scraggly hair dressed in black got under the truck on the passenger side. He spent about five minutes under my daddy's truck before his head popped out from underneath, followed by his body, and he was on his feet heading toward the Tool Shed Tavern like he hadn't done anything wrong.

"That man deserves to fry." Scarlet's voice was laced with venom.

Mateo and I looked at her, both of us surprised by the tone that was completely out of character for her.

"What?" she said. "He tried to turn my best friend into toast. *He* should be toast. A visit to Old Sparky in Huntsville is too good for him."

The corner of Mateo's mouth quirked. Old Sparky was the electric chair in the Prison Museum in Huntsville that was responsible for 361 inmate deaths. If Scarlet knew how bad that thing really was, I didn't think she'd wish it on anyone . . . even if Jimmy deserved it.

"I'm going to need a copy of that video."

"I can save it and give you access to the last twenty-four hours."

"That would be great. Thank you, Scarlet. I'm going to send in Detective Youngblood. If you could pause it and show him the clip, I'd appreciate it. The quicker we get Jimmy in for questioning, the more comfortable all of us will be."

We stood up and Mateo gripped my arms. "I'm glad you're okay. I wish I could—"

"But you have work to do. I understand. Go get Jimmy and put him behind bars."

"We will. Right now, I'm going to take your mayor to the hospital for some staples." Mateo leaned over and kissed me in front of Scarlet. It wasn't a passionate kiss, but it was tender, which said even more.

Scarlet could hardly contain herself when he left. "O.M.W. he's got it bad," she said as she fanned her face.

I rolled my eyes. "He didn't even react when he saw Cade and me walk out of the Barn."

"Why should he? The man is comfortable in his own skin."

"He could also be seeing ten other women."

"Wow, that would be exhausting for an unemployed man, let alone a man who works all hours of the day and night, to keep us safe—you safe."

I had to give her that, but I didn't have to acknowledge it verbally.

Mateo left with Cade looking like he was a member of the Marine Corp Reserve Detachment at the Naval Air Station Joint Reserve Base in Fort Worth. The wad of gauze he held to the cut on the back of his head and the loopy grin on his face, however, detracted from the warrior haircut. Maybe *distracted* was the better descriptor if the "ahhs" slipping from the lips of all the women in Hazel Rock were any indication as Mateo and

Cade walked out of the beauty shop. Even nose-to-the-grindstone Liza Twaine appeared to be a bit tongue-tied. Word had spread quickly that Cade was a hero.

Detective Youngblood came into the shop and recorded my statement, and then a crime scene tech took pictures of my dirty clothing and bloodied knees before I was allowed to clean up. She also wanted my shirt and shorts in case there were any trace amounts of the explosive material that had been used to blow my truck to smithereens. My word, not hers. She said smithereens didn't quite qualify because there was a shell left of the vehicle—including the tailgate that barely had a scratch on it.

Looking at my daddy's truck across the street made me want to cry, so I kept my gaze on other parts of the town, like the Tool Shed Tavern, or the Hazel Rock Diner, where crowds had gathered.

It wasn't too long before the action outside began to die down—only Detective Youngblood, a bomb and arson detective from the county who I'd never met, a woman in a suit everyone suspected was some type of federal agent, and one uniform police officer remained to watch over and prowl through the debris the fire department had left behind.

Daddy closed the Barn for the day and came back to the beauty shop. "I'd like to go see Isla—together. As her son and her granddaughter."

I looked down at my T-shirt and shorts. The pink lettering that read *All Day, Eyre Day at the Book Barn Princess* was a little tight, as were my jean shorts. I'd cleaned up my knees, but my appearance left much to be desired.

"I'll go clean up and then we can go," I said.

I turned to thank Scarlet for all her help when Joellen began yelling at the picture window. "That no-good son of a pistol is back!"

We all looked out the window and saw a white truck at the end of the street with Jimmy Shoemaker sitting behind the wheel trying to look like he belonged in my stompin' ground—he didn't.

A collective growl echoed through Beaus and Beauties and my daddy, smart man that he was, saw what was coming and raised his hands to stop the women from acting. "Ladies, let the law handle Jimmy Shoemaker."

His words were drowned out by a war cry that could have been heard from across the county. Ten women ran for the door, and he had no choice but to get out of the way or get trampled where he stood. If I'd been thinking, I would have been standing with him. Instead I was leading the fray with Scarlet keeping up with my every step in her five-inch heels.

We stopped in front of Jimmy's truck, and for a moment he sat there dumbstruck, not sure what to think of ten snarling women blocking his path. It was only when Sally Ferguson ran toward his truck from the opposite side of the crime scene, her police uniform a clear sign that he'd been caught, that Jimmy recognized how much trouble he was in.

His eyes widened and he reached down and shoved the truck into reverse as he turned around in his seat to look out the back window. His view was blocked by more women in town who'd witnessed the ruckus and weren't about to be left out. Liza Twaine was right in the middle, her phone up and recording the entire event.

"Get out of the way!" Jimmy yelled and revved his engine, but not a soul moved. It was a standoff Jimmy was about to lose. Because when the second line of women locked arms behind him, Jimmy turned back around to drive forward. His actions were too late.

Scarlet and I were at his driver's window. Joellen was at the passenger side along with Mary, and, bless her old heart, Daisy Mahan was there with them. I grabbed Jimmy by his shirt and yanked as hard as I could. He swiped at my arm and the truck began inching forward. Jimmy's feet, however, weren't on the pedals. They'd been lifted off the floorboard as Scarlet pulled on his left arm and someone else yanked on his hair. Jimmy Shoemaker was coming out of the window of his truck whether he wanted to or not.

His body slammed to the ground and a pile of women jumped on him, unleashing the biggest hissy fit pitched this side of the Mason-Dixon Line. In the midst of the fray, a little pink shell appeared and I knew Princess was among the women ready to put my attacker in his place.

Jimmy Shoemaker never knew what hit him.

Chapter Twenty-eight

"Get your paws off me, you stinkin' lawdawg!" The spittle from Jimmy's demand barely missed Sally Ferguson's uniform.

"Careful, Jimmy, or I'll unleash the beauties of Hazel Rock on you," Sally said as she pulled Jimmy to his feet.

But he wasn't as smart as he looked, and Jimmy Shoemaker didn't look none too bright to begin with. "That rat needs to be put down!" he yelled as he nodded in my direction.

It wasn't me he was referring to. It was the little pink armadillo I held in my arms.

"An armadillo isn't a rodent," I yelled back as I pulled Princess close to my chest.

"It bit me!"

"She did not!" I argued. Armadillos don't bite, but they do have claws that are meant for digging. In this case, Princess had left her mark.

Jimmy started to argue back, but Deputy Sally shut him down. "One more word and I'll make these women cancel your birth certificate. And just so you know, Princess is considered one of Hazel Rock's beauties— she'll be with them."

Jimmy glared at me and the rest the of beauties of Hazel Rock and clamped his mouth closed. It was either that or he'd end up with a matching scratch on his right cheek and a bald spot on the right side of his head to balance off the one on his left. I wasn't sure who ended up with a handful of his stringy hair, but I was glad it wasn't me. Just the thought of touching it made me itch.

I'd say none of the women of Hazel Rock had laid a claw on him to cause the deep gauges on his cheek, but that would be a lie. Somehow in the middle of the melee, Princess escaped through her pet door at the back of the Barn, made her way around the building, and did something I'd never seen her do—she'd attacked with her razor-sharp claws. She caught Jimmy across each cheek before I knew what hit him. How she got into the mix was beyond anyone's comprehension, but Jimmy's squeals of pain were probably what saved him from more female vigilante justice. Unfortunately for Jimmy, there was no magic coming from the experts at Beaus and Beauties like it had for Cade. Nor was there anyone willing to give him a towel to wipe the blood from his face.

Now Jimmy was being escorted down Main Street looking like the thug that he was with the exact opposite of a hero's welcome, and a center-framed video of him in all his glory for the six o'clock news to boot. It was a piece of irony we all relished. Princess was in my arms with a look of superiority plastered across her face. I could have sworn I heard her giggle.

Detective Youngblood had been the one to jump in the truck and stop it before it rammed into Cade's truck. Then he ordered a second tow for it so it could be processed for evidence. Daddy had been one of the men to run after the women ready to tar and feather Jimmy Shoemaker, but I think he got a secret kick out of the way we'd yanked Jimmy out through his window. As it was, the only thing that kept Daisy Mahan from drawing her gun from her pocketbook was the lack of a clear shot. There were too many of us in the crossfire, and I was thankful she had the presence of mind to leave it concealed.

"Go get cleaned up. I'm worried about Isla," Daddy whispered over my shoulder.

"Why?" I asked.

"The apple doesn't fall far from the tree." Daddy nodded toward Jimmy being driven down Main Street in the back of Sally Ferguson's cruiser.

"You think—"

Daddy shushed me. "I don't have any proof. Just a gut feeling that something bad is going to happen."

I believed in gut feelings. There wasn't any evidence of collusion between Jimmy's actions and his mother, Joan, but I wouldn't put it past the woman who'd walked into the Barn that morning. Especially after she found out that I helped her grandkids get into a shelter. I'm sure Jimmy worded the incident more along the lines of "that woman took my kids, and the cops wouldn't do anything about it."

"Let's go. I don't need a shower."

Daddy disagreed. "If it's nothing, I don't want to scare Isla."

"Fine, give me five minutes." I passed off Princess to Daddy before running for my apartment.

I took a two-minute shower and was down in front of the bookstore with one minute to spare. Daddy was parked on the street in his truck with Princess sitting on the front seat.

"Are we taking Princess with us?" I asked.

"Isla loves Princess, and I think it will do them both some good."

"Are you sure Princess won't claw anyone?"

"She's never done it before."

"But she did it today."

Daddy laughed. "I believe she wanted to make sure she wasn't the only female in Hazel Rock who didn't get her claws on Jimmy."

I smiled at that. "I'm just happy none of us got charged with a crime."

"What would they have charged you with?" Daddy asked. "No one hit him or kicked him. And as far as scratching goes, I don't think they can charge Princess with assault."

"Jimmy could demand she be quarantined."

"I think Jimmy has his hands too full to worry about a few scratches."

"Just for the record, they were gouges."

Daddy patted Princess on the head. "And they were mighty fine gouges at that."

It was my turn to laugh. My daddy was the least violent person I knew, but he was sure proud of Princess jumping in and giving Jimmy the what-for.

My phone rang and I pulled it out of the back pocket of my shorts. Mateo's number came up on the caller ID.

"Hello?"

Mateo didn't even greet me. "What old guy could have it in for Isla at Oak Grove Manor?" he asked.

"No one that I know of, why?"

"There's no one that you had a problem with out there?"

"No. Why do you ask?"

"Before Jimmy lawyered up, he said the old guy at the nursing home caught him cutting your tires last night. The old guy told him if he was going to do it, to do it right. Then he told Jimmy what website would teach him how to create the bomb. He went on to tell him exactly where to place the bomb to have the most impact . . . on the driver."

Holy crap. There wasn't one person who wanted me dead, there were two. And one of them lived with my grandmother.

"Daddy, you need to get to the nursing home now!"

"Are you with Bobby Ray?"

"What's going on?" Daddy asked.

"Yes. We're almost at Oak Grove Manor now."

"Wait for me, Charli. I don't want you surprising someone who wants you dead."

Daddy had had enough. "Put him on speaker, Princess."

I did as my daddy asked, and Mateo immediately took charge. "Bobby Ray, listen to me. Whoever was behind the bombing lives at the nursing home. All I know is that it's an old guy. I need you to wait until I get there."

"Are you telling us the man responsible for Ava's death, cutting me, and the bomb in my daughter's truck lives at the nursing home?"

"Yes."

"Have you lost your ever-lovin' mind?" I asked.

Daddy agreed. "Sorry, Mateo. We can't wait. My mama's in there with a man who has three gallons of crazy in a gallon size bucket. We're not waiting."

I hung up before Mateo could argue, although I was pretty sure I heard him say a four-letter word or two before I hit End. Daddy's pedal was to the metal and we were flying down FM 303 and hill jumpin' as we went.

"You would have had my hide if I'd driven like that as a teenager," I told him.

"Not if you were trying to save your mama."

I believed him, yet try as I might, nothing I could have done would have saved my mom. I hoped the same couldn't be said about my grandmother.

Daddy pulled into the lot and stopped in front of the portico. Neither one of us gave a rat's behind about the rules of parking a vehicle at the Oak Grove Manor. Nor did we stop to greet the old man in the wheelchair out front who shook his head at our rule violation.

Joan was sitting behind the desk talking on the phone—she was the last person I expected to see at that desk. She was supposed to be on leave, and something about that bothered me. But, from the look on her face, I could tell she wasn't a threat. She was all tore up. She looked as if her world had crashed around her and nothing was going to change it. When we caught her eye, her face turned deathly pale. There was no doubt in my mind that she had just learned what her son had done—the crimes he had committed. Words could never express her shame and her sorrow, and the only comfort I could give her was that I was here and not dead. I had survived despite her son's best efforts to kill me. It was little comfort for her, for she had just lost the son she loved, but it was great comfort to me.

I looked at the three amigos sitting along the wall.

Frank shrugged as if he didn't know why she was there either. "Mr. Andrews said she could come back to work."

I nodded and ordered, "Take care of her," to the three older men as Daddy and I ran for Isla's room, Princess in my arms.

What we found once we entered, however, was the last thing I'd expected. There was a gun, and the Judge, and Isla.

And Mason Andrews was ready to kill my grandparents before I even really knew them.

Chapter Twenty-nine

Mason rolled his eyes. "I should've known he couldn't do it. That numbskull."

"You're the old man who told Jimmy how to blow up my truck?" I asked.

Mason laughed. It was sort of diabolical. Not the type of laugh you ever want to hear while you're staring down the barrel of a gun.

Mason pointed his gun in the Judge's direction. "Move over next to the Judge."

Daddy and I did as we were told, and although the room was spacious, I felt claustrophobic. Princess did too. She squirmed and squealed and I held on tighter. Just as I thought I'd calmed her down, she jumped from my arms. I grabbed for her but missed and she landed hard on the floor.

She shook her head like a dog coming out of the water and then circled at my feet.

"That's what she did to me," Daddy said.

"That leap saved your life," Mason agreed. "Otherwise, my knife would have been buried in your throat."

I rubbed my throat just thinking about how close Daddy had come. Then I asked that age-old question every victim must ask: "Why?"

"Because of Isla," he said. Then he held his free hand out in Isla direction for her to take. "Come, Isla. I will protect you, since they have failed."

"How have I failed?" the Judge asked. I really didn't think he cared what Mason thought, but I think he did care what Isla thought.

"You left his mother on the floor for days with a broken hip and did nothing to save her," Isla answered.

I looked toward Mason and saw the pain on his face right before he hardened it. "I won't let you ignore Isla the way you ignored my mother. She died because you wouldn't let that deputy kick in that door for me."

The Judge stiffened. "You're Debbie Andrews's son?"

"Yeah. I'm the man that you took everything from. She was my only family, and now I'm going to do the same thing to you. This little family expansion you've had in the past week hasn't made it easy, but I'm ready to take away every person that ever meant something to you."

The Judge couldn't believe it. It was as if he'd never seen evil or senseless violence in his life, when in actuality, he saw it every day. "You killed Ava to get back at me?"

Mason grinned and nodded. "She was a pathetic woman. You should have never chosen her over your wife."

The Judge didn't deny having an affair with Ava, but I knew from the look on his face that he'd never felt anything beyond the love a father has for his daughter for Ava, and part of him was broken because of that loss.

"You tried to kill Bobby because he's my son?" the Judge whispered. Somehow, he still couldn't fathom the depth of Mason's hatred. I understood it all too clearly as Mason basked in the glory of his plan.

"And Princess?" the Judge asked. He wasn't talking about our armadillo. He was talking about me, and I couldn't help but warm up inside at the anger building in his voice.

"You probably didn't hear. I caught one of her admirers cutting the tires to her truck in our parking lot last night. I suggested a better way to be rid of the cancer in his life, but he obviously failed. Now his mom will have to take the fall for three murders instead of one. Joan can be a little passionate about cheating husbands and deadbeat sons and granddaughters who only show up to collect the money when the elderly die."

"That wasn't why I came by to see Isla!" I argued.

Mason laughed. "It was as far as Joan knew."

I thought about the way Joan's opinion of me had changed. It made sense that Mason was filling her head with lies.

My daddy joined the argument. "But Isla isn't dying."

Mason's grin was evil. "She is as far as Joan knows."

I looked at Isla to see how Mason's plan affected her. Her brow was drawn, and again I thought of those square pegs fitting into those round holes, but I could have sworn I saw understanding in the depths of her gaze as she made eye contact with me.

The Judge was still stuck on why Mason had targeted his family. "I followed our department policy," he said. "There isn't a day that goes by that I haven't thought of how I should have done things differently the day my deputy responded to your mama's house."

"You should have kicked in the door!" Mason yelled.

The Judge didn't argue. "You're right. I should have gone out to her house and kicked in the door myself. But I didn't, and we paid a substantial amount of money to you for the loss of your mother. I changed our policy because of my error. It was the biggest . . ." The Judge hesitated and looked at me. "It was the second biggest mistake of my life. Turning away from you before you were even born was the biggest."

"How touching," Mason said. "Well, now I'm going to take her and your son from you. But most of all, I'm going to take your wife from you. Because she deserves someone who will watch over her. Someone who will kick the door down if she doesn't answer the phone, regardless of the cost. Because it's the right thing to do when you are in charge of the welfare of others. It's the right thing to do." Mason's voice held the conviction of a zealot. A man crazed with his need to protect. A man who wanted to protect my grandmother from a family who loved her dearly.

Mason held out his hand for Isla to take. "Come. I will care of you."

Isla looked at Mason, the man she played Scrabble with every day, and then she gazed at the Judge. From the look of confusion on her face, I wasn't sure if she knew who the Judge was or if she'd chose Mason over him. Isla took a step in Mason's direction and then looked back at the Judge. She turned to the Judge and kissed him on the cheek as if saying goodbye one last time. I thought the Judge was going to fall apart that very moment . . . until Isla whispered something. Then it was his turn to look completely confused as Isla turned back and took Mason's hand.

A grin of superiority swept over Mason's face. He sensed victory—a bit too early.

Isla grabbed his hand and pulled with every bit of strength she had. It was the sign the Judge needed. He charged Mason and grabbed the gun, which exploded with a flash of white heat from the barrel. The Judge jerked back but never lost his grip on Mason's hand as Princess ran toward the fight and struck Mason in the shin with her head. The Judge, Isla, and Mason went down to the floor. Smoke filled the room as the gun went off a second time. Daddy jumped on Mason, wrapping his legs around his torso in a scissor hold while securing Mason's left arm with his hand. I knew it would be tough for him with his wounded arm, but the Judge was losing the battle for the gun despite repeatedly slamming Mason's knuckles against the tile floor.

Mason began kicking, trying to gain purchase with his feet, and I jumped into the tangled mass of bodies. I grabbed for the gun to ensure it didn't turn toward the Judge or Isla just as Isla began whacking Mason over the head with her cane—but she had terrible aim.

The cane struck Daddy's legs several times before it struck my arm, and I could have sworn it split my hand from my wrist. From the grunt my Daddy gave next, I think she hit him in the head. Then Mason swore, and I knew she hit her target—but not hard enough. I looked around for anything to hit him with and grabbed the nearest object within reach. I swung as hard as I could and struck Mason square in the nose. He yelled and blood flew. His grip weakened and the Judge gained the gun. Isla struck again for good measure, and this time, Mason was quiet. He was out cold, but Isla wasn't about to stop. She swung once more and missed her target. She got the Judge right across the bridge of the nose.

"Good God, woman! Isn't it bad enough that I've been shot? Do you have to cane me as well?"

Isla paused long enough to realize Mason wasn't a threat and the Judge was scooting back with blood covering his left shoulder. She dropped her cane, grabbed a towel from the shelves, and went to the Judge.

"Don't you die on me, you old coot," she said as she sat down next to him and applied pressure to his wound.

"I think that's what your granddaughter calls me."

"Well, if the shoe fits . . ."

"It used to fit. I'm a changed man."

"Don't you change. I love you just the way you are, Jacob Sperry." There was a smile on Isla's face, but a tear dribbled down her cheek and the Judge wiped it away.

"I love you, Isla Warren Sperry. I have from the first day I laid eyes on you, and nothing will ever change that."

I looked at my daddy, who still held on to Mason in case he became conscious.

Daddy took one look at me and laughed as Mateo and a deputy ran in the door with their guns drawn. I heard a chuckle behind me as Mateo took in the scene and asked, "Did you hit him with a bedpan?"

I looked at the object in my hand and dropped it to the floor. "Fuzz buckets."

Princess came out of nowhere and scooted the pan closer to me. I wasn't sure if she wanted to embarrass me further or make sure I was armed. I preferred to think she was still looking out for my welfare.

Mateo grinned and holstered his gun. Then he relieved Daddy from his hold and put Mason in handcuffs with the assistance of his deputy. Mateo instructed his deputy to use an ammonia inhalant to revive Mason, who immediately jerked his head upright as he got a whiff of the strong stimulant. He began to struggle but soon learned it was a fruitless endeavor.

"Relax. You're in custody now," Mateo said.

The Judge filled in the charges. "For the murder of Ava James. For the attempted murder of Bobby Ray Warren, and for conspiracy to commit murder of Charli Rae Warren." His last words were filled with the passion I remembered from my teens. "May God have mercy on your soul, because I hope to hell the courts don't."

Mateo and the deputy helped Mason to his feet, and a deputy escorted him out of the room.

"You got that all on video with your body cam, didn't you?" Isla asked.

Mateo looked down at the camera attached to his shirt. "I should have."

"Good. I need a copy."

Mateo's left brow rose and the rest of us looked at Isla.

"It was our first family movie, and I want to remember our teamwork for as long as I can."

Mateo was the first to speak. "That will be the best first family video in the history of family videos."

I couldn't have agreed more . . . except for the bedpan.

"Could you take our picture, Sheriff?" Isla asked. "I got one of Princess with the bedpan from behind, but I'd like to get one with all of us—together for the first time."

"Of course." Mateo stepped forward and took Isla's phone.

"You took a picture of me holding the bedpan?" I asked.

Isla grinned. I had expected the violence to confuse her even more, but instead, it had made her incredibly lucid . . . for now, at least. "Your daddy and you were working together. How could I pass that up? It's an incredible profile photo of the two of you."

I couldn't argue with her logic. I just hoped the video and the photo were family heirlooms and not put on display for everyone to see.

Daddy and I moved over toward the Judge and Isla—my grandparents—with Princess joining us as if she wasn't about to be left out, and the five of us posed for our first ever family photo.

"It would have been better if I didn't have a broken nose," my grandfather said.

"I think the gunshot wound is worse," Isla said.

"The gunshot wound is manly," my grandfather replied.

My grandmother and I rolled our eyes.

"Did Mason hit you?" asked Mateo.

"That's from my mother," Daddy said.

"Isla broke the Judge's nose?"

"And she hit Daddy's leg—"

"And my head." Daddy added.

"And my arm." I held up my arm to show the welt forming around my wrist.

Isla blushed. "That wasn't my intent."

"Darlin', you've never been able to hit the broad side of a barn with a shotgun filled with bird shot. What made you think you could hit Mason Andrews with your cane and not us?"

Isla looked affronted. "Well, I knew I would miss, but I thought my family was tougher than a few licks with a little old cane."

We all laughed and Mateo took the picture. It was a picture I would treasure for the rest of my life.

Chapter Thirty

It was moving day for two very important women.

After Ava's funeral, which was attended by even more people than her vigil had been, my grandfather produced Ava's will. A will he had encouraged Ava to make, because if anything happened to her, she would have the opportunity to make someone else's life better.

And she had. Ava's neatly kept trailer was now the property of Naomi Shoemaker, soon to be Naomi Smith once she obtained her divorce. Naomi's old rented trailer, which was no place for anyone to live, had been hauled away after the Department of Family and Protective Services had it condemned. Now Naomi, who had obtained a job as a receptionist at Oak Grove Manor thanks to a recommendation from her soon-to-be ex-mother-in-law, had a nice home with a great yard for her and her two kids, Lily and Jimmy Jr.

I couldn't have been happier for them.

It was moving day for my grandmother as well. She was moving home. Her hip was almost completely healed, and my grandfather had decided it was time to retire. His shoulder had healed nicely with a through-and-through wound that hadn't broken a single bone. He said he was more than lucky, he was blessed. With the help of a daily nurse, he wanted to spend as much time with my grandmother as possible before the disease took her from us once and for all. It was still difficult for me to think of them as my grandma and grandpa, but I was beginning to get used to the idea.

The book drive had been a huge success, and to go with it, I'd created a foster care library stall in the Book Barn Princess. The Ava James Library was only for children in foster care, and no one was allowed in the stall unless they were a foster child, or a foster parent. I hoped it would give those children a feeling of being loved and special in a world where they often felt lost and forgotten.

"That's the last box," Daddy said as we carried Isla's belongings into the house.

"Wait, I've got one more thing." I ran from the house and over to Daisy and Jessie's house to retrieve the package I'd left earlier that morning.

I rang the bell and Jessie answered the door. "Dagnabit, Princess. You just cost me five dollars."

Daisy came up behind him with her hand held out as Jessie dug a five-dollar bill from his wallet. "That's my husband," Daisy said with a grin and a wink in my direction.

I couldn't help but laugh. "What was the bet?"

"If you'd arrived five minutes later, I would have owed Jessie. I appreciate your punctuality." She took the five dollars from her husband and stuffed it down her bra.

Jessie's bushy eyebrows rose on his forehead. "Do I get a chance to win that back?"

"You get a chance to earn that back," Daisy said with a wink.

I laughed again and grabbed what I'd come over for. "I think I'll let you get to work," I told Jessie.

As the door closed behind me I heard a deep male "Yee-haw!"

Then I could have sworn I heard Daisy giggle and say, "That's my husband," as I left the porch and headed toward my grandparents' house.

I made it back inside as my family sat down for a glass of sweet tea, and I popped my head around the corner of the kitchen door.

"Close your eyes."

Three sets of eyes closed, but I could tell the Judge was peeking, and my daddy's left eye was open just a sliver.

"They're both cheating, aren't they?" asked my grandmother.

"I wouldn't—" My grandfather started to fib.

"Ah-ah-ah." I scolded. "Proverbs 12:22 says, 'The Lord detests lying lips, but he delights in people who are trustworthy.'"

Grandpa smiled. "I stand corrected. I was peeking along with your father."

"Speak for yourself, old man." Daddy struggled to keep a straight face as he winked at his own father.

Grandma grinned with her eyes closed. "He deserved that one."

"I learned that verse just so I could keep the three of you in line," I confessed to my family, then I gave them the best gift of all. "You can open your eyes now."

In the middle of my grandparents' table was a white Victorian birdcage containing Tweetle Dee and Tweetle Dum, who immediately began singing as if on cue. It was the gift of song that contained a memory of an aunt I never really got to know—Ava James—and not an eye was dry as we sat and told stories about the woman who was loved by all.

If you enjoyed *Lethal Literature*, be sure not to miss all of Kym Roberts's Book Barn Mysteries, including

Charli Rae Warren doesn't plan on striking it rich as the owner of an independent bookstore in Hazel Rock, Texas—especially one with a pink armadillo as its mascot. But when an ingenious advertising campaign puts her business on the map, it ropes in some deadly publicity . . .

Charli can't believe writer Lucy Barton has agreed to promote her latest Midnight Poet Society novel at the Book Barn Princess—or that there's only a week and a half to prepare for the signing. It's all because of the Book Seekers, a smartphone app created by her cousin Jamal exclusively for Charli's bookstore, which sends fans on a virtual scavenger hunt around town for a chance to meet the best-selling author. But as soon as it goes live, people turn up dead . . .

Someone's using the Book Seekers to track victims and copycat the fictional Midnight Poet Society homicides, and horrified locals suspect Jamal could be the mastermind behind the crimes. While Charli readies the Barn for a stampede of new customers, it'll take true grit to shelve the culprit before her brainy cousin gets locked behind bars, Ms. Barton backs out of the visit, and she finds herself up a creek—with a serial killer holding the paddle!

Keep reading for a special look!

A Lyrical Underground e-book on sale now.

Chapter One

"Your eye is twitching."

"It is not." My lashes fluttered against my cheek—twice. I rubbed my hand over my face and continued to deny the obvious. "I've got dust in my eye. Someone needs to clean this barn."

Daddy sighed. "You did that yesterday—on your day off."

"What? Yesterday wasn't my day off." I turned away from the view of an empty Main Street and picked up one of the delivery boxes from the counter. I'd put the box down when my ex walked by our store just now without stopping. Cade Calloway had strolled on by like he hadn't been promising to take me out to dinner for the past couple months after he got reelected as mayor—two weeks ago.

It was humiliating.

Obviously, we both remembered his invitation. Only one of us thought it'd been sincere. I started to growl and then covered the noise with a cough. My daddy didn't need to know that Cade had let me down, again. Cade and I hadn't been together since high school—and if I was being honest, he really didn't even rate the status of *ex*.

He was part of my childhood. Over and done with. Growing older meant moving forward. It was time I did that.

The front door of our bookstore swished open and the little buzzer dinged, signaling the arrival of customers. I shivered from the cool, damp breeze that came in with the two women. It was the breeze that caused goose bumps to form on my arms, not my anticipation that Cade had turned his all-American, apple-pie good looks around and walked into the Book Barn Princess. That was *not* something I wanted with every fiber of my being.

I also have a habit of lying to myself. My life had never been rosy. It'd been good, but not charmed. I yearned for charmed. Or maybe I just wanted a date…any date.

Daddy approached the two middle-aged ladies who were staring up at our over-sized loft filled with books and upon request, showed them our Poetry & Literature section in one of the Barn's old horse stalls. The front of the section was whitewashed and had *Poetry* painted in bold black letters with a tree growing out of the letter *t*. *Literature* was offset to the right in scrolling black calligraphy lettering with a feather pen and an inkwell emphasizing its beauty. It gave our rustic setting a touch of class.

I heard Daddy ask if they were looking for a present, and began to worry about being behind with our holiday stock. This was the first year in a long time that I actually wanted everything to be perfectly decorated to capture the festive nature of the season. For most of my life, holidays had always been a bummer with a capital *B*. I mean, sure, when I was a little kid, they were awesome. Toys and scrumptious food were in abundance, but the best part? My family was a family. My mom was alive and we would bake for hours, days, weeks…even months. The baking began in September when the holiday cookbooks would start to arrive at our family bookstore. My mom would open the boxes and her smile would light up her face.

She'd turn to me and say, "Charli Rae, I think we need to test these recipes before we tell our customers that these here books are full of recipes to die for, don't you?" In her voice, there would be that rich, heavenly tone she always had when we shared our favorite family holiday treat. It was like she was experiencing the burst of flavor on her taste buds as soon as she saw the covers of the cookbooks. It was the same look she had when my dad made peppermint milkshakes while we decorated the Christmas tree.

With one difference. If Dad was making his famous peppermint milkshakes, my mom would mosey on over to where he stood at the kitchen counter, her hips moving back and forth with a sassy sway, and she'd look up into my daddy's eyes and tell him no one could tempt her to sin the way he did as she took that first sip. Little did I know at the age of ten that her tone had more to do about the passion between them than the homemade milkshake. For me, it was all about the dessert.

I loved it.

There was nothing special about the ingredients—Homemade Vanilla Blue Bell Ice Cream, with milk, peppermint extract, and candy canes blended into one cool, scintillating dessert that I'd savor until the very last drop I didn't want to reach but couldn't wait to devour. To this day, I associate peppermint shakes with family and love.

All the wonder, however, disappeared after my tenth Christmas, after Momma died from cancer. Our first holiday was brutal. Dad made peppermint shakes in an attempt to give me normalcy. But I misunderstood the gesture and thought he was saying life would go on without Momma—nothing would change. I ended up throwing my milkshake, glass and all, across the apartment we lived in above the store. I shocked my dad as I screamed and stomped through the kitchen to my bedroom.

It was only when I heard him crying as he cleaned up the mess I'd made in the other room that I realized he was hurting just as much as I was. I returned to the living room and knelt beside him. He tried to hide his grief, but even at ten, there was no way I was going to let him. I needed to know I wasn't the only one utterly destroyed by her death…and for the next six years we spent the holidays sharing only one shake on Christmas Eve to remember my mom in our own special way.

"Are you going to open that box, or sit there and wait for the books to break out like Black Bart broke out of Hazel Rock's jail?"

I laughed at the lean man who had more gray than pepper on the top of his head. Daddy liked the Old West history of Hazel Rock. It was how my momma convinced him to settle in the Barn when I was eight.

Daddy returned to his worn leather chair behind the counter and sat with his feet propped up on the counter and crossed at the ankles. He rested his chin in his hand as he leaned against the arm of the chair and pondered what the blue blazes I was up to.

"You're supposed to be manning the register, not spying on me," I told him.

"If I was spying, I'd be asleep. Your life is about as exciting as the wind blowing."

"What's that supposed to mean?"

"It means get out of the Barn and live a little. Stop lollygagging around here on your day off."

"But the new books have arrived," I objected.

Daddy pulled his feet off the counter and stood. He was a handsome man just past his prime, with a laid-back manner and a twinkle in his eyes that belied his innocent expression. He was lean and fit, and could almost always be found wearing a plaid shirt with jeans and a pair of ancient cowboy boots. His skin had the weathered tan of a man who worked on a farm, or around a barn, like ours was before it was a bookstore. I'd idolized him as a child, demonized him as a teenager, and begun to appreciate him for the man, father, and husband he'd been as I approached thirty. He'd literally become my world once again.

Which didn't exactly say a whole lot for my social life. It was pathetic, and I was well aware of it.

"I'll have the new books on the shelves tomorrow when you come to work," he scolded.

"I want to open them today. Lucy Barton's book should be arriving any day…"

"And here I thought you were looking for cookbooks."

I grinned. He knew me better than I'd expected considering I'd run away from home to live with my aunt at the age of seventeen. It'd taken me a dozen years to find my way back to my hometown, but I wasn't about to completely confess my weakness for a good holiday treat.

Princess squawked from under my daddy's feet.

"If we're disturbing your beauty sleep, Princess, you should have stayed upstairs," I replied. "Quit complaining."

Princess stuck her pointy pink little nose out from behind the counter, yawned, and then disappeared from my view. Before moving back home, I would have never, in a million Texas years, believed that I would live with a nine-banded armadillo, let alone talk to one, but she intruded on our conversations like a little toddler dying for attention. Sometimes she smelled like one too.

I'd inherited the little creature from my dad when I returned home and moved into the apartment above the store on the backside of the Barn overlooking the Bravos River. Princess wasn't your typical pet; she was pink, sometimes stinky, and had a hard shell. A freak of nature abandoned at birth that my dad took in and gave a home. Then he gave her to me when I returned because she liked the Barn. As much as I grumbled about the little thing, I'd fallen in love with her beady eyes and cocky attitude. We were pretty much inseparable—unless she was out back digging for grubs…or stunk to high heaven and needed a bath…or I decided to get out of bed and not sleep all day long.

Daddy scooted across the concrete floors. He stopped in front of me as I struggled with my box cutter that was about as sharp as a pair of kiddy scissors. In other words, it wouldn't cut a piece of construction paper if it was perforated.

Daddy swayed his head from side to side and his lips curved in a smile of surrender. He'd given up on telling me to replace the blade. "Let me help you with that." He pulled out his pocket knife from his well-worn Levi's and bent over to grab the edge of the box.

"Don't cut any of the books," I warned.

His lip quirked but he said nothing as his knife made a clean cut down the center of the box, the blade slicing through the thick packing tape like it was butter on a hot sunny day. He made two more cuts at the ends of the box and I didn't wait for him to get out of the way; I immediately started pulling out the cardboard and paper packing that protected the books from damage during shipping.

Daddy's cell phone rang and I waited for him to take the call. I knew he wanted to see the books as much as I did. When his expression turned somber, a bad feeling stirred in my gut. Something was wrong. I listened for any hint of what the caller had to say on the other end of the phone. It was only when he said, "I'm sorry for your loss" that I knew how bad it was.

I pulled Princess onto my lap and hugged her tight. Daddy told the caller not to worry, that there was no rush, and asked that they put us on the list before he hung up the phone.

"What happened?"

Daddy clipped his phone to his belt and broke the bad news. "Matt Allen died this morning."

I couldn't place the name. I recognized it; I just wasn't sure who it belonged to.

Sensing my confusion, Daddy explained. "Matt was the electrician who was going to install the lights on the front of the store to light up the Book Barn Princess sign."

"What happened to him?"

"It seems he got electrocuted at a jobsite he was working on this morning. Now Warner Electric is short-handed and they're not sure when they can get someone out to install the lights."

"That's horrible. I hope they realized the lights weren't that important."

"Yeah, but they're a good, reliable company. They have a good safety record, and I know they must be having a hard time dealing with his death. Matt has been with them since he was a teenager. He was still just a kid, barely twenty-two."

We sat there for moment thinking of how precious life was and how quickly everything could change on a dirty dime. It was only when Princess squirmed off my lap that I returned my attention to the box and pulled out the latest Midnight Poet Society Mystery by Lucy Barton. A squeal may have escaped my lips. Lucy Barton had been my favorite murder mystery author since my aunt let me read her first Midnight Poet Society Mystery when I was seventeen. It was the perfect distraction from reality. When I was a teen, the gang of young dark poets became my best friends. It was also what we needed to keep us focused on the future right now.

I ran my hand across the hardback's cover sleeve. The sleek surface gave way to textured ridges across the title. The black and purple cover depicted a dark and eerie murder scene in a forest with a muted moon illuminating a dead body. The murder weapon was on prominent display in the middle of the book cover—an ax protruding from the bloodied chest of the victim, while forming the right arm of the letter X in the title, *Waxing Moon*. It was brilliant and spooky. Gruesome in thought, yet relatively tame in the actual image.

I *oohed* so loud, my dad couldn't resist taking a peek over my shoulder. I began to pull the books out of the box and realized the count was way off. I hadn't ordered that many books—in fact, I'd only ordered twenty because we had a midnight poetry reading scheduled for Friday night and were expecting at least ten people to be there. But from what I could see, there were at least thirty books in the one box.

"Something's wrong. I didn't order this many books." I looked over at the seven boxes that had been delivered. "Now that I think about it, I think this entire order is off. There's no way I should have this quantity."

The bell on the front door buzzed softly and the automatic barn door swooshed open, allowing a cool seasonal breeze to proceed the entrance of our customer.

"I'll get that," Daddy said before I could argue.

Except Daddy didn't move. His boots stayed rooted to the floor and I looked up to see what could possibly be the problem. His face had drained of color. His cheeks fell slack. But it was his eyes that really frightened me. They were full of pain—anguish that hit him at his core. A look I hadn't seen since my momma died—

I followed his gaze to the front door...and had the opposite reaction. Glee flooded through me, wiping away all my fear.

"Aunt Violet!"

About the Author

Three career paths resonated for **Kym Roberts** during her early childhood: detective, investigative reporter, and . . . nun. Being a nun, however, dropped by the wayside when she became aware of boys—they were the spice of life she couldn't deny. In high school her path was forged when she took her first job at a dry cleaner and met every cop in town, especially the lone female police officer on patrol. From that point on there was no stopping Kym's pursuit of a career in law enforcement. Kym followed her dream and became a detective, which fulfilled her desire to be an investigative reporter, with one extra perk—a badge. Promoted to sergeant, Kym spent the majority of her career in SVU. She retired from the job reluctantly when her husband dragged her kicking and screaming to another state, but writing continued to call her name. Visit her on the web at kymroberts.com.

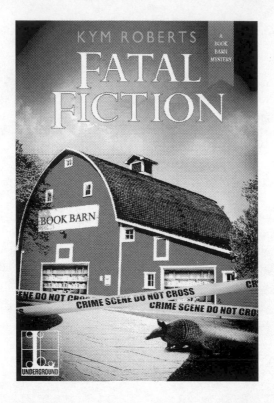

When kindergarten teacher Charli Rae Warren hightailed it out of Hazel Rock, Texas, as a teen, she vowed to leave her hometown in the dust. A decade later, she's braving the frontier of big hair and bigger gossip once again . . . but this time, she's saddled with murder!

Charli agrees to sell off the family bookstore, housed in a barn, and settle her estranged dad's debt—if only so she can ride into the sunset and cut ties with Hazel Rock forever. But the trip is extended when Charli finds her Realtor dead in the store, strangled by a bedazzled belt. And with daddy suspiciously MIA, father and daughter are topping the most wanted list . . .

Forging an unlikely alliance with the town beauty queen, the old beau who tore her family apart, and one ugly armadillo, Charli's intent on protecting what's left of her past . . . and wrangling the lone killer who's fixin' to destroy her future . . .

Charli Rae Warren is back home in Hazel Rock, Texas, spending her time reading, collecting, and selling books—at least, the ones that don't get eaten first by her father's pet armadillo. Running the family bookstore is a demanding job, but solving murders on the side can be flat-out dangerous

. . .

The Book Barn is more than just a shop, it's a part of the community—and Charli is keeping busy with a fundraising auction and the big rodeo event that's come to town. That includes dealing with the Texas-sized egos of some celebrity cowboys, including Dalton Hibbs, a blond, blue-eyed bull rider who gets overly rowdy one night with the local hairdresser . . . and soon afterward, disappears into thin air.

Dalton's brother also vanished seven years ago—and Charli is thrown about whether Dalton is a villain or a victim. After a close call with an assailant wielding a branding iron (that plays havoc with her hair) and some strange vandalism on her property, she's going to have to team up with the sheriff to untangle this mystery before she gets gored . . .

Printed in the United States
by Baker & Taylor Publisher Services